THE
BELLADONNA
INVITATION

The Belladonna Invitation

© 2023 Rose Biggin

First published in Great Britain 2023 by Ghost Orchid Press

ISBN 978-1-7396116-6-8 Paperback
ISBN 978-1-7396116-7-5 eBook

Text set in Garamond

Cover Design © Fay Lane
Typesetting: Lauren Cumber

THE BELLADONNA INVITATION

by Rose Biggin

Ghost Orchid Press
Cambridgeshire, UK

for E.G., who set an example

I

I

Look for me.

It starts with this: a distant figure, high and away in the finest private box.

Look for me.

A pull of magnetism, as thin and strong as filigree wire. It starts at the woman with the opera glasses, who sits gazing at the stage from on high, and ends with the woman who stands there watching, struck thunderbolt-still in the stalls.

Search me out. Go on.

Imagine if you were looking for me with those.

An opening night, the most prestigious event in the calendar; everyone is looking for everyone. The Opéra has them. Staring up at the box, with its bronze fruit and cherubs clinging on heavily, a young woman in a servant's dress, or something that passes for such, is jostled by the steady march of theatregoers to their seats. When they bump into her she does not even mumble an apology: she'll be reprimanded for that later, no doubt. But right now, all that has vanished along with everything else, and there is only this: the distant figure, all in black, in the finest box.

I have to be somebody that you're looking for.

The distant figure folds away the glasses with a neat flick of silver and turns to address an unseen companion beside her, disappearing from view in the movement.

It is a whole minute before the woman who might be a servant feels the tug of urgency to leave before the show begins (the final bell has already rung; she didn't hear it). Shutting her eyes she sees, in the darkness, the shape of the figure in that gown and those opera gloves, in dizzying white this time. A negative vision. She suspects such a woman would never wear white.

Leaving the auditorium she stumbles down velvet-lined corridors, carrying a crumpled fur stole in her arms.

*

'Forty-two francs on a mouldy old hat! What?'

The chatter in the cloakroom is muffled by the dense weight of fabric hanging in racks along that tiny space. Squeezing through the heavy fur coats are the shapes of people at work, with their neat system for organising other people's finery.

'Keep an eye on that cane, Michelle: the one with the handle with the silver wings.'

'Funny request, God knows. Why doesn't he have it in there with him?'

A young man is sorting through yellow paper tickets, his tall frame stooping to the task, his fingers as fast and virtuoso as those of a concert pianist. 'Too vain to imply he needs a cane, is it? Or showing it's for fashion and he doesn't really need one?'

'Neither. It's at the request of his wife. He bangs it on the floor to applaud; she's asked us to keep it here for the good of her toes.'

The sound of the orchestra comes briefly louder as the door opens: it's the overture's opening notes, long and low. Then the door closes heavily, and a new figure arrives breathless into the cloakroom. Her arrival gains tuts and minor shakes of the head from those who are hanging coats and sticking numbered labels into top hat bands, as they realise they'll have more to do.

'What's that, another fur? I'm very low on space for more fur.'

'Which seat was it? Did you at least get the name?'

The young woman who looks like a servant holds out the scrunched fur stole. It looks more like she is delivering bed linen.

A cloakroom attendant gives her a sympathetic look from underneath hair that's all curls. 'You're the printer's girl, aren't you? Why were you even in the theatre?'

A different attendant strides through, all efficiency and briskness. 'Never mind that. What did they look like? For heaven's sake don't say grand and old, we'll be needing more.' Swift hands snatch away the fur in the hunt for a crest or embroidered initial. 'Aha! There. It must belong to Mme. Desmarchelier. Put it with the other unknowns on that pile there. *Someone* will ask for it back no doubt and we'll do our best then won't we, without a ticket, thank you for your assistance.' This is spoken to the young woman in the plain dress, the printer's girl. She can only blink a little in response, but in any case, everyone has already gone back to their own business.

The printer's girl, F., looks at her skirts and smooths her hands down over her hips, an action of familiarity—as if trying to ground herself. She looks at the one remaining copy of the new playbills she has just delivered, freshly printed—now folded and bent—as if it were a map, and indeed all its landmarks are familiar. The title of the opera is there in large bold letters, the name of the Opéra itself surrounded by arabesque patterns, the singers named in various sizes according to reputation, and several beady lines of print for the finer details. Finally, the new addition, in letters big enough to threaten the bottom half of the page: the name of the conductor.

The cloakroom attendant with the curls, passing by again with an armful of silk, sees the print and rolls her eyes. 'I heard about that,' she says. 'Made a fuss, didn't he? I heard him in Monsieur Vernon's office, shouting that his name should be right at the top.'

'This was the compromise.'

'Well, a fine reason for you to be scurrying across Paris!' She rolls up a customer's cloak and squashes it under her arm. 'I'm Michelle, by the way.'

A great orchestral climax registers here in the cloakroom only as a muffle, the cymbals reduced to a distant *fsssss*. Such a wave comes through while F. takes a breath, before asking the question:

'Who's the one in black on the balcony?'

'Aha!' cries a tall fellow, bounding in from some hidden corner of the cloakroom. He stands beside his colleague with the curls and they smile at each other, leaning closer in than they might. The action of an arm placed around a waist is not performed but the ghost of it hovers in the room, and F. realises she is interrupting.

'Plenty of them in black, out there,' he says. 'But I bet I know which one you're talking about.' The cloakroom pair share a look.

F. nods, waiting for an answer. She doesn't mind having been easy to read, this time.

'She's a bit like royalty, really,' the tall fellow begins.

'Ha! Only if the *demimonde* is a realm. They say the Belladonna was once a star soprano, though that was before my time. Now she's one of the Opéra's best patrons. She always attends an opening night.'

'She's secretly married to Monsieur Vernon,' he adds, and softly puts his arm around Michelle; clearly they feel in the presence of a friend here. 'Actually, take that with salt and pepper. I don't know if it's true.'

'Of course it's true! What else accounts for it, Gauvain?'

'But there's no advantage to her in *marrying* Monsieur Vernon.' They fall into a pattern; clearly, this to-and-fro has happened before. 'Why chain yourself to *anyone* if you're in her position?' says Gauvain. 'Let alone an Opéra manager.'

'I *do* know she's always slipping into his office, though.'

'Well, of course. She's saved him from bankruptcy. More than once.'

F. watches these rumours dance about. In her mind pulses the image: *the Belladonna*, high in that private box.

Michelle and Gauvain are still arguing. 'Suitors are queue-ing. We're forever taking flowers and gift-boxes up to her box. No secret husband is going to tolerate that!'

F. remembers the flash of those silver opera-glasses catching the chandelier's light. 'But her lovers do?'

'Everyone's obsessed.'

'Or they're jealous. Or can't afford the company.' Michelle twists a curl of hair behind her ear. 'She's not as intimidating as you might think, apparently. But even if she were the loveliest person in Paris, I'm sure I wouldn't want to be trapped in a champagne toast with *La Dame aux Morelles*, what on earth would you say to someone like that?'

Every fact from this pair begets more questions. F. is about to ask something else, but she is knocked sideways as two women, in the same dark clothing that marks them out as Opéra staff, burst in and announce there has been a dreadful spillage in the champagne bar, and they'll be needing additional hands. The team responds and F. quietly leaves, with Act One stretching before them and her new friends freed from any more questions, at least until the late arrivals need somewhere for their things.

*

F. loiters in the foyer, not quite ready to leave, and in any case she should find someone who looks suitably in charge to inform them the playbills are delivered. She runs a finger along a curved picture-frame hanging on the wall and ascends the great staircase, moving invisibly up towards the balcony levels, where a series of carved doors lead through to the theatre's higher views. There are still a few people leaning against the red damask walls, chatting and not going into their seats. Instead they are seen in their jewel-coloured evening gowns, gathering elegantly to discuss love and art and war and ambition.

F. tells herself she was star-struck, that was all. Now some time has passed since the hot stroke of the moment down there in the stalls, F. feels around for her sense of perspective. *You were swept away with society's own joy at itself, going along with the excitement of it. You should know better.*

She's a person who likes to be certain. And F. is certain that the woman in the finest private box in this great shimmering building knows things and with more surety than anyone else. For a moment she wanted all that for herself. *But anyone would.* You heard what they said a moment ago. Anyone. All of Paris. You're not immune. At least now, having gossiped in the cloakroom and noticed her ink-stained hands, she feels more herself again, and she is just about reconciled to it, when a young man in a grey evening jacket overtakes her at a rush.

She has to veer out of the way, suddenly losing a race she never signed up to enter. He carries something bulky under one arm. The drooping usher beside one of the doors suddenly undroops himself and pulls a formidable authority from somewhere, conjuring it from the very spirit of the building: he holds one arm out before him and stops the young man in his tracks. The tone of their argument is clear before F. catches up with them: the young man's desperate wheedling, the usher's regretful firmness. The young man is breathlessly hopping from foot to foot in his shiny shoes, practically bouncing with anticipation. The package he carries is covered with violet crepe paper and tied with a black ribbon, and he is waving it rather desperately in the face of the impassive senior usher.

'Please, I have to give this to her! I was late. My carriage—'

'She is not to be disturbed, especially now the performance has begun. I'm sorry.'

'She'll want this though! They're from the right place. I know she *always* accepts these, my friend told me—'

The usher continues to hold out an arm as if it were an iron bar across the young man's hopes. 'We do not allow guests to be barged in upon, sir.'

'But I want to give this to her.'

'I cannot allow that.'

'Why you—' the young man's temper flares like a struck match.

'I'll take it to her.' Both men turn towards this new voice.

F. sounds more confident than she is, and she certainly appears calm as she walks towards them. But remember: her heart is beating with a power to make her whole body chime.

That's the way to her. You know it is. Here's a chance to go to her.

'I'll take your gift, sir,' she says again, surprised at the levelness of her own voice.

The young man looks almost alarmed and the usher becomes even more stoic, calmly waiting as if to see what the next assault on common sense will be.

F. says, 'Michelle sent me. She's catching up with some business in the cloakroom. We've unfortunately lost Mme. Desmarchelier's fur.'

The usher's eyebrow rises by a fraction.

F. turns to the young man and tries to sound as if she has said these lines many times. 'If I may advise, I would perhaps say that if she doesn't wish to be interrupted, you'd best not. Assuming you care to do as she prefers.'

The young man nods, deferring to her apparent expertise.

'But I can pass on your gift. And if you like I can … tell her you'd appreciate a private meeting after. Since you were unable to secure one tonight.' She lets a smile flash over her features, a smile that says, *I wouldn't normally say this, but* … 'I'll make a special case for you.'

'Mademoiselle,' the usher begins, but the young man leaps at the opportunity our girl has apparently offered him.

'Of course and perfect and yes!' he cries. He fishes in his pocket for a handkerchief to mop his relieved face, words coming at a jabber. 'I'm so glad you're able to help, my card's in there for a meeting and—good!' The gift box is pushed into her arms, the violet crepe paper a sudden rough presence against her chest, and the young man is gone.

F. stands there, holding the gift box. It's only her and the usher now, and what she's done reveals its absurdity. The usher will be suspicious, probably minded to call the authorities, certainly he won't be letting her up.

Fool. What do you think you're trying to do?

The usher leans against the door, looking down at her as if from a great height.

'New, are you?' he says. Then, all at once, the fight seems to go out of him. He takes his glasses off and rubs one of the lenses, sighing in a manner of bone-deep exhaustion. 'Oh, rot it. She won't object to a present, I'm sure. One word of advice: you might want to paint a little less thick on further promises. She has her own people for that.' He puts his glasses back on and waves her through. 'Well, go on up then.'

She clutches the parcel to herself and doffs him a small curtsey as she passes—a formality from one member of staff to another, *we're just doing our jobs, after all*—which he accepts with a polite nod.

*

F.'s thoughts as she finds herself in a new dark corridor:

So, this is it. Your first sighting, and now to see her up close on the very same evening. Could the world already be adjusting its boundaries, rearranging the furniture, making space for her?

She carries the package through into the private box, heart pounding as her hand opens an intricately carved door, then pushes aside velvet curtains. Boundaries upon boundaries: she half expects there to be to be a gate beyond the curtain that lies beyond the door, and for its key to be far off at the bottom of a well.

In. The opera box is lined with gilt and velvet and warmly lit by subtle light, the lamps with their discreet goldness, hundreds all across the auditorium. The audience in this place are never fully in the dark, especially not those who sit in the balcony boxes. It's a given that they are on display as much as any of the performers, but perhaps even more so: for the singers at least have darkened narrow wings to run away and hide in, the occasional brief chance to catch their breath before facing the next round of scrutiny. To be here, in the most prestigious private box any opera house offers, is to be held in everyone's sights, while on stage the bright pantomime of the opera plays on.

A woman in a black dress sits in one of the throne-like chairs. Her gown dips like a blade at the back, revealing a bare neck and shoulders, and her hair is piled high and decorated with—some flora or other, it's difficult to make out in the semi-gloom. Our printer's girl approaches, the pull of this mysterious woman making it quite easy to ignore the immediate offended recoil of the man who is also here, who leaps back in his chair as if F. has aimed a rifle at him.

F. makes her voice muffled, hushed, appropriate to the environment, and manages to say: 'Excuse me, pardon me, but I was sent to deliver this to you.' She clings to the words like a lifeline. She doesn't yet know how much will hang on this first exchange, how much weight her words will be required to hold. The ignored man adjusts his medals and mutters something about propriety; the woman in the black dress turns around.

Her delicate neck, her composure of grace and poise—this could be prepared for, easily guessed from the sight of her at a distance. Likewise, it's no surprise to see the intricate pile-up of hair, shining black as if each tress were a precious item— and which now, on closer inspection, is decorated with clusters of small round berries and a spray of leaves that are pointed and sharp. The defined cheekbones in the delicate oval face make for the perfect balance of softness on sharpness; her lips, open slightly in surprise at the interruption, seem made for the speaking of delectable words: all of this is beauty, and it's gorgeous, wonderful, yes, but not, perhaps, surprising; not, perhaps, overpowering in itself. The charm of this woman is held, handled, level, and F. can understand it: a woman like this in a place like this. But nothing is preparation for the exact nature of her gaze, and our girl is lost—utterly *lost*—in that.

Pupils the size of the entire iris. Or irises the colour of pupils.

The eyes of the woman they call the Belladonna look out at the world from a pitch-black place, they are dark windows to nowhere, huge and unnerving. Her gaze has the power to pin an onlooker to the ground where she stands. It is unscrupulous, both inviting and impenetrable, at once wholly open and devastatingly unreadable.

'Did I not ask for privacy?' she says, although her voice has a playful flute to it, as if she is interested in the reason for the breach, not angered by it. The man beside her is willing to cover the latter reaction and speaks a sharp complaint in Russian.

Still unable to look away from those incredible eyes, in the back of F.'s mind a fact waves for attention and, the message delivered, her arms finally judder into action. Those eyes. She holds the box out, its violet paper sunken to dark grey in the gloom.

'An admirer was very insistent that I deliver this to you.'

The Belladonna takes the box and smiles with Christmas-morning joy, a finger already twirling one of the black ribbons.

'Ah! Sugared black grapes, my favourite. He—and you—are most welcome, I'm sure. Thank you for bringing this to me.'

A flicker of a pause. Enough time for the Belladonna to take in our girl; her eyes, as much as it's possible to tell what she's looking at, slowly pass down her body and back up again. 'You're not with the Opéra, are you?'

No point in lying. *I want you to know who I am.* 'I'm not with the Opéra.'

'Well then what are you doing in my box?' A small sparkle

flits across her face, and there's a slight widening of the eyes. The man beside her is signalling that he wants this imposter removed. The Belladonna stops him with a lazy gesture. 'Might I ask how you came to be here?'

Little value in lying, but no need to open up about her simply risking a chance. She might object to that, and it would surely send the Russian beside her into a paroxysm.

'You were in need of me,' says F. There: that's true enough.

Her lips open, purse for a moment. 'I see.'

It is amusement. Barely detectable. It's probably amusement. It could be offence.

The Belladonna's hands pull languidly at the black ribbon around the box. According to the job, F. should really be making to go now the package is delivered.

Those impossible eyes take in F.'s hands. 'You're awfully smudged.'

'I'm sorry?'

'The ink on your hands. Have you been writing many letters?'

'Only delivering them.'

She looks down at the box of sweets, a merciful break from her stare. 'I empathise. I practise calligraphy, myself; take my advice and wear gloves. Especially black gloves. No sins show then.' She examines the crepe paper and nods, satisfied. 'You didn't get any on my present, at least. So that's something.'

The Russian's arms fling themselves up in exasperation as if to say, *Just how long are you going to chat merrily away to this interloper sent from a rival?* At this, the Belladonna seems to come back to herself, and responds as if to a cue. She taps him on

13

the shoulder and says, 'Will you go and tell the gentleman outside to call my carriage? Let's leave the Opéra and take in a more lengthy supper.'

He glares at F. as he leaves, not resenting her personally so much as the entire world she represents. While the gold beads on the curtain are still shaking from his rapid exit, the Belladonna leans forwards and looks at F. again.

'If you call on me another time, I hope you'll look after your hands. Or will this visit be enough for you? Have you seen what you needed to see?'

F. swallows, back in the prison of this direct look, which surely misses nothing.

'I ...'

'What is your name?'

'Flora.' It's an instinct: flinching from the woman's gaze and taking honesty with it. Honesty seems too exposing. So, an idea borne from those sharp leaves in her hair. It will do.

The Belladonna throws her head back to laugh. It's almost mocking but for the genuine happiness there in her open mouth, her closed eyes. (Her bared throat; except for the rope of black pearls around it.)

'How refreshing you are! I like you. Welcome back darling. Ready in one moment.'

The Russian re-enters the box, stalking in with a face of thunder. He sits down heavily and puts his feet up over the balcony. He might as well be waiting for a delayed train.

She, the Belladonna, seems content to ignore this small show of petulance. 'Flora, come here. I'd like to ask you something.'

She points with her full arm out over the balcony, drawing

our ink-smudged F.'s attentions to one of the more crowded boxes at the other side of the stage. A man in navy military dress is surrounded by young women and girls in dresses like white foam.

'Do you see him?'

'Yes.'

'That's the Grand-Duke Millares. From here, can you make out that shine on his breast-front pocket?'

At the far side of the Opéra. Away and oblivious to the scrutiny coming at him, Millares reaches out to pat one of the children lovingly on the head, and yes, something glitters there.

'That,' says the Belladonna, and she might almost be running her tongue delightedly around the words, 'is a diamond brooch, star shaped: a family heirloom belonging to his late first wife. They say he sleeps with it under his pillow.' She turns and aims her disconcerting gaze directly at F. 'How would you get it from him?'

It's as if a knife has been drawn, this sudden sharp scrutiny. F. backing away from it: 'I'm sorry?'

'And no cheating: you're not allowed to steal it, that's too easy. He has to *want* to give it to you. How would you do it?' A pause draws itself out. After a moment she adds, as if it remotely explains things: 'I like to know people who are capable of miracles.'

The Russian sighs and flops his crossed legs over again, but this goes unremarked. F. looks out at the far balcony.

Play along. And don't keep her waiting.

The Belladonna's fingers, sleek in black silk gloves, begin to tap, ever so gently, on the gilt edge of the balcony. Impatience.

Go on!

'Well …' F. frowns a little, feeling it out. 'You'd have to find out what he's willing to swap it for. Something he desperately wants. To prove his word, settle a bet, hush something down, avoid a difficulty. *That's* what I'd need to find out, what he wants … if I can do *that*, I can have your brooch here for you.'

The Belladonna nods once, some brief encouragement, but she is clearly also following the movements of the dancers down on the stage. Her attentions are being gradually sucked away from F., who tries to carry on and rallies herself, finding the thought experiment quite pleasing.

'How to find out what he wants … ? I would suppose a man like that is in no need of funds; couldn't make him pawn that brooch out of desperation for money. Or perhaps, actually, that would be the answer exactly: he could always be predictable and have a secret gambling habit, that shouldn't be too difficult to learn about.'

An image passes her vision, locks this plan into place: she knows who she'd ask, there's a boy at the print-house whose uncle has access to someone who'd know. She warms to the theme, working through different ways to obtain the brooch, slotting options in various orders like neat blocks of type.

'Or, his weak spot may be something more benign. Perhaps he cares deeply for the plight of the poor, or, even better! he wants to be *seen* to be. Or he wants to support a local beloved vineyard, various reasons for that, loyalty or love or shame or various deadly habits. So for that I might mention a new charity just sprung up, drop the names of those already courting to patron us, see if he takes to that bait. Ask for physical proof for the downpayment … ah, that might not be so plausible. Maybe—' Mentally she spills the typing blocks about again and prepares another arrangement.

'How would you get near him?' asks the Belladonna, her attentions still mainly on the stage below. 'How do you imagine being able to drop all these fine names about the place?'

This is so easily answered F. has to bite back on her surprise, lest she begin to sound too sure of herself.

'I can pass for an attendant dressed like this. I expect I could pass for much. Walk with the right amount of purpose, crack my voice with the right amount of desperation. Make it easy for people to let me through. If I were going over there right now, from here, I'd near enough burst into the box. Make it seem as if I only had a few moments before I were asked to leave. And there'd be a truth to that.' F. can picture herself strolling back into the Belladonna's box and presenting an envelope, the fine lady reaching into it and pulling out the brooch, slowly turning it over: the gleam of those diamonds against her black silk gloves. 'Only a small seed, you'd have to plant. If you knew what he wanted the most.'

'Mmm.' The Belladonna seems to be getting bored. She pulls open the lid of the box, then beams at the candies beneath. 'Oh, very good! This young man may certainly call on me again.' She picks up his card from within the folds of tissue paper, tilts her head like a bird to examine the name. With the other hand she gestures for Flora to keep talking.

'It might not work at one go, of course.' She can almost see it: the Grand-Duke desperately plucking the brooch from his jacket, accidentally pulling a thread from the lining, and presenting her, F., with the brooch, in a manner that tells her this is the last, most precious thing he could give. That would be very dramatic, but F. is one for practicalities. 'It might be many weeks, even knowing his weak spot. A man as protected as that. It could take some time to make him feel trapped into giving it up.'

'Mmm.' The Belladonna picks up her opera-glasses, swings them open again.

'It seems I … perhaps I could—'

The Russian prince laughs and says something very much *not* to F., gesturing to the Belladonna's opera glasses. She accepts his comment graciously, responds with a few phrases of her own. F. feels herself being pushed out of their private room, hears the click of a door locking.

So it was a game. You were an amusement and now she's tired of you.

'Of course there's always the long-lost relative angle,' she says, but she can feel herself flailing.

Whispers, then; the sound of actual whispers. The Belladonna is leaning towards her male companion, and he is mirroring the action; they form a close-knit company together, they are whispering to each other—our printer's girl hears more soft laughter.

A heat rises beneath her thoughts. Why *ask* at all, just to ignore the answer? This is someone very used to people jumping about at her whim. Somehow the indignity of this truth, of the Belladonna's sudden waning attention so soon after it was given, puts F. in a fit of annoyance. F.'s voice takes on a steely edge. She practically balls her hands into fists as she says: 'Or perhaps I could simply tell him *you* want it. That should work, no?'

Those dark infinite eyes look back again towards her. A moment stretches out, alongside the tenor's final note below. As the applause ripples politely through the stalls, she says: 'Thank you for the entertainment, Pallidiflora. You may go.'

Leaving the box she hears laughter, a silvery sound of excitement and, she hates that she recognises it, relief. She turns back at the curtain to see the two of them leaning in towards each other, speaking closely, their attentions totally upon each other, intimate and secret. The opened sweets box sits abandoned by their feet on the floor.

*

F. has dreams about the brooch, about dropping it into the Belladonna's lap. She has made the decision that she doesn't care at all, and she's certainly not to blame; people like that will have their fun and she was taken aback, briefly, in the moment. But she has recovered from that, because she is sensible.

But the dream says: you haven't recovered, and you're not that sensible.

In the dream she sees her in a monstrously large version of the Opéra lounge, a glittering centre of gravity as tall and thin as a blade, her black gown a streak of night-time among a crowd of admirers in garish colours. F. approaches her from behind, noticing her sweeping hair piled high, the paleness of her neck and shoulders. She imagines standing by the wall, watching the group who surround the Belladonna, knowing their bright chatter to be exquisitely cultured, refined, calculated to amuse—and the Belladonna turns, catches F.'s eye, and the movement of her glass being raised is so tiny, we can't quite be sure she made it at all. What we do know is an unknown passage of time clouds over until a heavy bell suggests the opera is about to recommence. And then, we are in the box, and here is the presentation of the envelope.

'You have it.' Belladonna stares down at the brooch, a bright piece of the heavens held in her gloves of midnight. 'You brought it for me.'

'Of course,' comes the reply. F. can hear herself saying it, far more casually than she could ever manage in real life. 'You asked me to.'

Even in this impossible dreamland she half expects the Belladonna to take it in her stride, throw the brooch away and say *now for the real challenge*.

And yet, as she reaches into the envelope and pulls the brooch out, and slowly turns it—once more the gleam of those diamonds against her black silk gloves—F. knows Belladonna's absolute surprise; she can taste it, vivid on her tongue like ice. When she wakes up, which always happens shortly after this, she'll chastise herself for getting pulled under again. But in the moment there's no denying it.

Belladonna looks up at her in the dream, and those bottomless eyes widen in surprise. She gets the brooch out of the envelope and turns it in her hands. The dream can keep the turning going on for eternity.

'You brought it to me,' she says.

And F. nods and says: 'Of course. You asked for it.'

II

F. is working at the printing press when the letter comes. It's an important moment for her, and not only because its appearance ushers her into a new world. But because it is her first glance at the signature.

She is lining up her blocks, concentration narrowed to metal ridges and tiny lettered walls, when she becomes aware of the whispers, of her colleagues gathering around her. Suddenly by her side is a stiff-looking gent, his silver waistcoat buttons bearing the crest of the Opéra. He presents the letter sealed with a small blob of dark wax. A looping hand on the front spells out her real name.

'Says here I've to give it to you personally.'

You brought it to me.

Breaking the wax and unfolding the rich paper is the work of a moment and the other apprentices gather, watching beadily from within the shadows of the churning rollers. Her eye is drawn, before any of the content, to the great B, after which the rest of the letters follow naturally as a river. The word sits purple-black on the thick, expensive ink with a deepness to the tone, practically still glinting; if she were to tilt the paper surely the name would run and drip into a dark pool on the dusty floor. The signature carries the quality of having been done quickly without a thought, which only adds to its authority. F. could no more disobey its summons than she could pin it to the moon.

*

The brasserie is busy, which is not unusual for this hour of night. Customers sit in lines along the tables, chattering over their bowls and plates, bread and wine, seated with people they didn't arrive with; the hubbub of gossip, of old and new acquaintances. Soft spots of light are held by brass fixtures, and a rail runs along the place, bulky with customers' hats and coats. F. is heading towards a table at the back; the waiter looks sceptical, but leads her there.

Here the noise is a little more muted, for parties that wish to remain on their own terms and can happily pay for it. The Belladonna, all in black, is sitting alone at a round table set for a dozen.

They are shrouded by the play of shadows, the subtle café light glinting off the cutlery and clean white plates rimmed with gold. There is a spray of violets in the centre.

And the Belladonna is smiling at F.; no question of that. And the smile is beaming, wide, glowing beneath a ghostly skin. It's as meaningful and sincere a smile as F. has yet seen from her, even accounting for those eyes that make every expression too heightened to be real. It is unclear if her eyes also smile. Distracted by this thought F. stalls, then makes a hedged move to sit across: which would put her miles away on the other side of the table. Rescue comes with a gesture of an arm, once more clad in opera gloves, motioning for F. to sit beside her.

'Wouldn't have you come all this way,' the Belladonna says, as F. sits, 'for you to then sit over there. I'd be squinting at you.'

F. moves a fine-pronged fish-fork a little with one finger. '*Je vous remercie*, though I should let you know,' she says. 'My employers haven't been delighted to receive personal messengers at their premises.'

'So may I thank you for coming.'

'My real name on the envelope—'

'Well, you're getting straight down to business. It was easy enough to obtain it.'

F.'s internal compass spins; she must take care, or she may be thrown off course. She may not be, she realises, master of this conversation: she must work to be even an equal party. Otherwise she might as well have been bunched up in one of the brass coat racks for the Belladonna's convenience.

'Only to say that it was somewhat strange, seeing it addressed that way,' she says. 'I haven't gone by that name for a long time.'

'Well I apologise for that; in response I might wonder why you came into my private box and then didn't give me any of your names. But there is no great mystery in how I found that one, and it seems to have done the trick. First off, I'm quite good at seeking out people I want to find. Secondly, lest that make me sound overly vigilant, there really aren't many printing houses in Paris that cater to the Opéra. It became a matter of asking the right people the right questions. And I only know the right people.'

She can't imagine it, this woman setting an investigation into her, however leisurely it may have been conducted. 'Tell me what happens now you've found me.'

The Belladonna's face does something strange at this point, but it is a strangeness F. will find difficult to explain to herself later on, trying to pinpoint exactly what happened, how it moved her. In effect she looks at F. calmly and with a gaze of quiet interest; but it is not, or not only, the gaze of one waiting for a respected acquaintance to speak, or even a dear friend. It is a deeply personal gaze, of an intensity that is impossible to shake, and it wraps around F.'s awareness of herself. The effect is that, if only for this moment, you're the only person in the world the Belladonna would dream of talking to.

'Yes dear, we'll come to that.' She takes a moment's pause. 'When I asked you that question about the brooch, you spoke of leveraging desires. And, do you know? I liked that.'

'That's curious. I thought the opposite. Or that you weren't interested.'

'My darling, I can spin more than one plate. I was listening, but I had to keep that gentleman onside.' She runs a silken finger around the rim of her glass. 'Wouldn't do to make him feel there was a joke he wasn't in on.' She looks at—into—F. again. 'I'd hate to feel a door was closed to me. Wouldn't you agree there's nothing worse?'

F. thinks. *How to survive this?* 'There's value in negotiating your place. It can teach you something.'

'You're trying to tell me the right story, aren't you? Very good. But I've seen a side to you already and I'm not entirely convinced. I don't think you appreciate a barrier any more than I.' She shrugs, without breaking her gaze. 'But either way.'

F. casts a glance about. Usually she'd expect to be bothered by a waiter by now and nudged into placing an order, beneath a suspicious frown that doubts her ability to pay. It feels like quite a power for them to be left alone.

'An honest occupation isn't easy to come by. I should feel lucky,' says F., 'to be working at the print house.'

'You should, but you don't. I can see it doesn't suit your gifts. Not all of them, anyway.'

'I don't expect my work to give me everything.'

It's true, there's a tranquillity to working with thousands of metal letters, lining them up to give neat meaning to things. But that's too intimate a detail to tell her now. It might reveal too much.

'Lack of expectation is a curse. I'd never recommend it.' The Belladonna leans in a little, her raised eyebrows opening her face further to the question. 'Why skulk about the Opéra unless you're seeking excellence?'

F. feels her own defensiveness as a rising heat. *But remember: she asked you to come here.*

She does not say how she came to be in the theatre at all, stomping into the stalls of the greatest opera house in the city, and on an opening night, of all the nights to choose. How she'd come from the long room with its low beams and air full of dust and ink, churning metal and wood, the blocks of paper. How she'd run through Paris bearing the playbills, the ink still fresh, how she'd squeezed through heaving crowds outside the theatre, getting splashed by the horses who stomp in the puddles. Through the foyer, its great marble columns and shimmering gilt becoming a blur, no time to admire that luxury now—through the doors into the stalls (a rich old woman dumping her fur stole into her arms, identifying her as staff by her quick walking pace, but monstrously confusing the role)—and finally, fulfilling the errand she came here for, with a single heaving heartbeat; giving the papers triumphantly, and with no time to spare, to the conductor who'd demanded his name in larger letters, his face still stuck in its rictus of desperate waiting.

So, F.'s dash to the Opéra, determination packed down neatly like the papers she carried; F. running through the theatre foyer and into destiny. Taking a moment, finally, to look across the heat and plush of the theatre, spinning a little and craning her head back to take in the whole place and then, her eye caught by a movement, the briefest of glances up to the box.

And there.

The sight of La Dame aux Morelles high up in the balcony, and F.'s desperate reach towards prettier dreams.

Wishing you would search me out. And you did.

But the Belladonna needn't know that, not in this moment. *Keep your cards close, or she'll have you well-marked.* F. swallows the memory down and says: 'I had to be there on a professional errand. I was as obliged to be at the Opéra as you were.'

'Ah, but you absolutely, positively did not *have* to be in my box, as I did. That decision was all yours.'

'Someone needed to deliver your gift ... ' *That* story trails off under the darkly infinite gaze. F. knows they're not talking about sugared fruit. 'And I wanted to be the one to do it. Everyone was staring up at you. I wanted to know exactly who they were looking at.'

'They do enjoy a display. Opéra nights can be demanding in that way.' She looks down at her plate. The effect is of coyness, but the precision is uncanny.

'So now you've seen me, *exactly*, you can go back to your print shop satisfied.' She asks the next question down to the plate. 'Or are we missing something?'

F. waits, some invisible force pressing her into the chair.

'I have been thinking upon a certain matter,' the Belladonna says quietly. 'I wouldn't say I'm wanting. Nor would I say that I'm disorganised, or lonely. I'm not one to wait and certainly I'm not lacking. But when one is always in demand of one sort or other and I've said as much before, quality requires its maintenance. And more's the matter, it can be much nicer if there's someone else to share the blame.'

She adjusts her necklace.

'I have people informally of course, but they come and go. I want to formalise it. It's time; it seems to be time.' A sigh is arrested before it begins, then she continues: 'It'll be a role that pays, of course; more, I expect, than you're getting plodding away at paper. I can't promise it won't be demanding. And it may not offer you everything. Although you tell me you don't mind at least a bit of that.'

The world turns; ideas shift and shuffle.

'I need to know you would be passionate about the idea of such a position. After that, well, there's plenty to explain, but if you're interested in the *sense* of it, that's the most important thing. All else follows.'

F. had come here expectantly—to what end she did not know, perhaps exile. Perhaps a city-wide test to scrape the barrel of her moral character; she'd already stooped to depriving a duke of his prize jewels. Instead she finds the key to the city pressing its weight into her palm.

The Belladonna's gaze remains downcast as she speaks. 'I've often said to girls, "oh yes, bring me Millares' star and it will prove you love me," and anyone who answers as you have is someone I can trust. Or at least someone who'll be afraid of losing my trust.'

F. tries to take everything in. There must be something hidden away. You don't simply receive such an invitation.

'So perhaps you'll work for me,' says the Belladonna. 'And we see a lot more of each other. What do you think?'

She raises her eyes and looks straight at F. The effect is extraordinary. The Belladonna has the ability to make her face into the plainest of masks, a look almost melancholy in its devotion, straight into you, to hold the two of you alone, together, at the centre of the universe.

She keeps the gaze a moment longer, not letting F. off the butcher's hook of it. And breath *does* catch. This is a gaze that says: *that* was all a social performance, everything I did before. And wasn't it good. But what you're seeing now, this is me. All for you. Yours.

'It's like …' F. breathes, the statement trailing off before it can even be unsaid, and her heartbeat makes itself more known in her chest.

The slightest raise of an eyebrow: *It's like what?*

Adrenalin shoots. Her heartbeat becomes a source of power, an urge: say it.

'It's like—'

Say it.

'You look like—'

She knows the words she wants to say, but her throat has become a hard lump, and the words have clustered together on the furthest side of it.

Her face waits impassively, gorgeously impassively. 'Yes?'

F. opens her mouth, and in spite of her common sense about what sort of conversation the Belladonna must surely be used to, an urgent admission dives between her thoughts and her tongue.

Don't: you'll have her running from the place.

But then she is looking deeply into F. again and how, how can it be ambiguous?

F. says it, all at once: 'It's like you want to kiss me.'

A pause. The moment beats, like the pulse in F.'s neck.

The Belladonna's face maintains that impassivity for a long moment, then her brow furrows a little. It is about to knock her expression into total confusion, as if F. has just announced that the opera house has been built upside-down, with a large lake in the roof.

'What do you mean?'

'Sorry. I didn't mean. Excuse me. I shouldn't have spoken. It's just … when you look at me like that. It feels very particular.'

The Belladonna laughs, the peal of a bell, closing her eyes and bringing her hand up somewhat self-consciously to her hair.

'I have a somewhat intense stare, you mean? Oh yes, there's truth to that.' She smooths a tress of hair down, lending deliberation to what was—for a moment, F. was certain— genuine disorientation. 'But I believe it's a common reading of that expression: don't worry that you've overstepped. It's not that I'm not listening, or listening too much, I find it's a side effect of the …' she performs a gesture that seems to encompass her whole head. '*Visage.*' She looks at the jar of violets and narrows her eyes. 'Hmm. Does it also work on flowers? Can I get them to wilt right now, do you think?'

F. feels quite boneless with relief. She too looks into the forest of stems, that in the candlelight seem to dance about, waving at them both. The relief makes her brave.

'You'll have to teach me how to do it,' she says. 'Despite my best efforts, sometimes my thoughts can be easier to read than I'd wish for.'

'That won't do at all, in our line of work. But I can teach you.'

'Not that I could ever do it like you.' Come to that, F. wonders if she would want to. Powerful as those eyes are, don't they hurt?

The Belladonna draws herself up straight, putting aside any further discussion about the power of her face and how it sits.

'Now, I'm thinking that I want this to happen quickly. Sometimes, you see, I decide on something and become terribly impatient. Can we move you in tomorrow?—or, that might be too soon but I'd rather it were days than weeks—' As she goes—rattling off dates and times, gradually squeezing the days closer until yes, *yes*, why *not* tomorrow?—she pats her hands elegantly onto the table, as if approving a signed contract. Although they are alone within the busy restaurant there is something public, ceremonious, about the gesture, and there is a feeling of ribbon cut with scissors, polite applause from an assembled audience. They have moved from the intimacy of a meeting between the two of them into something much more far-reaching, something momentous.

The rain has become heavier by the time F. leaves the brasserie, and she passes the windows smudged and glowing with warmth and activity. Her mind busily replays events as she walks, searching for mistakes and potential slip-ups, and as she makes her way through the overflowing gutters the evening is rewritten as a patchwork of regrets and misfired comments. And yet. The result. The agreement; the arrangement—the decision that she will visit the Belladonna at her private apartments tomorrow as a forerunner, gloriously, to *becoming her companion*—this cannot be distorted by memory, the result cannot be budged. It glows steadily from beneath the dark spots that make up the rest of her recollection of the meeting, immutable and true.

She only thinks lightly about how she never actually *said*: '*Yes, I'll do it, I'll come to you, and let it be tomorrow.*' The world simply changed around her, a cloth thrown up, and as it settled into a new configuration this was where she happened to be. This is how things are laid out, now.

The journey home takes no time at all, in spite of the rain—in weather like this the long walk would normally be interminable. But time has galvanised itself and she barely notices returning home, climbing the endless rickety stairs, or pulling off her shift; all she wants is the flat comfort of a bed coming up to meet her, at last.

But it won't happen that way. There is someone she needs to talk to. Who is currently sitting up in the bed, waiting for her to come home, like they usually do.

*

'If you take the role, what happens to all this?'

A hand gestures in the darkness at the room, which exists, for now, in this slice of time before dawn, long before the morning peers in properly. Many hours lie ahead, mercifully free of either the print house, or will it be the opera house?— and here are two bodies, loosely entwined on a bed, discussing the future. The stillness of this hour comes in through the rafters, dressed as chilly moonlight. We are in a high attic room, somewhere in a poor part of Paris. The room is cheaply lived in: this is clear from the mess, picked out in silhouette. There is a chipped basin, a water jug of burnished copper, a pile of old skirts to make do for towels. An hour unlike any other: the piano bars have stopped; the night owls have left. If either of the bodies on the bed were to stand, go to the window and peer down into the Paris street, they might see a few early risers picking their way along the roads. But the bustle of the city's nightlife has paused for a moment and Paris sits expectantly, waiting for the day to stretch over it. Entwined on a cheap bed, it is the time for conversations like this one.

'This work, it's not so easy. You'll be living there. You won't be free to decide what to do in the same way.'

'I know it will be different …'

'But what I really need to know is what happens to us?'

No pretending this time. F. has an ache in her wrist from supporting her head, but there is such intimacy in facing each other this way, postures mirrored across the bed. It would be unthinkable to do something as drastic as, say, rolling over onto her back and bringing that to an end.

'I suppose,' she says, slowly, 'we'd take things where we could.'

'You suppose,' says the other person. 'Would I see you at all?'

The silence stretches out between them.

And here, it is F.'s lover who breaks the position, flopping down onto the threadbare pillow. 'I fear this will be our last night together.'

F. pulls herself forwards and wraps her arms around her lover's trembling body, which is giving out heat like a furnace. F. likes that quality. She herself is usually the cold one. Their bodies press closely together.

'I might not actually move as soon as she wants—'

'It doesn't matter when it happens,' comes the rejoinder, from a head pressed firmly into F.'s chest. 'Things are changing.'

'You're asking me not to do it.'

'Don't say nonsense. This *grand dame* won't keep you around if you go about saying nonsense.'

F.'s lover sits up on the bed, and F. follows. The blueness of the dawning sky comes in at the window. The light troubles their eyes as they crane their necks up to look, but it's a welcome respite from staring at each other for a moment.

The lover runs a hand across F.'s back. 'I'm not asking you for anything.'

The hand over her back trails up and down.

'Of course you're going to take it, and perhaps you won't be able to see me, at least not in the same way. But I know that if you didn't, and stayed, how much you'd resent me for that. We wouldn't want to be together in that knowledge.'

F. nods. 'I will still see you.'

'I don't know how that can be true. Although I'd rather it was.'

F.'s voice is barely above a whisper. 'I love you.'

'I know. You'll soon be attending all manner of splendid occasions. It will be wonderful for you.'

F. begins to say, 'Please,' but her voice is stopped by a sudden movement as her lover leaps onto her, hugging her tightly, and F. is pressed down onto the dull mattress. The springs push into her back.

The blue morning shows some mercy; time lingers in that bedroom for longer than anyone would have thought natural. It is as if the clock paused itself to observe, keeping the night in a suspended state. In the darkness F. raises her face and tears run down it.

'You know I have to,' she says, through a voice that chokes and wavers.

Her lover has a hold of her hips. 'I do, but that doesn't make it any easier for me.'

F. snaps, with a strength of resolution that surges up like a wave. 'I can't just stay here and keep to what I know. I have to at least try. I want to see.'

Her lover says, '*Shh*,' but not loud enough for F. to hear. Eventually F. comes back into the embrace, and her breathing turns into something calm and regular. She has loved, confessed, betrayed her way to sleep, her lover knows, stroking F.'s hair and watching the shadows of the room around them.

In the morning they dress silently. At the door, F.'s lover turns and leans against the frame. 'I hope this works out for you. I really do.'

'We can make a plan to meet once everything's settled.'

'No, stop saying that. This can't be a goodbye like that.'

They watch each other.

F. breaks the silence. 'What will you do?'

'I'll write to my brother. He's always said there's rooms if I'm in need. Well, I'll take the bed space and see how long I can put up with him while I find something. Don't worry.'

'I'll write to you,' says F. 'I'll tell you everything that goes on, and I bet I can find a way to bring you in.'

'I will say this,' says F.'s lover, making a point of ignoring such promises. 'You're willing to give up a lot for this woman. Be careful. Not many people will do the same for you. Don't let her take advantage. Keep hold of who you are.'

What's this? Keep hold of the person who just broke two hearts for the sake of a ride in a carriage and the chance to deliver more love tokens for someone else? That person? Oh yes, I'll want to keep a tight hold of that one.

'I *will* write to you,' F. says.

But she knows there can be no pretence: the pale sunlight seems to lift the cobblestones and shines on the old wine barrels in the street, standing in a row outside the building where they no longer live. F. pushes a tress of hair from her face—it is already escaping her plait, done in a rush.

F.'s lover has gathered any remaining possessions into a small bundle, wrapped in a woollen cloak against the chill. F. watches them disappear through the crumbling buildings. It had only ever been a temporary arrangement, perhaps due to run its natural course soon enough anyway … The sunlit cobblestones are suddenly blurring in F.'s vision, and her eyes are hot, brimming with tears.

But remember the Belladonna's eyes.

She goes upstairs, sits on the bed and knows she won't come back here again. But then the dull sadness clears before her to reveal a stretch of excitement and anticipation, clear as water. She's doing what is needed. And she will be the Belladonna's companion, there to do what needs to be done.

*

The apartments are to be found on the top floor of the grand hotel, which is called, extremely suitably, Le Grand Hôtel, a gilded stone's throw from the Opéra itself and tended at all times by dozens of staff in starched black and white. F.'s first thought is that it hardly seems worth the cost to insist on the top floor, if those thick damask curtains are always to be kept closed. At all times it might as well be the middle of the night. The apartments are lit by candles and lowered gas lamps, giving the atmosphere a delicate fuzz. It's not only to flatter, as F. begins to understand. There are costs to having such sensitive eyes.

The Belladonna greets F. 'The preparations went smoothly, I hope?' she asks, taking her through to the drawing-room, gown trailing behind her. She is already dressed for an evening soiree.

F. remembers her lover. She nods. 'I'm all here,' she says. 'I'm all yours.'

'Very good.'

Without too much ceremony, the Belladonna gives a brief tour. The apartments. High ceilings, bouquets freshly delivered, chandeliers, grand piano in the salon room, enough floor space to cartwheel in. Yes, yes. And then?

'*Very* special clientele make their way here,' she adds, leading the way into the bedroom.

The bedroom. How many gifts are given, invitations sought, parties crashed, from the desire to know what happens in here? Over the threshold. There: now you know her.

No delicate interior design in the bedroom, unlike in the rest of the apartments—where entertainments may be as respectable as they are refined. No. The bedroom has more of a gravity to it, as if the room could sink under its own weight. Dominating it is a four-poster with curtains and canopy of fine black, tied off to one side to reveal sheets and pillows of silk, a dark blackish-purple. A finely painted mural of a monstrous plant almost entirely covers the far wall.

'That's an impressive picture,' says F., her eyes flickering over the branches, calculating the painter's time with each delicate twig—then she realises the Belladonna beside her is saying nothing, only smiling. She's waiting for something. F. looks again at the plant and in the semi-darkness La Dame aux Morelles always lives in, her mind fights against seeing the truth of what is there.

Finally F. sees it, or her mind allows her to.

It is not a painting. On the far side of the bedroom is a black wooden cabinet, on which sits a monstrous growth of deadly nightshade. The leaves have spikes, the flowers look like monstrous dark tulips.

La Dame claps softly in her silk gloves when she sees F. get it, then she leads her through another door. F. follows, but keeps her eye on the plant for as long as she can.

The spacious dressing-room is larger than F.'s entire

allocated bedroom. Adjoined to the Belladonna's private chamber is an architectural shrine to the idea of the wardrobe, the walls completely lined with black gowns in rich fabrics: lace, silk, beaded velvet. The deep black-on-blackness of the formal gowns with their jet beads and dark pearls. An array of boxes open forth to display diamonds, jet, opals, concoctions of glean and shine; moonstone and amethyst, some set in silver, some in ebony; necklaces and brooches made from thin cast iron, delicate as lace: recurring across the jewellery is the sharp leaf of nightshade, the roundness of the berry. Feathers, plucked from songbirds, for the hair when stepping out; the cloak, a whole swirling cloud of it, for visiting the Opéra. Mirrors throughout the room gleam back an endless display of this opulence, and the full-length one shows F. as she stares.

'There's a drawer of wrist-length gloves at the back,' says the Belladonna, standing behind her, watching her admire the clothes. 'Take a pair for yourself.'

That's the first thing F. learns about being the companion. For the Belladonna herself, opera gloves are an integral part of the silhouette. For the companion: black gloves to the wrist. Soon she'll barely know her hands without them.

Back in the bedroom, the Belladonna explains the routine: the visits from the hair-stylist, the daily walks in the late afternoons, the nocturnal patterning of the hours.

And: 'We tug that for the concierge,' she says, gesturing idly to the pair of bell-pulls in the corner. 'The purple one.' It is made of damask silk, fringed at the edge.

F. swallows, distracted by the second bell-pull, the black one: little more than a skinny, fraying strand of rope with a knot at the end like a fist. 'And the other one?'

'That's for emergencies only. And—mark it—only to be pulled by the Belladonna. Think of it as a private alarm. It's more for show than for use, to be honest I doubt it is still connected to anything. Remove part of your dress for me, I want to get to your arm,' she adds, gesturing for F. to leave the bedroom. Behind F., she walks about, to the far end of the room and back again; there is a faint sound of silk.

And F. suddenly feels a gentle touch, barely a tickle, floating across her upper arm.

It becomes a patch of hot pain. She looks down, too surprised to cry out.

A faint red mark is visible, spreading even as she watches. A pain borne from such a gentle, intimate touch.

'What was that?'

The Belladonna there, brandishing one of the leaves from the plant. F. rubs the burning mark on her skin and stares at her, stunned.

'Even the leaves hurt,' she explains, slowly and carefully, as if delineating the rules of the house: the washing goes *here*, the coal is kept *here*, gloves to the *wrist*, and now let us briefly discuss the plants. 'So don't even brush up against it. Keep your distance until we can agree you know what you're doing.'

F. finds some words for response, clasps desperately at them. 'You wear those on your dress? In your hair?'

She looks at the plant. *You harvest it, knowing it does that to skin?*

La Dame aux Morelles shakes her head. Her voice has a smile to it. 'The ones I wear,' she says, 'are not real.'

F. runs a hand over the mark on her arm. It is still red but the burning has softened into a tingling wash. The pain is intense and short-lived.

The Belladonna breaks into a fluting laugh. 'I'm not about to hurt myself in the name of decoration. Remember our role here.' She takes F.'s hand in hers, then presses her silken fingers cold and soothing against F.'s burning skin. 'The effect is what we're after.'

*

F. prepares for her first evening accompanying the Belladonna to see a select group of friends, a meeting for supper and fine conversation, and an easy first experience for F. as she'll mainly have to be quiet, when a letter arrives bearing the Opéra crest.

'Well he's awfully keen,' La Dame aux Morelles says, when F. brings the letter to her. She is sitting at the dressing-table, clustered with powders and brushes and crystal vials of scent. 'I thought he might at least wait until tomorrow.'

'Who?'

'Monsieur Vernon of course. You can call him Vernon too. He'll answer to M. Vernon or Vernon, but nothing else.'

'So Vernon is his family name?'

'He likes that nobody is certain.'

'Do you know?'

'No one does. Or if I once did, I've forgotten.' The Belladonna smiles. 'In time you'll forget you don't know his real name. The point is, I mentioned your coming over; it seems he wants to meet you straight away. Tell you what: get ready now, go and see him, and come and join me at the brasserie after.

We'll inform the carriage of the route.'

A personal summons from Monsieur Vernon! Now, *that's* news. An event to turn any gradually settling perspective upside-down yet again. Manager of the Opéra; the one everyone thinks the Belladonna has secretly married. Although F. doubts this can be true, it's impossible not to feel at least some ceremony as she knocks on the door to his office, that space so central to many of the whispers.

He is hard at work, the wide desk filled with papers. He looks up and smiles.

'Watch yourself standing there in the doorway! You'll get carted off and stored with the props if you keep standing there like a cut-out.'

This is M. Vernon, master of ceremonies, whose life, he would have acquaintances believe, is akin to being ringmaster of a frantic circus, and his role a risky high-wire act all of its own. But he has more control than that implies, of course he does. It's clear from the moment F. sees him.

His top hat sits over the corner of his chair. His hair is combed to accentuate the natural curls of it: no pomade for him, his is a natural talent. And he takes up space with it; F. can easily imagine him calling out for more champagne in a booming voice while laughing at his patrons' jokes, sometimes cajoling, perhaps convincing, always cavorting: making the place run all on his own. He is, after a fashion, doing so at the moment, for the Opéra is closed to visitors.

F., still standing there in the doorway, feels herself on a new threshold, knows that she is somehow on the verge of something. M. Vernon probably sees this too, as he beckons her in.

'That's it, come on and sit down. Needn't worry about getting bitten.' He knots his fingers together at the desk and sits up, immediately changing from casual to formal. 'Sit yourself down and for heaven's sake, spare me the gossip of what the soloist said to the stage manager or anything like that, we've far too much to talk about.'

F. sits opposite him across the desk.

'So. Brass tacks. I hear you're the newest favourite of our own favourite, is that right? Not happy with your current set-up, I suppose? She plucks you out and offers the chance to spend the season roaming around her closet instead? Am I close?'

F. is blown here and there by the buffeting forces of his assertions. She still cannot see what any of this has to do with him, didn't-you-hear-they're-secretly-married or no.

'I'm going to be her companion,' she says.

'A new venture: yes, I'm sure you'll learn a lot. Well, I'd say she's chosen a little rashly, for me to be meeting you *now*, but if she thinks you've got what it takes who am I to differ, eh?'

F. is wondering that. *Who* are you, to have an opinion on this business at all? Yet she can see it does matter, somehow, that he is satisfied.

'I will do my best,' she says. 'I confess, I want to know more about her. She seems so *effortlessly* elegant.' Too late, she's said it. She didn't mean to say something so … so flattering, but it's true. And there's something about Vernon's personability, solid and unmoving as bronze, that inspires confidence. 'I don't expect it's all to be spent in the closet,' she adds. 'But even if it is. I'll do whatever she needs.'

His fingers drum on the wood. 'Thank you for obliging. And good to hear it.' His eyes flick to one of the papers on the desk, and he frowns slightly at a column of numbers. 'Those totals are uneven, actually.'

He pushes the paper aside, letting it crumple under itself. Here is a man who is quick to displace things that have been found wanting.

'As we appear to be in accord,' he says, 'I suspect we'll get on. Here's some literature for you …' he opens a desk drawer, pulls out a ledger. It lands with a satisfying thunk on the desk. 'Proof of expenses and full accounts of the last two seasons; time spent, when, where, with who, column for any relevant notes …' he opens a page at random and runs a finger down a narrow list of figures. 'Oh yes! This was a good one. Comte de Rennes challenged his own brother to a duel over who'd accompany her to *Figaro*.' He looks up at F. 'Many a long night's reading here.' He hoists the book upside-down to show her a figure at the top of a column. 'The wine we ordered for her last private salon. Very exclusive; only four guests. This is the date; this is the price; this is the amount by the barrel.' His finger taps the neat handwritten number. 'That's almost what the whole orchestra received for performing here that same evening.'

He sits back at his desk again, satisfied. 'We try to ensure the Opéra nearly runs by itself, or at least it staggers along by itself. It's a drunk you don't *quite* have to prop up. My main role, at least as I conceive it and in terms of emotional commitment, is the management of the Belladonna's career. Both calendar and social standing. We work together. If you're to be assisting her, you and I will also be working closely.'

All that rumour evaporates, leaving a few beaded drops of truth. F. frowns a little; this sounds a little like the Belladonna is under somebody else's control. Is she to be taking orders from this man, instead of those at the printing-press? Little difference.

Monsieur can see her thinking this. 'I'm not the one in charge. You see this is why I don't go about announcing it from the rooftops, people don't understand. If you're to join us you absolutely must understand.'

F. casts an eye over the account book. 'So who works for whom?'

'We're partners. Together we manage her business.' He sees her disillusionment and chuckles, not unkindly. 'You think she's doing it alone? Everybody thinks that. All this *effortlessly* floating through life, making the best of it? Of course there is infrastructure.'

He grabs his top hat, runs a finger around the band. When he looks back at F., the serious sentiment behind his eyes is clear. 'Forgive my brusqueness. I know what you meant by it. But this is what I'm trying to get you to understand. It isn't fate or coincidence that she's always in the right place at the right time! That she manages everything she must manage, attends the right events, puts in the right appearances, manages potential lovers with finesse, that sort of thing. You can't live a life like that without income; certainly not without a *schedule*.'

'People pay to love her?'

He beamed. 'You've actually put your finger right on the question. Yes and no. The nature of our work is the maintenance of her success. People pay for time in her company, for the honour of her attending their event, for the gift of being seated beside her; for her endorsement, shall we say?

Her full-time occupation, her work, is to be who she is. Why else does she inspire this mix of fascination, adoration, some confusion, the occasional spot of moral outrage? People think it happens, out of the air! As for intimate relationships … well, that's up to her, it can be managed. But that's my point. It is *managed*. Nothing is accidental. And now—and let joy be unconfined, and give me every third Monday off!—she wants you to join the team. An extra pair of hands, an ear to the ground. Not to reduce it all to body parts.' He smiles.

He puts the heavy ledger back into his desk drawer. F. wants to laugh; all those theorists of secret marriage are closer to the truth than they know.

'Of course the true test will be how you handle our special private salons,' says Vernon, gracefully bowing her out of his office. 'Won't be long now. Soon as the berries are ripe.'

F. remembers the first time she saw someone fly. Onstage, the dancer stepped off and drifted effortlessly into the air, taking small steps through smoky light across a backdrop of painted stars. F. had gasped with wonder along with everyone else.

Now it is as if she stands in the wings seeing the ropes and pulleys. Far from diffusing her excitement, learning the true nature of the Belladonna's existence, she finds herself invigorated by it. *Starstruck. The effect is what we're after.* This is more than a glimpse backstage: she finds herself desperate to pull on the rope.

*

'Join us, we're getting oysters.'

This is what it means, to be The Companion. The material benefits: the fine carriage pulled by a pair of beautiful horses, hung with those same damask curtains. The shimmery darkness of the apartments, with its high ceilings and luxurious furnishings; the private box; the gilt-edged invitations; the chef's own table at all the best places. F. is being ushered towards one now, a long stretch of balcony where a group of wits lounge like cats among the wine glasses, ready for a whole merry night over lemon and ice.

F. sits in one corner, an onlooker to the party. The Belladonna has come over and offered a gloss: *that's* a poet from Leipzig; *this* is the son of so-and-so; *those* are friends of mine from … just watch and pay attention. F. nods, and although a few of the party look over and smile politely, they continue as if she isn't really here. The Belladonna is holding court at the table; she has, remarkably, been following several conversations at once, and she interjects into one:

'And whatever did you say to him?'

'I told him melodrama was best suited to the stage,' says a young Lord, fingers twitching over his short beard, 'and then I left. I've no time for tempers.'

'He must have been surprised at you,' says the poet from Leipzig, wide-eyed. 'And after the critics were so warm about his work on hermeneutics!'

'That may be so,' continues the Lord. 'But if he asks me to read his latest volume he's going to get my latest opinion. Unfortunately for him, I'd settled on it years ago.'

All of this delightful business does not float along; it must be made to move. Coal must be continually shovelled into the boiling engine. To be the companion is going to mean accessing a whole new raft of knowledge: F. already intuits, and tomorrow she'll learn, what each young chap is paying to attend this supper tonight.

The poet, who has a profile like a hawk and a stare to match, leans forwards and says: 'So my lady.' His words come purposefully, having consumed a few drinks. 'Not to discredit this fine establishment, when will you next kick your heels and host for us again? I'm ready for another Belladonna salon, if I say so.'

The Belladonna smiles. 'Oh well, if *you* say so…'

There is a change of energy, people leaning in all about the oyster table.

'Oh yes. We're due one, aren't we!' The chatter rises out into the night, fogged breath going with it, and opinions become strong, anticipation brews, and F. watches.

La Dame aux Morelles laughs, tilting her head. 'Very soon,' she promises. 'I believe I'll be ready to host a salon within the month.'

The table ripples with excitement. The young Lord's eyes widen in meaningful surprise: 'The berries are soon to be ripe, then?'

The Belladonna gives a nod, and murmurs grow around the table. F. frowns slightly: there's a shared reaction here, spurred by the very mention of the berries, that she doesn't know how to read.

There are a few more remarks about the berries as the night lengthens. Eventually threads of orange creep into the sky and the party briefly pretends to consider retiring, before calling for another round of oysters.

So. The immediate future for F., as it stands:

There will be more of these socials as the next weeks pass, and these nocturnal hours will gradually shift her sense of the day off-kilter. She will rise late in the afternoon, dress for engagements in the evening, go off to enjoy them all night. It almost seems effortless. She'll see so many mornings break she'll forget, or nearly forget, how it felt to see that final dawn with her lover.

And then, for weeks, *this* will be what it means, to be the companion, to be alongside and in the company of, La Dame aux Morelles. It means a new wardrobe. ('You must be difficult to place, and therefore capable of anything.') It means a new vocabulary. ('Monseigneur first, after that he's fine with Romuald. Oh, and never call le Duc son Altesse "his highness" once he's onto his second drink. It will aggravate him impossibly.') It means preparations for effortless recall; sometimes entire stacks of novels. ('He loves them all and is bound to ask. Help me prepare a few insightful things to say.') It means singing lessons: sometimes F. is explained as an old friend from the Belladonna's performing days. ('You don't need to be good. It just needs to be plausible that you were good *once*.') The glamour, the social breeze, yes, it means all that. Witnessing the arrival of many gifts; not for F., but she gets to deliver them, and they open them together, so it's practically as good as: assessing the jewellery, reading the card aloud in silly voices, laughing at the china dog— and once, unforgettably, sharing genuine joy at the basket of paper fruit that reveals itself to be real fruit wrapped in paper money. It's enough to make F. feel she belongs in this world, that somehow enough time has passed to give her the broad measure of the life of the Belladonna.

The reader of a poem perceives the end of a line of verse as simply a space, a stretch of blank paper: this seems so obvious, they'll barely notice anything after the words, they'll simply think 'nice ending' and send for more oysters. But in fact, that emptiness must be carefully designed. A thin blank bar is fitted in alongside the letters, so the poet's words sit in the page appropriately. What a reader perceives as a few lines of verse requires a whole block of busy activity, most of it invisible, holding the letters tightly into place, pieces that structure everything but make no mark themselves.

That's the companion. The blank piece that juts up against the words and allows them to work: and if the job is done well, its efforts won't be seen at all. F. understands now. A decadent world this may be, but she has a sense of it, more or less.

So when the Belladonna, as F. fastens a jet brooch to her bodice, utters casually that there may be a few surprises at the salon they're about to host, F. barely gives it a thought.

III

A recurring dream begins about this time: F. has become something like a governess in a large house. The house itself changes. Sometimes it isn't much more than a crumbling pile with ivy spooling in through shattered windows. Sometimes the place is more pristine, with neat rugs by the fire and a sense that the owners have just gone out. In the dream she is looking for something, running from room to room. Growing frantic, she finds a chest in a darkened hiding place and pulls open the top drawer. In the dream she often has time to notice that the handle is ornate brass, and that the drawer itself is patterned with mosaic tiles. She pulls open the drawer and leaps back—with a heart-buckling lurch that jolts her awake—at the sight of moonlight glinting on steel, smooth as a mirror. The soft drawer is filled with knives. Blade after blade, heaped.

And no rest for F. now either, surrounded as she is by salon conversation.

'Now don't get me wrong, the composition itself is gorgeous, no doubting that. Exquisite. However … I'll come straight out with it, since I'm among friends. My daughter's spaniel relieves itself every morning and it keeps better time than that conductor who waggles his baton about like he's trying to get something off his fingers.'

A quirk of a sceptical eyebrow. 'Is that so?'

'I couldn't say, could you? What's the good in even attempting such a repertoire if you're sloshing your rhythms about like you're bailing out the *Mary Rose*.'

Private salons at the Belladonna apartments, though rare, come about seasonally in a small flourish.

Salons: like this one.

'Met them at the Juniper, must have been a year ago now. Curious pair; it's a challenge to say anything they don't turn into an ornate poem. You can ask them any ordinary question and not get the answer until it's published a year later in verse.'

The Belladonna apartments have a heady scent of flowers and cigar smoke; you can practically see the atmosphere swirling about the place. Occasionally someone plays a sparkling tune at the piano. The salon contains about four dozen people of extremely well-cut cloth and, deprived of any name for most of them, F. is working out from first principles who they are. Quickly, though, there's too many of them to follow it all. F. is treading water in all the chic.

Belladonna appears by her side. 'I count that as everyone now here; there's both a soprano and a talented composer from the Opéra, later on I'll ask them to perform for us. This is part of the act, of course, them having already agreed to do so.'

A pause, then Belladonna closes her eyes briefly. This is a tell F. recognises as the onset of a headache, and it's terrible news that it's come on so early. She brings her hand up to her forehead, and the way she rubs her temples shows F. this is going to be one of the bad ones.

Then La Dame aux Morelles comes back again, refreshes her smile like turning the page of a book.

'Come and meet some friends.'

She steers F. to a group artfully arranged beside the fireplace.

*

Before this salon began, F. had finally been permitted to see the process which is the secret of the Belladonna's eyes. The final stage of dressing being completed and the jewellery chosen F. would normally be dismissed for a moment, but tonight the Belladonna instructed her to stay and observe. She had seated herself at the dressing-table and reached over the clutter—jars, brushes, ropes of dark pearls, scattered clouds of lavender powder, the dressing-table so full F. can hardly see the wood—Belladonna had reached her arm across the table and taken one of the two bottles that stand at the back like overbearing guards.

They both contain clear liquid: one is topped with a purple gem, a rich crusted amethyst; the other is darker, like a crystal trapping smoke, an opal of midnight. She took the bottle with the purple crystal, threw back her head—a sudden sharp movement, as if she'd just heard the tread of a foot in the ceiling—and quickly tipped the bottle, a drop of its liquid into each eye, then breathed out slowly. Finally she ran a hand delicately over her eyes and leaned forwards to replace the purple bottle. In the reflection of the mirror she had caught F. standing there, and she had smiled and said something about not having to re-do it much, these days. It's reached a point where that endlessly dark stare is almost permanent. If her eyes ever fully returned to normal, she couldn't be sure how she'd manage. But oh, the need for dim light, and always, the headaches. But one look into her eyes and yes. It all does seem worth it, yes.

*

By the mantlepiece, an actress is towering over the group—an actress surely, F. thinks, gazing up at her, she can be nothing else. In trousers and a bow-tie, she pulls on a cigarette she carries in a long holder, and, flickering her eyes to the Belladonna to acknowledge her presence, continues the story she is telling.

'We were just outside Le Havre. I was performing some *Hamlet* pieces with the charity show, but the skull had been hidden by a member of the company I must have unwittingly insulted. After much searching the manager of the receiving house found it in a hatbox and we hit it off immediately. She's so jovial and a loving one, and keen to be helpful—which is a bonus in theatre, let me tell you.'

'I've never known you commit offence unwittingly,' puts in La Dame aux Morelles. 'Don't tell me you've been forgetting yourself?'

The actress pulls on her cigarette, heavily. 'If only I could.'

'Well, you certainly have my permission. At least an audience never forgets you. Those incandescent memories blazing, the shadows you leave us with. We don't stand a chance.'

Only the slightest tension in the Belladonna's jaw reveals the headache, now clamped like a vice at either side of her temple, steadily turning.

F. whispers, as they move on: 'Wasn't that Celeste Favrerie?' F. has seen the name spelled out on a stack of playbills; most of Paris has heard great things, revolutionary things, about her Phaedra. But in the heat of the moment the more sensational gossip boils over first. 'They say she sleeps in a coffin. Is that true?'

'Ha! *She* says she sleeps in a coffin. Wonderful ruse. Wish I'd thought of that.'

They are distracted for a moment by the blustery entrance of an older woman in pink feathers, brandishing a piece of paper about—Belladonna quickly deals with that business, folding it neatly away and motioning the woman to greet someone at the far end of the room. When she has gone, Belladonna offers F. a low explanation for the awkwardness: 'invitation only' oughtn't be acted upon so literally.

They move on. Sitting up at one end of a chaise longue is a young man with an eager expression. He is discussing prayer with a lolling playwright, who sprawls on the rest of it to the fullest.

'You communicate with each of the Holy Trinity at once?' asks the playwright, with an undercurrent of amusement.

The thin man frowns. 'I suppose, naturally,' he offers. 'Otherwise I'd be picking one, and that kind of favouritism wouldn't be on.'

The playwright shrugs. 'Isn't it crowded?' As he moves, his jacket shows filigree gold patterns: the garment, which seemed to be the standard black of a gentleman's evening wear, is actually velvet, expensive. F. updates her view of him.

The playwright has become aware of his audience: not only of the Belladonna and F., but the small group of the kind that always tends to cluster about him. He looks into his glass.

'Here's the question as I see it,' he says. 'When you experience religious ecstasy, are we talking onanism or *ménage à trois?*'

The other man turns to him, shocked. 'I beg your pardon?'

'I always find it vital to know exactly which sin one is committing. The guilt becomes so much simpler to deal with. There is nothing more judgemental than a clear conscience.'

'M. Renaudière, I do believe you are quite wicked.'

'A devil does whisper at my shoulder on occasion. It tends to ask for advice.'

The group by the chaise longue breaks into laughter, and the Belladonna swiftly moves on, catching the attention of another guest who needs greeting. The whole fabric of the salon seems to be patterned as an intricate series of connections, and the woman with infinite eyes is its most gracious weaver. Soon they are discussing ballet secrets with a dancer, who is shaking with the ambition of achieving a principal role next season even as she assures La Dame aux Morelles that frankly she could take it or leave it.

A new figure arrives and pushes into the group, with such verve his presence seems to refresh the energy around him. His hair sticks out at all angles and his wide jacket is far too big for him, the gold tassels of his epaulettes flapping as his arms open for an embrace with the Belladonna. It looks more as if he's raided the dressing-up box than he belongs to the actual military. La Dame aux Morelles, with only a slight wince across her features to betray her migraine, looks him up and down.

'I took you for a rake,' she says. 'I thought, why is this implement arriving at my party? Perhaps he is here for the lawns.'

The rake turns to F. and offers an elaborate bow, as ornate as the rest of him.

'This is M. Marcelin Capet,' says the Belladonna. 'He's holding dalliance with the—*le quatorzième régiment*, at the moment?' She treats herself to a hand pressed briefly to the temple. 'Marcelin, this is Flora, she's an old and dear friend from the Opéra.' She turns away to lightly cough.

Showing respect in the presence of an artist, Marcelin adds a further flourish to his bow. '*Un plaisir*, Flora.'

Well yes, the name Flora is fitting ever better. Why not wear it for the party.

'I'm delighted—'

But the Belladonna coughs again and this time it's a deep sound, wrought directly from the centre of her. Concerned glances are passed delicately across the room.

'Take care of each other for a moment,' she says, her voice strained between coughs. 'I've come over juddery. I'll sort it out.' She disappears through the door to her bedroom, where Flora knows the medicines she will swallow, the creams she will rub on her temple to assuage the throbbing. The guests who see her leave turn to look at each other a little confused. At a Salon, the Belladonna is the centre of gravity.

Marcelin takes Flora by the arm. 'Now Flora, since my lady has so elegantly paired us up for the time being, I wonder if you could settle an argument for me.' He leads her towards the group gathered by the fireplace. He looks at her seriously. 'Hugely important subject.'

The group is indeed in a state of intense debate.

'Let me try to catch you up,' says Marcelin. 'We were speaking about the various attractions to be found at the *Foire du Trône*. Now, the issue we've arrived at concerns fairground mirrors. Eugène here suggests that few things in life offer a truer reflection of who we are.'

Eugène—the playwright from the chaise longue—nods approvingly at this summary. 'Precisely,' he says. 'A contorted picture presents a much *truer* likeness than whatever sits over one's dressing-table. The latter is merely *accurate*.'

'Whereas our friend Celeste here,' Marcelin gestures to the actress, who is moodily twisting a new cigarette into its holder. '*She* says the world is so distorted already, one can hardly tell what novelty mirrors are supposed to *add*.'

Celeste holds the cigarette up to her face as if inspecting the smoke. 'Close enough. What I said was, *we* are all distorted. When I look into a fairground mirror, I don't see anything I don't already know. But show me a plain reflection, make me look at what the rest of the world sees, and may foolishly take to be me—yes, Eugène, the sight over my dressing-table—*that's* the true horror.'

'But to claim this you're implying something about a person's nature,' interjects Eugène, 'and I must surely stop you there. Fairground mirrors are human-made things. They have been formed to reflect your own twisted self back at you. Say it's nothing but your own nature you're seeing and you reduce the crafting hand in the whole thing. The *design* of it.'

Marcelin puts in. 'Art offers a distorted view of humanity, an exaggerated view—sometimes this gets written off as *play*. But only in the most grotesque art can we see true beauty.' Some of the others begin to nod.

'You can't mean that!' cries a young lady in peacock blue, who sits up further from the armchair, diamonds sparkling in her ears as they swing in alarm.

'Certainly I do. I might say that all of art is fairground mirrors. Presenting falseness, that we might know truth.'

Marcelin looks at Flora as if to say, *Isn't it a wonderful game?*

'We should set up a merry-go-round in every gallery,' he says. 'Watch the pictures spin by. Could that be the best, nay the only way to look at art? Upon heady rotation?'

The actress's voice has a barb to it. 'You may rotate yourself right around, I'm sure. But my question is *how* do we distinguish one from the other? It's all very well to say, present falseness to know truth. I do that all day. But you could just as easily say art shows us the truth of the world, so we might distinguish it from the falseness that gathers all around.'

Eugène looks casually at his mostly empty glass. 'Like growing storm-clouds.'

'Quite. Art might not show us the real, but that doesn't mean the same as untrue.'

'You should meet my friend Lucian,' says Marcelin thoughtfully. 'He thinks fairgrounds are beautiful places. Mind you he's a very open soul, finds beauty anywhere.'

The woman in peacock blue sighs, her eyes shining. 'Some people can. Oh, what a dreadful burden for them.'

The actress rolls her eyes. 'Nothing pretty about a fairground. Jolts of life, that's what they give you: coloured lights to dazzle your eyes, music to stupefy your senses to everything else, rides and jostle to make you so aware of your own stomach and the blood rushing about your head you'll question why you ever wanted to bother.'

Eugène drains his glass. 'Sounds like a perfect distillation of life to me.'

'That's my objection,' says the actress. 'It's too much of a distillation. Too much experience at once when there's enough about naturally, and where's your truth in that?'

Suddenly as one, they all turn to Flora.

For a moment they are a perfect tableau arranged about the fireplace, an image almost inviting itself to be painted. *The Enraptured Audience*, she'd call it. *Or The Carefully Laid Trap.*

Marcelin's eyes are glittering with encouragement. Eugène's face is harder to read. Celeste looks interested; so does the lady in peacock blue, and all the other onlookers forming a cluster around this circle of intense bohemian debate.

She shrugs. Oh, may as well be on with it.

'I suppose it's like this,' she says slowly. 'Lies are bound to reveal some truth somewhere, and truth, of course, is the one thing worth lying about.'

She is treated to a course of immediate laughter.

'A-ha! There, you see? She's got it!' Marcelin shouts this good news over the din, as the whole group raise their glasses to her; the damn of mirth breaking and pouring over her. Marcelin slaps her on the back. 'You'll fit in here.'

'She's got it indeed,' says Eugène. 'We seem to have a bout of it.' More quietly he adds: 'We can only hope it doesn't make her *too* ill.'

A movement in the swirling bodies of the soiree catches F.'s attention. The Belladonna has returned and is going about the room, and ripples of endearing goodbyes spread among the guests as she subtly ushers them out.

The golden wrought clock on the fireplace is stopped at midnight, so time is free to whirl about untethered until the apartment has mostly depleted. Suddenly, the black silk swirl of the hostess is by F.'s side, waving goodbye to Marcelin, Eugène and the others, who are chattering about the possibility of one last trip to Lilie's brasserie before the closing hour. Or have they already missed the closing hour? They'll go and see. Belladonna clasps her hand to Marcelin's arm, enjoying his company too much to let him go.

La Dame's attitude is business-like when she returns. The apartment is not, however, empty. Three guests remain, seated on the armchairs. Between them is a low table with intricate brass legs; the surface is glass. Light from the candles distorts the shadows onto the floor through it. On the table sits an empty crystal bowl.

The Belladonna approaches her remaining guests and looks steadily from one to the other, biting her lip in a calculation that somehow factors F. in, too. Then she nods, a small professional decision, bends and picks up the crystal bowl from the table. For a moment she stands there, over her guests, cradling the bowl. F. adjusts her gloves, picking at the lace around the hem, and refrains the urge to put her arms protectively around herself.

'Are we all comfortable?' the Belladonna asks. Receiving a trio of nods: 'In that case,' she says, tasting each word like slowly sipping wine, 'I can inform you that they are ripe, it falls only for me to harvest, and I shall return in a speck of a moment.' A hot prickle winds its way across the back of F.'s neck as the Belladonna disappears through the door to the bedroom.

They sit in silence for a moment, until an older woman breaks the tension. Her hat has a tall feather in it, pale pink.

'Have any of the rest of you done this?' she says. 'I haven't, but I've several friends who have. They say it's the must-do thing.' The pink feather trembles to a nervous halt.

After her awkward arrival at the party, brandishing the piece of paper, F. had been surprised to learn that this woman is the widow to the sole heir of a great raft of perfume factories. Her wealth must stretch deep and low, like a great cave filled with amethyst. Her presence in this world confuses F., never mind her presence in this room now. How could all that scented money accumulate in one person, sitting there now holding a glass of champagne like it's the most ordinary thing in the world, like surely everybody understands?

The larger man sitting in the next chair says something about trying new experiences then examines the wallpaper; the third guest, a slight young man in a silk patterned waistcoat, whom F. was told is a promising entrepreneur, picks at his beard and says in a voice near a whisper that it *is* quite a shock but he's sure they'll get used to it. Both men seem nervous and such apprehension is catching. The perfume widow begins silently playing with the feathers of her shawl. The silence remains strained and frightened as the Belladonna sweeps back into the room and places the crystal bowl onto the glass table, where it is now filled with shining berries, small and smooth and round and black.

F. leans forwards to look at them, and she is not the only one. The company crane their necks towards the bowl, not experiencing pleasure in the encounter so much as judging it. The berries sit there as innocent as sloes picked for gin. Someone makes a joke to that effect, and the Belladonna laughs in response, flopping down into the remaining chair, and the conversation trips (almost gratefully) into inconsequentialities.

The bowl of berries in the centre of the table now has its own gravity, pulling everyone in, distorting all conversation. People look at them without looking. Eventually she chooses her moment, waves the entrepreneur's sentence away while he's halfway through speaking it, and leans forwards to pick up a berry. She raises it high as if inspecting it, holding it delicately between thumb and forefinger. Partially obscured by candlelight, she holds what appears to be a bead of pure darkness.

'A few rules,' she says. 'I know some of you may know them. I repeat them anyway.' She looks around the group with importance. The light splash of her salon manner has evaporated, leading them all into more sombre territory.

'The word to summon the doctor, if you think it is necessary, is *Venus*. And you must only take one. Never more. Follow the second rule and you shouldn't need the first.' Belladonna looks around the room, and with a quick, swift movement places her hand over her mouth.

Permission granted. The perfume widow puts hers in whole and swallows it like a pill. The men take their berries more slowly and chew, screwing up their faces at the bitterness.

'It's so sour,' manages the entrepreneur, already beginning

to distort in his chair. The widow is taking deep breaths, staring up at the ceiling, clutching at the arms of her seat.

The Belladonna makes a slight, flicking movement with her hand and back again—a movement designed for F. to notice while the other guests do not, busy as they are being wracked with unpleasantness of taste. The gesture reveals to F. that La Dame aux Morelles is still holding the berry.

F. takes a berry—the surface is cold and dry. It sits there innocently, a hole in the middle of her palm. If she touched it, perhaps her finger would go straight through …

The entrepreneur has wrenched himself sideways, curling up against the back of his chair. 'Going to be sick,' he manages.

'You won't be.' The voice of the Belladonna comes through calm and low, as if the berry itself has been given a dry voice. She continues to speak, slowly, keeping her watchful gaze upon F. Her face is still but half smiling: she looks deadly. 'Concentrate on the feeling in your mind.'

With a brief nod she gestures towards the berry in F's own hand.

'What's that up there in the chandelier? Is it a bat?' cries the widow, staring up at nothing.

The Belladonna nods, still concentrating on F., who stares back, and the voices are clear in F.'s mind as she decides:

You don't have to eat the berry, remember.

But it would probably benefit to know.

And that's what this is all about, isn't it? Knowing?

She closes her eyes and tips her head back; the tasteless bead comes further into her mouth and she crunches it between her backmost molars—and a juice of pure foulness immediately enters her mouth, which is suddenly the driest place in her body, and her face closes around it, her mouth pulling her cheeks, her eyes, inwards towards itself; her face is turning in on itself; her hair must surely be in her mouth, then, how come it isn't, where is it? A great pounding sets in behind her eyes, arriving like an unwelcome guest, and it sits there, in the forehead, pushing out from behind her eyes, knocking at her skull.

She manages to say something like '*oh*,' and possibly '*vile*'—but too late: the bloating pounding in her head has become all-encompassing, a discomfort too big for her mere skull; this delicate, useless skull, too thin, too thin for a bulging pain like this—it must come out, the ache must come out and be free to rush about the room—a heavy juddering now through her throat, and an astringent thickness fills her senses, becomes a foul pillow pressed over her face, and her mouth is smeared with liquid she tries to wipe away, but her mouth is strange, her numb lips are like touching a distant piece of cold meat, and the feel and scent of the vomit is only faintly registered, a mere loose fact with no thought attached.

F. presses herself into the back of her chair and tries to see the room again, tries to look past the burning that now spreads through her chest, up into her throat. There is a heavy sound, a thump: someone a few miles away is landing on the floor, they have fallen from their chair and are curled up on the floor—and a flock of birds, too dark to be doves—swallows?—spin upwards and lose themselves in the chandelier, and its crystals have begun to melt and are dripping down into the bowl, and the splashes of liquid glass, when they land, are black and the berries are everywhere, and nausea rises again and a fresh convulsion shakes her—

This is my body failing. This is what it's like.

—and the dark shapes beyond her blurred vision somehow combine into a figure, elegant in soft black, beside her, and there's a comforting hand on her arm—the smooth, cool silk of it on her burning skin like ointment. F. looks up and through the pain in her head into the shifting outline before her, the vision of a black dress becoming two, then three, then one of itself; her sight blurs as her tears heat up her eyes, the taste rolling through her in waves, as she focuses as much as she can on the woman kneeling by her side.

'Look at me,' says the blurring image of the Belladonna, over the quiet groans in the room.

F. focuses her attention on the sharp neckline of the gown, the exquisite Belladonna fabric a vivid slash against her pale skin, and—here's a thing. F. is dying, she knows this, her heart is going to beat itself open, this whole event is a drawn-out convulsion, a great desperate rattle—her body is currently, unquestionably, dying—but even so it won't, *somehow*, after all this, be dead. And her body knows this— and here's the thing; in spite of the blur, and the heat, and the shaking, curtains sweep aside to a heightening of perception, and details stand out and declare themselves to her parched senses, and she can make out each individual thread of silk in the dress; the light on each dark pearl threaded across the gown— and for a moment the world is still, and she and the Belladonna are at the absolute centre. And then each pearl is a berry, a knot of blackness she cannot untie, and bubbling acid once more rises up from her stomach to press against her breastbone, and her body is burning with pressure that makes breathing impossible, and the shadows lean in closer and, on top of everything, here is a sudden calm pressure on her head: Belladonna's hand gently, lovingly, stroking her hair, and to this, F. submits; the pain is too much, the gentleness is too much, and she opens herself to the beauty of this. She is dying, and the Belladonna is the bringer of the darkness, and She rises and Her long black dress is endless, and F. dives into it, and is gone from there.

*

Strange visions with a backdrop of thunderous night: the most waking sleep she's ever had. The Belladonna crying black tears from those distinctive eyes; an entire libretto that reads as one agonising scream. The grand piano opening like a coffin. F. wakes in a room she does not recognise, and it takes a minute for familiar furniture to assemble itself from the jumble. She lies there, in a state that might be called awake. She stares blankly at the wall, which seems to be the only unmoving thing in the room.

Eventually her body suggests sitting may be more pleasant than sickly lying down, and she raises herself up, her arms delicate and fawn-like—ridiculously weak, *what's this now, can I not even support my own weight?*—sheer stubbornness propels her into a sitting position but her eyes stay closed. A new headache is attempting a solid, gradual push against the back-most edge of her sight. It's as if to open her eyes would flout some new rule: to even think about focussing on anything requires her body to perform an unpleasant drumroll first. Many thanks for that.

Eventually she can look at the table beside the bed, reading several times over the note there. Signed with the lush B, as sprawling and grand as ever, it advises her to ring the bell when she wakes. The bell in question is small and silver and sits there quite innocently. It takes a few minutes more of mental preparation before F. feels ready to will into being any actual sound.

Its tiny peal cuts right across her tender head, a sharp sting and a flash in her vision all at once. It grows and grows until it's a thunderous echo, painfully reverberating through everything. She closes her eyes in the intensity of it, then, as the last of it rolls away, the Belladonna is at her bedside.

'Good morning, merrymaker.'

She is alert, watching F. carefully. She seems as put together as ever, and it must be late, very late afternoon. The coiffeur will have been; any signs of the salon will have been cleared away. She must have had to do everything; this thought must come into F.'s expression, as the Belladonna waves it away with a sweep of her hand.

'Not to worry. Besides, next time you'll palm your berry along with me.'

F.'s mouth feels like a ball of crinkled paper. 'I've never felt anything like it.'

'Forgive me for springing it on you, though in many ways we know I didn't. It's worth experiencing once, is my belief.'

F. frowns and struggles to sit up further. Incandescent questions fire across her mind, then fizzle out in the face of the Belladonna's expression. Dull memories become brighter: the perfume widow blustering in with the paperwork, waving the contract about; a gaudy mistake, the Belladonna had acted fast to quash it.

'She wasn't committed until the very last moment,' the Belladonna shrugs. 'That woman's afraid of herself.'

It all makes sense. The looks between those who know; the cavernous stretch between those and others who merely wonder. The second salon hidden in plain sight within the first. F. leans back against the headboard with its swirls of brass.

'Why do they do it?'

'Why should I ask? Besides, it's either obvious or I'm sure I don't wish to know.' She seems to flick the question away. 'Your guess is as good as mine. You saw them too.'

F. picks up the jug of water and pours herself a shaking glass, watching the surface tremble: a fine clear skin stretched over an invisible world. 'How often does it happen?'

'*Extremely* rarely. It's not the climax of all my salons, if that's what you're thinking.' She looks at F. seriously now. Despite the shards of head pain, F. is back at the brasserie: it's impossible to turn away from the Belladonna when she looks at you like that. 'Naturally, Vernon and I hope you wish to continue. As I say you shan't have to participate again. I don't see you having that particular wish.'

F. finishes the water—letting its coolness spread down her painful throat—and puts the empty glass back onto the table. It lands heavily on the note, and a wet ring begins to smudge the writing on the paper; the large B morphs into a shape like a devil. She looks back into the Belladonna's face, which is all concern and studious worry.

'I'll stay,' she says, 'but I'd rather not take a berry again.'

'Very good on both counts. Now I'll leave you to further

recover.' She rises, lightly rubbing her hands together: on to the next job. 'Take your time, I've no socialising tonight. I've put it about that I am far too exhausted.'

At the door she stops. 'I hope you weren't too afraid? I doubt you could have been.'

'Why do you say that?' *I felt my body failing. I reached the limits of my own existence—afraid doesn't even begin to scratch at it. How can you doubt I was afraid?*

'Some people take the berries to lose themselves, and find themselves that way. But I suspect you've never wondered who you are.'

The door neatly closes as F. is formulating a response. She frowns, looks down, lets her vision wander the gentle stripes of the wooden floor around the bed. The experience was terrifying but if she'd been asked why she wouldn't take another berry she wouldn't speak of that fear, nor of the foul taste. The lack of control was the unrepeatable thing. Contrast with the way the Belladonna had guided everyone through it: the thrill of that. The thrill of that.

*

Knowing what she knows of the berries, knowing the secret of the Belladonna's poison salon, allows the world to change. F. can finally hear things she would otherwise miss, understanding what they refer to. She has learned their secret language.

For example, in the interval at the Opéra, the Comte du Foix had twisted in his chair and said to her: 'I heard there's quite a waiting list? Perhaps it is possible,' his tone becoming urgent, 'for one to circumvent it? Could you possibly have a word?' She now understands what he was asking.

A brightly dressed *gandin* on the Champs-Elysees, cane in hand, had once come up to her and said: 'Hey! You're with *La Dame*, aren't you? My friend says you're the one to talk to about getting into the death club.' Before this, she would have put such talk down to a critique on the morbidity of all that black.

She also can speak on the secret herself. When Celeste Favrerie visited the apartments, F. asked if she'd ever taken a berry. 'Once or twice. But you know,' the actress took a long drag on her cigarette, 'it's never enough for people. Not for what they really want to get out of it.' She stubbed the cigarette out on a silver dish. 'Tell you what though, it was *wonderful* prep for doing Juliet.'

And the perfume widow had put her hand on F.'s shoulder on the Rue Royale: 'I haven't lived until now. Everything is a dull haze. Do you understand? I must do it again. Can you organise that for me? Can you do it? It's love. I cannot wait—*how* long? No. No.' F. had shaken her off with excuses in the end, but her grip had been desperate.

Now it's clear to F. that this is all part of her role, Vernon also has notes: 'My dear, you're going to have to come out with something more original than "I thought I was going to die." Sell it to them!'

*

The Companion is visible, and The Companion is unseen. That's a particularity of all this, it's a strange dance in and out of the light. It's a duet, a two-step.

To be the companion, you must be prepared to do this dance. To be less visible when beside her—practically non-existent, when beside her. Everyone wants the attention of the Belladonna and there's no space here to be looking at *you*. She is the storm, and you reside in the centre with her. You are a ghost: helping, reassuring, whispering answers, and nobody else gets so close.

A two-step. The second step: people see her whispering something to you, and you will briefly become the centre of attention. *Who are you to be her chosen confidant?* people will wonder. *Who are you, and what do you know?* When that happens, you must be aloof enough for this intensity of gaze not to change you, and you certainly must not look back into it. You must act as if it were not there, and in time they will forget about you. The illumination is sudden and sharp, like a strike of lightning, and then it fades back to nothing once again. The key point: you must be comfortable to bear the anonymity as well as the scrutiny.

The Belladonna, of course, has only the option of visibility, and lives within that halo of attention. Difficult not to wonder what it must be like to forever exist at the other end of society's glare. No wonder she adapts her eyes, makes a discomforting gaze of her own, goes out only in the darkness of evenings. It's hard to imagine how daylight would treat her, or what exactly would show if bright light ever shone on her world.

F. resembles any other young girl. Standing in the doorway of one boutique or other, the owner stomps towards her, face shut like a bolted door, ready to inform her of the imminent closing, and then: something reveals it to them. Perhaps they notice F. is wearing a subtle pin in the shape of the leaf, or perhaps the comb in her hair has a certain quality to its making that gives her away. Perhaps she stares at them with a power similar to her mistress, certainly she wishes she does. In any case, a welcoming smile takes over when they realise what F. represents and who she is there for, and then she is warmly greeted: the shopkeeper will throw an arm over her shoulder as she is whisked into back rooms to be demonstrated the latest fashions, led to gaze upon quality, be offered for free the most cared-for and precious items. In moments like these—F. is the most visible person in the room.

Leaving the boutique—the gargantuan order to follow behind, delivered in the owner's own carriage—F. always reminds herself: they weren't actually seeing her. They were recognising La Dame. Her visibility passes through F., and it always leaves.

And so, almost silently the question comes, spoken by a shadowy presence at the back of her thoughts, a murmur in her own voice she does not explicitly permit. *Where will I be if this isn't enough?*

II

IV

A theatre of horror. Who in their right mind would seek such entertainment?

'More people than you might think,' she says, as they rattle along in the carriage.

'And not a small portion from gentile society, indeed. Many secretly adore it. There's more on show in five minutes of these ghoulish pantomimes than a whole night of *La Tosca*.'

Flora shakes her head, pushes the damask curtain aside to watch the city trotting past the coach, the regular dot-dot-dot of the street-lamps in the darkness. 'I don't believe you think that.'

Belladonna laughs and leans back into one of the tousled cushions, a position that threatens to squash the intricate pile of hair she's wearing tonight, or at least distort it.

'You've caught me running my lines too early. It's the sort of thing I expect people to say if I don't express it myself. And there's certainly plenty on show if you watch the *audience*.'

The last alleyway is too narrow for the trap; they must get out and walk. The respectability of this part of town wobbles this way and that, like a heat haze. There are plenty of grandly dressed persons here, but many walk with a slightness, as if they'd rather not be seen. A dancehall stands proudly on one side of the street, alongside Flora as she steps over the cracked edge of a green bottle, and on the other side a row of absinthe bars put out their chalky-liquorice sweetness.

At the far end of the alley is the theatre itself, all thin columns of stone and delicate ironwork. The shapes are distinctive: it takes a moment to see it.

'Are those church windows?'

The Belladonna nods and smiles with a sense of belonging. 'It's a temple of blasphemy now.'

Inside, the theatre is all shabby wooden panelling and the close smell of liqueur; we are far from any grand foyer, where if someone approaches you'll have a few minutes' warning. No, this is a space where people creep up on you; where they leap out and surprise. The walls are lined with lurid posters done with thick expressive brushstrokes: bodies contorted into absurd positions, blades sticking out at all angles, black and white and red. Wounds everywhere.

There's no private box for them tonight; they squeeze into the stalls with everyone else.

'It bears saying,' says the Belladonna, as they settle into their seats, 'you may not enjoy this at all. On the other hand, you might. It's personal taste in the end.'

This revelation tears Flora's concentration away from the ragged curtain. She had been imagining this was a rite of passage: the companion of the Belladonna must surely show some commitment to the macabre. It seems that every month La Dame aux Morelles will come here, to show that her company isn't exclusively for the gilt-edged.

With dark eyes lowered, she explains: 'You're here to vet the newcomers in the interval. I haven't been seen here for some time, so make sure we're not overrun with them between one show and the next.'

Her voice has lowered, so Flora has to lean in to listen. She sees attentions flick in their direction; whatever are they whispering about, the lady and her companion?

'I believe I saw Marcelin circulating tonight, Flora. I rather hope to catch him.'

'Catch him out, perhaps.' Flora knows that Belladonna likes to play with Monsieur Marcelin Capet like a cat with a mouse, and she also knows that he believes he is playing the exact same game.

'Ha! Let's do what we can.'

Far above, carved stone cherubs look down on the action disapprovingly: acrobatic tortures, horrors as absurd as they are obscene; a parade passes before the jeering hooting audience, juggling jellied balls for eyes; flinging a fake severed arm into the front row; dousing everything with perfectly recreated blood, thick arterial and the thinner red of surface wounds, and it congeals in real time—it's an exact science, it's an art, we're in a temple to the artist's craft. The faint smell of incense hangs over the audience like an angel—always that sweetness of smoke, the holy incense absorbed into the building's very stone. Impossible to get out, a ghost like that. When an actress dressed in a nun's habit comes on to cheers from the crowd, and turns to reveal the butcher's knife she's hiding behind her back, Flora half expects a thunderclap to shake everyone out into the street.

'So, what did you think?' Belladonna asks, when they return to the raucous foyer for the interval. La Dame had been laughing and clapping along with the rest. Flora begins to answer, raising her voice against the hubbub—but her attention is caught by a confident movement in their direction.

The Belladonna spots it too, a split-second behind, and together they assume an aloof facade. It drops over their faces like scenery flats—perhaps a painted graveyard like the one onstage.

There are two of them: one striding ahead, already removing his hat and beginning to bow. The other follows, more hesitantly, somewhat reluctant, shy. The fellow in the front is immediately recognisable. He reaches them and bows with a flourish, or at least as close to one as can be managed in the bustling space.

'What has the Grand Guignol done to deserve the attentions of *La Dame aux Morelles?*' says Marcelin Capet, his face full of surprise.

Belladonna smiles, her face otherwise closed. 'A pleasure to run into you, Marcelin,' she says, her voice clipped, 'although I might ask why I'm only seeing you now. Have you been avoiding me?'

'No one can avoid you, my dear, even if they desperately desired it. When will you host a salon again? I've been wanting for refined conversation and all I get in the Regiment is … well, it's not to be repeated.'

Belladonna's smile grows. 'Yet grotesque theatricals bring you to me?'

'No choice, since I had to see you,' he says. 'I know what you like. Speaking of which, I've a friend wishes to meet you. May I introduce…?' and he brings in the dark-haired, nervous-looking fellow who until now has been loitering slightly behind him. 'This is M. Lucian Delamarre, my lady.' (That's how casually he says it, how easily he brings Lucian into their lives, just like that. Stunning, really.) 'Luc is a good friend of mine, fresh from—what did you quit most recently, medical school was it? Or the bar? Never mind me and all that, the point is, he's been awfully desperate to make your acquaintance for some time.'

Flora examines this Lucian, sizing him up. Marcelin stands back and grins as if he has just pulled off a magic trick, which perhaps he has.

Lucian's hair is the first thing to notice, with its volume and hint of curl. A stab of envy at the sight of it: there's plenty who would spend a long time with an iron and still not achieve that. Not quite as dark as the Belladonna's, of course, whose hair matches her eyes, but almost: and a shadow over his face. Not the fashion, this halfway house; do you have a beard, or don't you? And nonetheless, he chooses ambiguity: that's interesting. Certainly something the Belladonna would enjoy. This same face is flushed at the embarrassment of being introduced, and the overall effect is of a young man wrapped into his father's coat to go out. It's hard to tell, on first glance, what might be made of him.

He speaks: 'Mademoiselle … *La Dame aux Morelles*. I'm so extremely delighted and pleased. This is an honour, and you look simply divine.' His voice suppressing a wobble. This could be a standard line of his, could even be a practised wobble: again, it's difficult to tell. It might be affected charm, but he looks utterly starstruck, genuinely so.

Lucian takes a small bow, then reaches out to take the Belladonna's hand: 'I've been so desirous to make your acquaintance. Ever since I first saw you at the Opéra in fact.'

Excuse me?

The unease starts low in Flora, becomes a feeling shifting through her body. Like her organs are moving about to make space for something new, something foreign, something she is already braced to reject. She cannot quite understand the sensation enough to say: *You can't say that. I feel that way for her. That's me, not you.* But the recognition is there, prickling beyond a place she can perceive. If she were a cat her back would be arching.

The Belladonna smiles, an open and warm expression. 'The Opéra, you say? How wonderful that you're a music lover. And by frequenting this establishment also, you enjoy culture's full range. When you're not leaving various professions.'

Marcelin smiles, as if to say, and that's it, my job is done, they are away! But then, unable to resist intervening, he adds: 'Oh, Luc hasn't seen one of these horror-plays yet. We're going to go in for the next one tonight and *that* will be his first.' Luc looks dubious, so Marcelin shoves him in the ribs. 'I keep telling you. You'll love it! See? *La Dame* loves it. Always going on about wanting some exciting new experiences aren't you. Well, this will be it. A totally new style. It's called naturalism. Won't he love it?'

The Belladonna shrugs off the question. 'Some acquire the taste.'

Lucian laughs nervously and the Belladonna smiles again, providing the necessary reassurance. She looks about the tiny theatre, busy with revellers.

'If you haven't seen what they do here, I wonder how to do it justice in words. Monsieur, somehow they really *do* depict exactly how it would be to have one's eyes gouged out and the sockets jabbed with rose stems; the actors play how it would truly really *feel*, emotionally, to place a decapitated head upon your own father's blood-splattered tomb. I'll confess I never found myself wondering before, but now I've no doubt I really *know*. Say they produced "The Bloody Flower" as an opera. You might get a sense of the great themes, but could you say you've really obtained a sense of *how* you might cut off somebody's limbs? Isn't it curious how art can open up our world to take in others?'

'It's amazing,' Marcelin interjects, and adds some helpful detail. 'Whatever they make their skin out of, creates an extraordinary sound as it's pulled apart.'

Lucian mutters something in polite agreement about the wonders of naturalism, and looks around as if desperate for inspiration, or possibly a way out. The movement allows Flora to see him more fully, as the foyer lights have commenced brightening and dimming—a quick pulse, hurrying the dawdling audience back into the theatre. And in that bright light she sees it: his hair looks mahogany, she had pinned it as dark, but its movement reveals a rich ore of copper. Lucian's hair is lifted by a unique shade of reddish gold, a secret until you see him right. Hidden treasure, this one.

She looks between him and her lady and feels she is admiring a set of earrings, a pair of deep-coloured gems, glittering when held up to the light.

Lucian starts as if he's forgotten something. 'Oh! I've brought …' He pulls out a small box wrapped in crumpled violet, just as the bell rings to signal the next performance of terror is beginning, and the crowd streams back into the closeness of the auditorium. La Dame aux Morelles stands unmoving, with no intention to attend. She nods approvingly at Marcelin and Lucian (*you may call upon me again*, her expression says) and wishes them a pleasant experience. They both look disappointed, but neither press the issue.

A short time later, rolling home in the carriage, sitting in silence that has stretched out a little. The Belladonna's face has become still, suggesting that pain descends, and Flora is replaying images from the evening over and over: the scenes that make her feel the most uncomfortable are the ones she is most drawn to. Not all these images are things she's seen in a play. The Belladonna, her eyes still closed: 'You didn't want to stay for any more, did you?'

'Not at all.' That rich copper hair, the slightly clumsy way he'd held the present out to her, practically exposing a vein.

Raising a hand to press at the pain in her forehead, the Belladonna leans back against the wall of the carriage, fussing up her hair. 'That's good; I wouldn't want to pull you away. I felt we'd done enough business for the night, and I didn't want those two circling us a second time. A very brief impression was more than enough for Lucian. Wasn't it?'

Certainly.

*

She signs her name with a flourish. 'Certainly he may enter.'

With a bow, the servant leaves; he'll take the autograph to a hopeful devotee and, crucially, deliver the message to the admirer waiting below. (And if this servant remembers Flora from their brief meeting in the cloakroom, he makes no hint of it.)

They are sitting in their box at the Opéra. Opening night, first interval: a prestigious window for receiving guests. The fringed curtain is pushed aside and there Lucian stands, feet tight together as if trying to fit across a narrow ledge. He holds the violet crepe box out and Belladonna leans towards Flora and whispers, and this is the beginning of a standard manoeuvre between them—see how it plays.

'Perhaps we come back to this later do you think?' she says—and Flora, in black wrist-length gloves, puts her hand over her mouth and laughs gently, eyes to the floor (seemingly to regain control), then she—and oh, it's expertly timed—sneaks a look back to Lucian. The ruse works as intended; he rocks slightly on his heels, his centre of gravity displaced. Belladonna and her Flora are a united front, and he is no longer sure how to proceed.

Taking the gift from him results in discomfort for Flora, because it leads to the sight of the Belladonna eating sugared grapes. It's something she cannot seem to get used to, the way the sweets uncannily double the nightshade. She even has replica berries scattered in tonight's hair. Eyes closed, head thrown back, baring her neck to eat handfuls of the things at a time—no wonder the salons are rife with whispers and rumours about her invincibility to the poison. She thanks her new admirer for the gift, politely answers a few of his comments, then dismisses him. So far, so simple.

Soon, Belladonna is accepting another invitation for Lucian to call. Collecting her at the door, they stand close and whisper together, a brief conversation of nothings—that's usual enough. Except, Flora perceives that something is different. The nervousness Lucian came with has gradually shed away, and now she feels herself too present in their company. She can't perform her duties as the invisible Companion, it's not enough to keep discreetly out of the way; it seems too much that she's there at all.

In his oak-lined office, Vernon frowns and taps the top of his desk with an ink-stained hand.

'La Dame is seeing rather a lot of this one,' he says. 'Poet, isn't he? That doesn't bode well. Not many spends from him, to justify all this personal attention. What's your verdict?'

'She's almost exclusively in his company,' says Flora. 'And it's still not as often as he'd like; often she'll tell him not to come, and I've written enough apologies for her illness to him I can do it without looking.'

'But she's not actually ill?'

'Thankfully no, it's her favoured alibi. But she's not seeing anyone else, either.'

Why one person and not another? Flora wonders this as, yet again, Belladonna is collected at the door of the hotel by Lucian, pluming himself up in readiness to show her to her carriage—and then suddenly becoming rigid. A sigh passes through his body, as visible as if he'd written it out, as Flora's approach reveals that she, too, will be going with them. There's tension through the rest of the evening, mirrored by how he holds himself—in the carriage, through the meal, during noncommittal goodbyes, as if there's nothing for it now but to wait for the damned evening to be over. Why one person and not another: why not Marcelin, even, or any gentleman from the salons? Why choose the one with this strange aversion to Flora's very presence, who makes her feel as if she's about to be pushed backwards out the door?

La Dame aux Morelles decides to ignore his letters completely for a few days, and Flora finds herself operating with an improved energy, as if some deep pressure has been lifted.

*

What you see: and what's really there.

Rumours grow ripe on the branch (*the Belladonna and that poet—what's his name, the youngest Delamarre son … I heard they're never apart*) but it would not do to pluck one down and examine it. Besides, this sort of chatter is expected, it is designed and encouraged, it lends a sense of reality to the whole thing. A cunning illusion, expertly drawn.

It's early afternoon and La Dame, as always, has not long arisen. She finishes a leisurely breakfast and announces that the time is right for appreciating culture. The Musée des Artistes Vivants has a new exhibition of illusion painting. 'I thought Luc might enjoy it, all that trompe l'oeil.'

So, she wants to play further games with reality. Flora knows Vernon would advise against encouraging Lucian further, and she doesn't at all feel up to trudging silently through a gallery, sensing his impatience at her presence.

'I have an idea, though,' the Belladonna says, seeing Flora thinking this, 'for making it a bit more fun. Here's my development.' She leans forward, her expression widening.

'Instead of the three of us, why don't you take him on your own?'

'I'm sorry?' Further sense of dread at that, she could sink all the way down through her chair: what, cart his sulking self all the way around an art gallery *on her own?* Oh yes, what a joy he'll be when there's no Belladonna at all. Verily, she can hardly wait. But the Belladonna coughs again and it shakes through her whole frame, and the suggestion takes on a different context: these new, stronger coughing fits. No doubting she'd better stay away from the roaring fog of the city. But still, why push Flora into it?

The Belladonna explains further, her hand at her head. 'I'm going to invite him to come, then baulk at the last minute. I've already declined an offer of supper with the faithful Madame Guilliard, so the news will soon get about that I'm not seeing anyone. And I think it might complicate things nicely, for you to take him.'

'So, La Dame, it will seem that you intended to go with him, but couldn't. And after not replying to him for over a week! He'll be very disappointed.' *A very disappointed Lucian Delamarre. I could not hope to envisage better company at a gallery.*

'Shall I come out and wave him off, do you think?' the Belladonna asks.

'A little cruel, on top of everything else,' Flora says.

'You're probably right. But it's honest at least.'

Dressing, then, for this brief moment: very like La Dame aux Morelles to put in all the usual effort for an appearance of only a few seconds. When Flora gets flustered choosing her lady's jewellery, the Belladonna comes to the rescue, swooping into the dressing-room and finding Flora caught looking at two very similar necklaces, lost in the differences.

'There are nuances,' says the Belladonna, making a decision and picking up the sharper oval. She holds it to her throat, standing before one of the full-length mirrors.

Flora feels the tension of her own indecision. 'You're right,' she says. *Why one person and not another? Is one simply fitter for purpose?*

The Belladonna nods, looking at her reflection—it's possible to watch her become her title in that moment, in the way she examines her face in the glass. Those eyes … Then she smiles, reaching up to fasten the pendant about her neck.

Lucian is waiting beside the carriage, and as the hotel entrance reveals Belladonna's sharp silhouette and Flora stood beside, he smiles, and holds the carriage door open for them. The Belladonna refuses the invitation, turns and goes back into the hotel, leaving Flora to take charge of matters.

By the time Flora reaches the carriage, any surprise he might have expressed has become something firm. He looks closed, his face holding an irritated question: would you provide an explanation, please?

'My lady is indisposed,' says F. And the carriage ride to the gallery is swallowed up by gloomy silence.

The trompe l'oeil exhibition is the first of its kind, a series of experiments brought together into the Galerie Georges Petit, a thin building stripped of its furnishings for the purpose. *Le Journal* has been abuzz for weeks with writings, even presenting some intricate previews in its full-colour *supplément illustré*: breathlessly anticipating the arrival of so many paintings that mimic objects from life, and the puzzle a building full of them would surely present to the senses.

F. and Lucian walk through the rooms, and although they take a determined silence with them, there are wondrous things to look at. F. would believe there really *is* a viola hanging from the wall, accompanied by its bow and sheafs of sheet music. She feels she could reach out and touch the cavalier who points his finger at them from the inside of his picture-frame, that she could heave herself through the gilt border and dwell in the space beyond.

One room has been painted such that, for all the world, you'd think yourself looking at the carnage left behind after a great wrecking-ball had swung on a chain and shattered the brickwork; in another, it is only when Lucian stands over the gaping hole that the architecture of the floor and wall loom up out of the darkness, making the vision waiver: he floats, he stands, he floats. F. breaks into laughter and although she quickly covers her mouth it flutes high, given the nerves she has been suppressing all the time they've been making their way about together; and the sheer absurdity of it all seems to break Lucian out of his shell.

'I'm getting dizzy,' he says. 'Why don't I plummet?'

'Ha! That's all very well, Lucian, but how do you suppose I feel? I shouldn't be able to see you at all. How are you there, and yet still stubbornly living?'

He puts his hands on his hips, but his expression is warm. Floating one moment, anchored to the floor the next. 'It would be easier for you, I suppose, to have me out of the way.' And he looks at her with what seems to be genuine friendliness.

Something is changing between them. F. feels certain; she knows it, she wants to dance. *Don't look at it directly, yet;*

just enjoy it.

Lucian steps off the precipice. 'I'm glad we've come here. I wanted to ask…' He casts around, gestures at the painted emptiness that never, in the end, swallowed him up. 'Does the Belladonna tell you about me?'

'No, not at all. Why should she?' *She doesn't tell me everything the two of you get up to. I see enough already, and I don't want to know the rest.*

'I haven't spoken to you before, have I? Not properly. You know you could have gone off anywhere else today besides the gallery.'

'But now you can tell her all about it.'

Her toes nudge the edge of the precipice over the floor.

He lowers his head. 'You're happy sacrificing yourself for her?'

'Of course. As are you. I know it's more entertaining if she's around.'

'An undeniable truth.' Lucian holds out his arm and beckons F. to step over the painted void. They smile at each other; does the smile linger?

As they walk through the next rooms the paintings, for all their eerie realness and forced perspectives clamouring for attention, can no longer compete with her inner feelings. Her imagination reels and the paintings sink into the background. She and Lucian have somehow broken through the deadlock, like it was never there, and in its place is an opening for friendship. And they seem to take it up with enthusiasm.

'You know, I originally thought Marcelin was having me on—about meeting the Belladonna. The both of you surely wouldn't be seen somewhere that ghastly. I don't know how you manage to stomach it.'

'I have a harder constitution than it may appear. But Lucian—where *would* you presume to find me? Now we've spent the afternoon and you're an expert in such matters.'

'We're discussing a moment on your own, theoretically?'

'If you had to place a bet.'

'I wouldn't presume. It's an interesting thing, I'm realising now—I'm sure I couldn't find you if you didn't wish for it.'

Something in the next room catches his eye.

'Look at that.' He points to the painted aura that spreads over the gallery wall. 'An angel descending!' The angelic figure appears to be bursting through its gilt-illusioned frame. 'They really are among us.'

She squeezes his arm. 'Might we end up with too many?'

The redness that glints through the darkness of his hair is an aura too, of a kind.

She wants this moment to carry on. F. has sensed this longing in others who surround the Belladonna, the way they lean in to disclose great secrets, how she creates a sense of intimacy and privacy for them: with F. sitting right there, of course. F. has watched all this happen between other people, but now, with Lucian, there is a difference to the feeling. She is seeing it from the inside.

Not long after the tromp l'oeil trip, La Dame aux Morelles decides to cut Lucian off again. It's a long-term plan: make him wait, stretch the rumours out, display her availability for other callers, open up invitations to other events. F. agrees with the strategy but worries at the loss of his company, no sooner than it had opened to her. The whole thing is a lot to ignore. His letters grow from daily to twice a day. He asks after the Belladonna's health, wishes her good morning, offers further invitations, asks whether he has offended, expresses confusion, wishes her good night. F. pictures him, she remembers the hole, wondering if he fell in after all.

*

It is at the next salon when Flora sees him again properly. At the Belladonna's pleasure the apartments have been opened once more to her selected guests, who have been ushered through the damask-lined rooms and now sit among the candles. Conversation drifts through the place, with the smell of incense and flowers delivered that morning (in the shadows it barely matters what species they are). The piano has been newly polished and sits there impressively. An esteemed pianist is in attendance tonight, and we should be lucky enough to catch his performance.

The Belladonna is in close conversation with a young man, and Flora pretends she doesn't recognise Lucian until he rises in laughter at some comment or other, and she sees the flash of red as he moves through a soft pool of candlelight. He wipes his face with the back of his hand, still laughing, and the Belladonna leans against his arm slightly. How can it be that the two of them have immediately returned to such intimate relations? Flora makes her way through the party until she hovers beside them, her stomach sinking. She *knew* it would be like this, and it is.

Belladonna gives Flora her reluctant attention. 'Are you needing something to do?'

'Just the opposite. We're ready to announce the music.'

At this news, Belladonna's expression dissolves and she claps her hands. Lucian looks momentarily thrown off, unaware of any such plans.

La Dame speaks excitedly. 'Fetch him, Flora; oh, there's no need. There he is. Franz!'

She refers to the man in the violet suit who is coming towards them. There's something cat-like in his movements as he adjusts his collar, in conscious display of those famous hands. Tonight he is going to premiere a new work, a *coup de théâtre* for both himself and the hostess. The triangle that is made up of the Belladonna, Flora and Lucian must, impossibly, accommodate a fourth corner.

The pianist bends to kiss her outstretched hand. As he rises he towers over her, while she stares up at him adoringly.

Child prodigy and now an international touring star, Franz has had a career like a comet, and recently returned from a wide and rigorous campaign on the continent, melting crowd after crowd with rapturous playing that, by all accounts, seems to introduce the piano (properly, at least) to the world. He bows and greets Flora with courtesy, and on hearing she is an old Opéra friend of La Dame aux Morelles—and therefore a friend of art itself—he takes care to ask intently after both of them. His face has a freshness as if he has just come off stage, and experience lends wisdom to his eyes, seeing broader horizons than the rest of them. Here is a person who has pursued what he wants to a level of world-class excellence, and thinks, why doesn't everybody?

'Look at this. The first time I met Franz—where was it again?'

'Montmartre. *Le Divan*, in Pigalle. I know you can

remember.'

'You were playing those incredibly fast scales with one hand, and toying with that girl's hair with the other, showing off! And I, excited thing as I was, dared you to compare hands with me.'

A smile like love. 'And I, dazzled, couldn't begin to think what you meant.'

'Let's do it again, show Flora. Flora, I want you to see. Look at this!'

The Belladonna holds out her hand, fingers spread, and the pianist puts his hand to match, touching hers palm to palm. His fingers spread far past and beyond.

Her dark eyes widen, a perfect impression of childlike wonder. 'Incredible!'

Lucian has taken a few steps backwards, and now he stands as if trapped in an alleyway, forced to watch this exchange between pianist and Belladonna as it plays out before him. Although his disapproval is clear, it appears he cannot bring himself to leave either. Flora ought to rescue him, take his elbow and ask a charming question while leading him gently away: perhaps she might ask about Lucian's own musicianship. Or enquire about his family affairs—although she stops herself asking something personal, perhaps that might be something for between them on a good day. But she doesn't rescue him, doesn't do any of this. Instead she remains still, witness to Lucian being pinned into position, trapped in a state of awkwardness uncharacteristic of him and so even more distressing to see. She's just as trapped herself. And the Belladonna, effecting an apparent obliviousness to all this, is clearly ignoring Lucian's distress as she enjoys the pianist's fingers dancing before her, letting him move closer as they speak excitedly about the particular charm of the concert halls in Belarus, the dignified approval of the crowds in Berlin, the queues of lace-draped ladies begging for signatures in Rome. The Belladonna is being her operatic self, experienced and otherworldly, well-travelled and fully rehearsed. It is required, to match the swirling tempest of life Franz brings with him.

Lucian's sad eyes gaze across the group and catch Flora, bisecting the rapt attentions of the other two. Willing her face blank, she stares at him. He looks defeated.

Yes, she would say to him, if she could speak freely. *That's what it's like for me, too. It comes to all of us. It happened to me when she first met you.*

Lucian is finally given the attentions of La Dame aux Morelles, who clutches his arm and takes him off to be introduced to people: Flora hears him entertaining guest after guest throughout the night, his voice and manner returned to him, working quickly as if to make up for time. His presence at the salon is a full success: he listens carefully to a dowager duchess's list of woes and charms her with his sympathies; he is able to join a tricky legal dispute and even recall the dates correctly, if not the Latin. The famous playwright Renaudière, whom Flora had impressed at the previous salon, sneaks up to ask her where on earth he'd been discovered. He smiles at Flora meaningfully and tells her to make sure the Belladonna doesn't lose this one: 'not before the rest of us have had a chance to find him.'

Later, after the piano concert and its fizz of applause, after Franz has bid farewell to the guests, who practically break out the trumpets to see him off, and after the exodus of the rest of the guests, including Lucian who does not look Flora fully in the eye as she stands by the door; after all this is completed and the next stage of the salon is underway, after the berries have been eaten and the drawing-room has taken on the bitter smell of vomit, the Belladonna looks up to her companion and speaks.

'Plays devil on this carpet.' Her voice is precise and careful, to make itself heard over the low moans that fill the room like steadily rising water. She is kneeling, and in one arm she cradles the head of a troubled young woman whose agony has been audible and constant from the moment the berry took effect.

Flora is passing with a vase under her arm, to tidy the flowers the poisoned woman just knocked over with an involuntary kick of the leg.

'It's all right,' the Belladonna whispers to the guest. Then, louder to Flora, she adds: 'Lots of soil, and it's gone under the table; you'd better bring the brush.'

Flora was walking towards the spilled flowers. Of course she'd seen the soil; and this gives her irritation a final push.

It's out before she can think about it. 'You were uncivil to Lucian tonight.'

From the floor the Belladonna radiates disapproval which Flora picks up on, so she speaks quickly to get through the heat of it.

'You know he could tell it was deliberate. You ignoring him like that to go about with Franz. We could all tell, and quite frankly I don't see there was any need for it.'

'Very well, you're right it was deliberate. But I do also

adore Franz. Two birds … and we both know Luc has been spoilt. He's had plenty of attention, he has to *know* how this works. Besides, he seemed perfectly content the rest of the time. There's much that was a thorough success this evening. Don't fixate on a negative.'

'But I think it's not so simple.' *You saw his expression as he left. You'll force him away, playing games like that.* 'He felt humiliated. Do you think Lucian will allow himself to be treated that way?'

'We'll need the brush.' Her face is closed: there is to be no further discussion. There are more important things to be done. 'There there,' she adds softly, returning her attentions to the young woman in her arms, whose eyes roll with visions from the berry.

*

In the daytime, especially when the sky is clouded over so the light is soft and non-insistent, and the Belladonna has risen in time to take advantage of the cool air, she is known to take the carriage to the Rue des Martyrs and walk out alone. It is a reliable enough habit, in a fashionable enough spot, that crowds gather to watch her from a distance. Today the light is dark and smudged, as if the whole city is under a thick glass bowl, and so the Belladonna has gone for her walk, and F. sits alone beneath the awning of a cafe, reading a letter from the jewellers: a family business La Dame keeps on retainer.

The letter says much that she expected. The necklace the Belladonna asked for is being constructed as quickly as possible; the jewellers hope that La Dame will be pleased with the purity of the diamond. Well, of course they hope that. Folding the letter neatly in half, a movement catches her eye; she looks up and sees Lucian coming towards her. Her fingers momentarily twitch to keep going with the paper: fold it twice, thrice, four times, turn it into a swan, even— anything to look busy.

'Flora! Well, good afternoon, what a surprise.'

The sincerity of his voice is convincing, and it seems for a moment he is genuinely pleased to find her there. Seems and, who knows, perhaps he really is. F. lets herself admit that possibility. The Belladonna is off on her afternoon walk, after all; he would surely know where to find the lady herself if he were looking for her. The result of this manner of reasoning is that F. allows herself to accept Lucian's company, and then finds that they are strolling along the boulevard together, in and out through the great shadow-stripes of the trees.

'I don't have too long,' says F., mostly to quell her own thoughts: even as this pleasant moment begins, she is telling herself, remember it will be ending.

'You'll have your duties, I understand,' says Lucian politely. There's some attentiveness there, too—for he notices her putting a hand to her lower back.

'Should we find another place to sit?'

'I'm perfectly fine,' she says. 'A lot of correspondence to be dealt with, which is very good at keeping me still.' *Too much time spent leaning over a printing press*, she supposes. But it won't last. And it's nice of him to ask.

'You mustn't understate it. Laudanum can help if needed.'

F. giggles. 'What sage wisdom you have, Monsieur Delamarre! Your friend Monsieur Capet said you were a scholar in the field I believe?'

Whatever happens, she is thinking, *don't turn this to a discussion of coughing or headaches. This time is for me.*

'A fair rebuttal. But if you recall Marcelin saying nice things, then your memory is exaggerating in my favour. He would have said I *stopped* studying it.' He laughs, a little strained, and lightly kicks a loose stone: it rolls lumpily across the shadows over the ground. 'I find myself between schools. My family wanted law; I wanted art, sculpture; poetry certainly isn't going to pay, that's one thing I do know. We settled on medicine, briefly, but I've given it in.'

'May I ask why you did?'

'It wasn't …' he gestures as if his arm would take in the whole world, '… enough.' He laughs at himself. 'You know I don't think I can get any closer to it. Is that too romantic, would you take me seriously if I said it? Nevertheless, I challenge anybody with a sense of their own survival to see that world and want to donate their lives to it.'

Lucian pulls at the lapels of his coat. 'And, I felt my professors may have loathed me.'

'I've known professors and they're too busy to hate, so it certainly wouldn't be that.'

A young artist passes them by with a scorpion, walking it on a leash. All the interesting people are out this afternoon, it seems. F. refuses to give this one the attention.

'Well they certainly had little time for me,' says Lucian.

F.'s eyes widen with realisation. 'I've known medical students,' she says.

'It seems you've known many different sorts of people.'

'Perhaps. Is it not the case that such students have to work with dead bodies, have to dissect cadavers? And, in fact, I remember you not looking too delighted at the talk of blood.'

He smiles, briefly. 'All right. You have me. But it wasn't as often as people might think. And it's very controlled. It's not the dregs of a night at the absinthe house. But it most certainly isn't for me.'

The shadows of the trees move over them as they walk on. *No more questions to you. I need you to ask something of me. I require it.* F. makes the resolution to wait.

'Well. Enough of my self regard,' he says. 'Forgive me. I've been wanting to know … '

A satisfaction swells within her.

Come now, ask after me!

'Surely you're not from Paris? I have a theory that nobody is.'

Is that what you have? Is that your question?

The relief F. had felt dissipates quickly. 'I don't know about your theory but in my case, you are right,' she says.

'I want to leave Paris someday.' He sighs. 'And I worry that's something the Belladonna would never do, which makes our relationship quite complicated.'

And there it is. No matter how wide the boulevard it will reach the same, inevitable destination as if they'd all squeezed down the narrowest of alleyways. For a moment she allowed herself to believe that just maybe … but no. Foolish to even think.

She lets a gap in conversation strain out between them.

'How long have you been her companion?'

'Long enough.' That's right: don't give him anything.

He laughs, and has the grace to be self-effacing. 'Me too then, I suppose. It doesn't take long to be enough, does it? I know I'm fortunate to have her choose me.'

'We're both lucky then.'

She is facing a complete blank. How does the Belladonna do this? La Dame and this one can speak in whispered half-nothings, rippled through with laughter, tied together by an immediate understanding and a shared joy, within seconds of meeting and do it for hours; why does she, F., find her hands tied the moment it comes to doing the same? Never mind that the Belladonna can do that with *anyone*.

He nods to himself as more silence slots between them, as if they've both admitted to sharing the same secret.

She finds herself wishing she could confide in him: about important things, her previous life, so different compared to now. For a moment he'd asked her story; she would have been ready to tell him. But now she sees it: what would any of it be to Lucian? It's from the time before the Belladonna, and so can be struck out.

Not even a glimmer of conversation arises now. The boulevard is long, she has no real sense of destination: all that possibility has drained away, as if the Belladonna stuck a pin into their time and drew out all the fun. It's spiteful. All F. is left with has been gummed into silence, the better to not give him anything at all. They pass a shop window filled with bonnets and Lucian stops and mutters something about having to leave, having to be somewhere; F. casts an empty gaze about the bonnets in the window and nods, says a few vague words about going in for ribbons.

That voice again at the back of her mind: where has this hardness come from? Resent him, then feel sorry for him, and now this determined nothingness. What is it? That the Belladonna is between them. Or is it that Lucian is taking F.'s place? This distinct feeling, as imprecise as it is uncomfortable, that somebody is in the way.

He takes a step in the direction of the road to call for a carriage. It might as well be a ten-acre leap away from her.

To say it is painful would be too much, but it's a jolt to know he's abandoned her like that, and even though she suffered in his company, she's sorry there isn't more of it. So it is only now that she fully realises.

Maybe I'm the one in love here.

So that's it.

*

She is unsure what to do. For a while she puzzles it over, turning it around this way and that. She has cultivated feelings for Lucian; she knows that. But is it *love*? How could it be possible when she is so swayed by the dark charisma of the Belladonna? Does she love her mistress? Is that what this is? Does she simply need the attentions of the woman she so admires? She wants, more than anything, to be in the life of the Belladonna. That much hasn't changed. So perhaps, she thinks, this new tangle concerning Lucian is nothing to do with Lucian's own charms. And yet, charms she sees. And she wants Lucian, just as much, to see her. Such confusion. What will happen if she simply accepts the lot? If she decides upon a world where she does, yes, love Lucian, and also the Belladonna, she can put it all aside by knowing her closeness to La Dame is hers alone: a closeness based on their maintaining of that exalted position. And so, she presses herself into it. Lucian's clumsy infatuations become easier to live with; in fact, it brings them closer together.

They both know what it is like, to be in thrall to the woman with the pitch-black eyes; and the three become attached. A dynamic that is guided between them, secret knowledge that allows such good friendships in fact, that F. thinks, *maybe Lucian is feeling these things for me, too.*

And new approaches are tried.

*

She had expected the realisation to add to the pressure, but for a while things are strangely easy. The Belladonna and Lucian go for their long walks, visit the theatre, take late night suppers and whisper secretly together, and Flora runs the messages, organises the meetings, consults with the carriage-driver, scans, adjusts and sets the menu; but her presence to them is welcome, as is theirs to her. The three of them together, no longer a source of frustration.

The trio, then, in the Belladonna apartments. Flora sitting between the two of them. Lucian has kicked off his boots and they are all admiring some of the Belladonna's larger jewels. With a moderate frown of appraisal, she is idly draping across her neck and collarbone a necklace the size of a lace napkin, a concoction of diamonds as far-spreading as if a regular necklace has split, and the gems run everywhere.

'I've never found a use for this one,' says La Dame aux

Morelles. 'Somehow it always seems, just a bit too much.' She pours it back into its box with a sigh, then briefly brings a hand to cover her eyes.

'What's that, are you tired? I should take my leave,' says Lucian, and slowly begins to rise. He is not permitted to, of course, and they both wave him back, until he is once more lounging on the chaise.

More champagne instead, delivered by a smirking hotel-boy in a cap fringed with gold. As they raise their glasses for a triumphant toast, Flora imagines Vernon angrily pacing: why weren't they present at the ballet tonight? Does she think rumour won't start? Does she think, after he's been promised her attendance, the Baron de Lavictoire won't notice her absence? Oh, but she wouldn't be the Belladonna if she didn't ignore an invitation once in a while. She mustn't be seen to be at anyone's beck and call.

There are always more requests. Speaking of which. Lucian says: 'When will you sing for us?'

She stops, and affects to be shocked—her hands in those silk gloves lifting another frothing pile of diamonds towards his head to pile them on top for amusement. 'I beg your pardon?'

'I'm desperate to hear you.' He rises, is heading to the piano. 'My parents battered lessons into me, I bet I can remember at least something.'

They follow him to where the instrument stands, grand and silent, surrounded by the closed curtains, as if threatening to rise. The Belladonna leans onto the piano, Flora can see her shaking a little. 'All right. But I won't begin alone.'

The three of them stumble together through the *Habanera*

aria, and the Belladonna's confidence grows—by the end of the first verse, she has opened her chest and sings with defiance. Her voice lilts through the apartments and gathers strength as it goes, as if her throat were a flower that had not opened for a season, stretching to the sun. Flora and Lucian give their own flourishes to her melody, joining in with additions of their own as they gradually cast themselves as the chorus: by the end, they all collapse laughing. Lucian stands at the piano, putting himself into an awkward half-crouch, fingers still on the keys and stretching as if he also wants to reach her.

'Your voice!' he cries. 'So delicate, but what beauty!'

Flora is wildly excited. The three of them can act like this, perfectly happily, and the world won't end. In her euphoria she puts words to the image that has just come to her: 'You ought to perform at your salons.'

The Belladonna waves the suggestion away. 'I am their host! They come to relax, not be pressured into applauding my every idea.'

'Oh but really!' Lucian and Flora inch closer together in their giddiness: now the idea has been introduced, of the Belladonna doing this for a wider audience, the two of them are momentarily drunk with it:

'Just think of it!'

'Everyone would love it!'

'It's true!' says Flora. 'Imagine you on the Opéra stage! I can picture it.' The image lights up her mind, as fanciful as it is. And yet somehow tantalising.

Then Lucian's hand finds the top of Flora's arm; they look at each other and the space between them is warm, welcoming. Here it is again, as if an excellent sparkling wine has been uncorked between them.

The feeling rises, rises until it's all she's made of. The Belladonna is leafing through some sheet music, apparently oblivious; Lucian and Flora look at each other, caught, in a position that's practically an embrace. A tiny voice in the back of her mind says: *but look, oh god, this is dangerous; this is not my role. And he's completely for the Belladonna, you do know that don't you? You're actually watching that happening. You're helping, for heaven's sake.*

And another voice answers: *but, no, perhaps … perhaps the world can spin backwards. In fact, yes: I do believe the world is spinning backwards. How else to explain this?* After all, she's not invisible in Lucian's presence anymore, more than that, she's *so* visible now. She can't possibly be imagining this.

'You must let more people hear you sing,' says Flora, finally sending her attention back to the woman at the piano. 'There's always been rumours, everyone has a story of your voice, imagine the joy when they hear it for themselves!'

Lucian moves back a little, towards the keys; the warmth of his fingers leaves her arm.

The Belladonna's smile is enigmatic as she traces a finger along the piano lid, where another great name is spelled out in a delicate gold script. 'I don't know about that. For you two it's different, as my dearest friends … let's do another, it *is* freeing,' she says.

Lucian claps his hands and reseats himself, begins a few trills on the piano.

The song quickly develops into something new and made up, charged by the freedom of the drink; Flora joins in and the earth reels in reverse, she doesn't even feel her barely trained voice is misplaced as somehow the three of them all combine to produce something wonderful, their own parts making sense in the whole, like magic.

They reach a spontaneous finale in a mad flourish of notes and come together in a wild celebration, half in a hug, half in a huddle. The Belladonna is short of breath as she replaces her corsage and straightens the collar that had come awry.

Lucian says: 'You are a marvel.'

Flora agrees silently: she is a marvel. But so too are you. By the time he and the Belladonna retire into the bedroom, and Flora is waving them off, looking as happy as either of them, the voice within her is able to say: Well, of course he goes with *her*.

That's only to be expected. But I newly think I am right, that he'd happily go with me too. Also, or instead: I mean, if our places were different.

And that's what gets her through the night, thinking about the secret space between herself and Lucian. He's courting the Belladonna, of course: naturally he is. And yet.

So, three it is. And Flora looks forward to every visit, and each smile and laugh and slight glance from Lucian feels like a gift. She collects them; she has enough to make a raft. Impossible to sink anyway, with hope keeping you up.

*

'A country house retreat? Am I hearing you right?'

The three of them are gathered in the Opéra office, and Monsieur Vernon's mouth has dropped open in shock. With no anomalies arising and everything seeming to be above board, the Belladonna dropped the stone of this suggestion into the meeting just as she and F. were rising to go, and now it looks as if passion has drawn them all from their seats.

Vernon stalks around the table, avoiding their eyes and staring straight ahead, as if there's a centre of gravity in the room he won't be caught in. 'Terrible idea,' he says. 'Bad, bad, bad. It's early for you to do anything on that scale, especially with that one. Plus, we have *le Prix de Diane* just after. Treads on the toes.'

'It wouldn't be for the month. Three weeks at the most. And my being away would create some intrigue.'

'Bother to that. We need you *here* for those weeks. And what about supper with the Comtesse two weeks over, do you think she needs the mystery? And the Baron has been asking questions again.'

He has performed a full circulation of the desk. He does an about turn, goes around it the other way.

The Belladonna is watching his movement with a steady, gentle turning of the head. F. is reminded of an owl making the necessary calculations before the plunge. 'We may have to delay the Comtesse.'

'May we buggery. You know we can't and you're just saying that to wind me up. But regardless. I just don't think you should leave the city, for that long, at this time.'

'Luc has put himself through some difficulties to raise the funds, through appeals to his family, whom he says are not in a position to easily acquiesce.'

'Do they even know what they're raising funds for?'

'Time away for taking the air. For his health.' A triumphant smile warms the tone of her voice. 'Once he got that idea into them, he tells me his mother practically pushed him out the door. They are more caring than they are financially stretched, it seems.'

Vernon shakes his head, more in wonder at the audacity than rejection of it. 'I do like the potential for a certain flavour of scandal. But as I say, we've too many other commitments. Not to mention there'll be no further income through that time.'

The Belladonna speaks sharply. 'We aren't hand to mouth exactly, are we? He found the place himself, secured the lease. I have assented to go with him.'

'Unassent.'

'Unacceptable.'

'You shouldn't have committed in the first place. What, did you think it wouldn't come to this?' Vernon stops circling and they face each other, the desk between them a thick wooden impasse.

It's unwelcome to F., the sight of a genuine disagreement between these two. In the Belladonna's expression, she sees why: regardless of how she ought to be *seen*, La Dame wants this.

F. is speaking before she fully realises. 'I know a way to make it beneficial.'

Whose voice is that, cantering into a battlefield and waving merrily at the livid troops on either side?

They turn their eyes to her. Vernon's voice expresses interest, though his face remains cautious. 'How so?'

'I think it could be made to work, even the things that don't work.' Seeing their frozen expressions, she keeps going.

'Let me explain: the inappropriate timing, the late notice. It could all be used to our advantage.'

Vernon rolls his eyes and the Belladonna loosens a little and begins knotting her fingers together, as if reconciled to waiting this out before resuming the crossfire between the two of them, the parties who actually know what they are talking about.

F. addresses Vernon, as the Belladonna's disinterest is too off-putting. 'We go all the way, we welcome the damaged reputation, all the lapsed invites, sudden cancellations. We push everything as far as we can.'

He shakes his head, but isn't forcing the idea away: it's concentration, turning the idea this way and that, he brings up his hands as if to hold it out before him, testing its weight. He does trust her. 'So we do the trip, and on return, issue a barrage of apologies—'

'No apologies at all.'

His hands freeze in mid-air. 'I don't understand.'

F. looks at the pile of ledgers, still lying fat and open on the table, the exposed pages filled with columns of neatly written prices and dates. 'We begin to put it about—that the Belladonna is thinking about resigning the life. Hence no apologies, no notice of absence. We say she and Lucian are, possibly, we think, it *seems*, in love—I mean can you believe it—and running away to leave the city. The Belladonna has been convinced, through finding him, to surrender wholly to love, and we know she was *going* to attend your supper, Comtesse, but she's gone.'

The Belladonna's hands have become still again. F. feels the weight of both of their attentions on her and doesn't even notice which of them says: 'Go on.'

She goes on: 'For then, this is it, you see: when the scandal comes, it will be around the question—could it be true? Has the Belladonna really gone? Is she leaving the city for a bucolic existence in the rumpled dungheap of some small village? Can we really imagine *our* lady of the night swayed by the passions of one young poet among so many? Is she really going to give up the moonlit boulevards and Opéra premieres to strut about in daylight in a summer dress, go boating with him on the duckpond? With a *parasol*?'

She flips the ledger closed with a heavy thunk. 'Then, three weeks later, we turn up at the *Diane* races. No apology for the moment of madness, and things go on as usual. Perhaps we never say either way. And they'll wonder: *was* it love, *is* it true, all that about giving everything up. We never say how close she came to the edge.'

The Belladonna speaks: it would have to be her, because Vernon would never ask this. 'And what about Luc himself, what happens to him?'

F. doesn't quite know on whose behalf she's acting, but she wants this trip to happen, the three of them together—why not?

She says: 'Perhaps Lucian believes the story too, I'm sure he'll happily believe in it all. That your relationship has grown to the extent that, yes, this begins a new life for both of you.'

It's all become hypothetical, a game where the object is to make the trip happen. And they seem convinced: the three of them might just get to go, and *they'd* be courting, it's to be expected, but *she*, F. would also get to be with Lucian when the Belladonna's headaches descend. She adds: 'Or you can bring him into the story, let him play it out alongside you.'

Her micro shake of the head. 'That wouldn't work.'

Vernon, coming in with practicalities, flinging them in like heavy suitcases: 'You'd have to officially end it with him, when you return. Especially if he really thinks there's a future for the two of you. Either you've changed your mind or—I don't know, better offers have come up. Bit of a cruel game, this.'

The Belladonna nods, face closed, thinking. There's an urgency boiling within her that F. can practically see, pushing La Dame towards irrational decisions. F. sees it now, clear as the nightshade bottle.

'We'll do it. Let society think I'm in danger of leaving forever. Some quarters will be delighted at the prospect, I'm sure. And the others may wait.' She smiles, and her face meets Vernon's, where there is a matching expression.

F.'s happiness brims: let the *after* take care of itself.

As Vernon and the Belladonna begin speaking practicalities, drawing up lists on fresh sheets of paper—deciding who will be the first to be informed of her shock disappearance—F. dimly registers that her work has just grown considerably. But it's a thought that's much obscured by the vision of the country house, waking up to a day of peace stretching ahead, the three of them, without having to break off for a card party, a seance or some other such jaunt.

Later on, back in the apartments, the Belladonna says: 'I sometimes wonder if I am in danger of leaving forever. Perhaps this gives me a chance to test it.'

F. laughs, suspecting La Dame to be playing. But she knows many playful things are said in truth, so she also says: 'I hope you don't enjoy it too much, then. Many people prefer you in Paris. Including me.'

She smiles, and her tone is reassuring: 'I'm not going to be cruel to him, by the way.'

'You don't have to promise me anything.'

'But I know you like him, and the two of you get on. And I know it was … tricky for the two of you, at first.'

'It took us time to work out where we both stood, that's all.' *Turns out it was wherever you wanted us to stand.*

'I promise you, Flora, this is going to be a caper. The rumours of love are for the rest of society, Luc won't fall for them.'

'I think he likes you very much.'

'Yes. I do love him dearly. But abandoning our way of life to be with him? Come now.'

A voice inside F. says: *You see? It isn't love, with Lucian. Even though she said it was.*

*

F. blinks, a thought coming upon her suddenly as she folds an underskirt, so the fabric sits hanging in her hands, mouth suddenly dry, her heart thudding. She remembers that first feeling, early in their acquaintance, which evolved into something more like patience—when the Belladonna and Lucian began to wish for privacy, quietly and gently desiring her to leave. And then, more recently, when they stopped even wasting time on that, their relationship so close they *could* have it fully in her presence, totally sealed off in a soft space of their own making.

How can she be sure of anything? Maybe the Belladonna and 'Luc' really are in love and planning to elope and all of these promises are empty …

But Lucian always has a kind word for her, too. It's the three of them, isn't it? He's courting *her*, the Belladonna, but that's only to be expected. But then …

There's an optical illusion F. sees, of two faces that flicker between looking like a vase or a candlestick. A fizzing pop in the mind's eye that's as enticing as it is perplexing, the way it's impossible to see both at the same time: each image must give up its authority to allow the other to come to the fore. No, it's more devious than that, the onlooker must give authority up, they must decide what to see. First F. is in the far distance of Lucian's feelings; sometimes she must surely be in the front. Then a dizzy-making reversal again. It throws her, as one used to understanding the composition of images, to be so unable to distinguish between figure and ground.

She has a sudden vision of Lucian standing over the painted nothingness on the gallery floor, vividly about to plummet and his face full of abandon.

And a small voice says: *Don't lose him. You might be about to.*

She shakes that image off, decides to see the other. Her heart beats quicker with him put back in view.

*

The Belladonna is at a soiree across town and Flora is alone in the apartments, facing some administrative paperwork long into the night. So there must have been a mistake, because Lucian surely knows the Belladonna is out—but the note, presented neatly at the door, announces that a Monsieur Delamarre is waiting outside. Will he be shown in?

He comes as a blur, stalking directly to the fireplace, turning, walking again back and forth. Not quite as if it were his own home; he moves through the rooms as if being in them is a precious commodity. Must not waste the time.

'Do you know what I … ?' He screws up his face, looks to his shoes, shakes his head. His voice also wavers, as if he needs to gather the strength for desperate words, as if the effort exhausts him. It's so clear he's in a state of extreme upset that he might almost be pretending, but Flora has seen scripted spells of upset, and none of this is scripted. It reads, but it's far too messy. 'I've come because there are things I need to say.'

'You know the Belladonna isn't here?'

Finally he looks up and into her, comes towards her, for a moment a gesture indicates he is about to grab her by the arms. But the gesture fades even as it doesn't appear, and in any case such a move isn't needed. He has Flora's full attention.

'Yes, I know she isn't here. Damn the knowing! Even when I try not to read the papers, the news will reach me. Yes, I know she's out.'

Flora's mouth opens, shuts. Her heart swells. For a vivid moment Flora thinks: *so you knew I'd be alone.*

Lucian is almost shaking, with stress or something like desire. He says: 'I have something to say to you. I wanted to see you tonight, only you.'

Flora would go to him, push him backwards until they reached a wall or the mantlepiece, begin something. *But he has to say it first.*

Lucian takes a deep breath in. 'You're her loyal friend, aren't you—I know you'll share secrets between you. And I know we haven't spoken much you and I, not alone anyway, not about anything serious ….'

It's happening. He's here. He's about to tell you he's yours.

'But I think you can help me if I just say it. I know it's all fun and games between us, I know she's playing, with me, the salons, everything; I know she's bound to treat me a certain way. But the two of *us*, you and I, I mean, Flora, I think we have a shared understanding? So perhaps I can say.'

Flora leaps off the cliff. 'You can say.' *Oh, God, you can say.* 'Say, and I'll help. What do you need to tell me?'

He turns, begins pacing again. 'I've never known anything like this, Flora. I cannot bear the torment. It's every day, you'd wouldn't think it's possible to be in such a dreadful bind *every day*, but she and I, between us, we've driven me to that place.'

Flora, listening.

He stops pacing. 'I live with her in my mind, Flora. Constantly. It's a prison I've built of my own thoughts. She owns my every attention and affection; she is always there. There is a sort of—double of her, that inhabits my mind only—' his arms move quickly to illustrate his vision, as if he were reaching for a pommel-horse. 'This twin of her is a sort of trap laid across my thoughts. Not simply existing but everywhere with me, like a scarring memory. My burden. I haven't come to ask you whether she feels this too, by the way.' His tone becomes more neutral, as if the passion has drained away and left a husk behind. 'I believe she cannot, for how many of us, really, have ever felt like this?'

She blinks at him. Her own private outrage is pushed somewhere deep, deep down. She can hear it wailing, but can't bring herself to listen. 'Go on.'

He laughs bleakly, shakes his head. 'I don't know how else to explain it. Flora, I cannot function. I cannot eat or smile. It's the wanting. I don't know what I can do but I can start by confessing to you. We have an understanding, don't we?'

Oh, yes.

'The invitation to the country… people are talking, Flora. They ask me what I've done to have a hold on her. But—she holds *me*, I choke! My heart; when she approaches I swear everyone can hear it, and my body seems to fill up with something cold.'

'It sounds dreadful.' *Oh, dreadful.*

'When I'm with her, Flora, you must have noticed I am in a heightened state, I must capture everything. I have to collect and remember, you see, every fleeting moment, in my memory I have a whole library of fragments. Single words are enough to set them off, and when I wake I've lost hours.'

Flora's words come from somewhere else, a set of letters already slotted into the printer, and all she is required to do is press. 'You'd say, perhaps, that you love her.'

'When I don't hear from her the walls might crumble in around me. And when I am near her, every utterance might be chiselled into stone for the attentions I afford them.' He closes his eyes, exhausted, grips the mantlepiece with one hand. But he must finish the telling. He forces the rest out, his eyes on the dying fire.

'When I know where she is: when I've heard she's attending

some supper or other, I become a nervous bundle as much as if I myself were going, and the moment comes and I'll think: now she'll be donning this dress or that, now she'll be stepping into the carriage, now she'll be in the carriage: what might she be thinking in there … perhaps she leans her head back against the board, closes her eyes a moment, rests—I see it, Flora, as vividly as if it were happening. Then I realise I don't actually know whether it happened at all. The carriage could have stalled, or fallen down, or been set upon by thieves … or—' he speaks with exasperation '—for the love of God, maybe she walked. I don't actually know. And then, well, I have lost some of my own time, joining her in a dream that she knows nothing of. And I am devastated at the loss.'

Flora, standing there before the fireplace, helpless: remembering an endless dream she herself had about giving the Belladonna a stolen brooch, and thoroughly, thoroughly understanding.

'It comes to this, Flora. I have to know what she is doing: not knowing is agony. And I know it isn't my right to know. How does one exist through such a paradox? Even if I am enjoying myself, even when I am at my happiest, I am not: for I don't know what she would do, or say, were she present! Can you imagine?'

Flora's mouth opens, closes.

Yes, I can.

On the table beside her, the account book sits open. Flora observes its blank columns as a steady, straight-ruled reprimand. Somebody should really enter the true cost of Belladonna's carryings on.

He's finished, or finished for now. The silence stretches

between them. Flora can hear his heavy breathing, sense his relief at finally sharing such tortuous thoughts, the sheer horrible ecstasy of them.

He speaks in a low voice: 'Between us, you and I, I've sensed a kinship coming from many shared sympathies. It's as simple as that. With her I am still overawed, to my disesteem. But you, I can tell things to.'

Something is raging deep within Flora, she can feel it opening its ghastly maw.

'I do feel better for telling you,' he says. 'All I know is, I want her to feel the same, and I suspect she doesn't, and those two irreconcilable facts are breaking me.' He seems to shrink, right there on the carpet, as if she could pick him up whole. 'I want to know everything,' he says, his voice defeated. 'Where she keeps her least important things, how she prefers her food. I ache that I do not know. Shouldn't I know, by now?'

And suddenly a dizzying vista of understanding opens, dazzles her mind with the expanse of it. Because she knows. Which bottles stand on the dressing-table, what each is for. For food; yes, she runs over a few recipes in her mind. Any of those would do. Depending on the wine, or the weather. A wave of heat rises through her: it feels something like triumph. She takes care with her facial expression. There is power in the room, she feels it as cleanly as if the floor tilted under her feet.

Never mind her other lovers: they don't know her truly, like you want to, so you don't mind them. But me?—I have what you want.

He looks at her and for a dreadful moment these facts are clear to both of them: he sees it and his face opens, she can feel his longing, she could tug it between them like a rope, pull him about on it. The feeling is unambiguous and solid, knowing how sick, how unmoored she was, even moments before.

His voice is flat: no use pretending now. 'Everyone else seems perfectly able to play at love, what's happened to me?'

'She has this effect on people.'

'Except you. And Vernon. And every person who's ever spoken to her except me … no, no, I know that shouldn't be true—but I feel it.'

'It will mature, or fade, with the natural course of things.'

'But it won't. It can't. It's love, it is.'

Oh, horror. 'You barely know her.' *I barely know her*, and that's a truth to stick in the throat: Flora can imagine a raging tumult of her own, losing her control to waves of adrenaline and fear and desire just like his. She stands there unable to move, one hand resting on a pile of blotting paper, good for tears.

Speaking of which.

'I am being a fool, I know.' He squeezes his eyes closed and there they are, spreading over his cheeks, adding to the image of boyish hopelessness. He runs a hand across his face—Flora's hand twitches to join him in that action. She could stroke his head, perhaps that would be a helpful thing to do?

Helpful for who?

'You're not a fool,' she says, looking briefly at the account book.

'I love her.'

'You haven't got a person to love; you don't know who she is.

You love an outline, some charming party conversation.' *The feeling of being at the centre of her attentions; never mind that everyone she looks at feels that way.*

'Then I'll love the mystery. If only I could resolve to know and keep that unknowing, if that's what you say it is—God, I want everything.'

'You're contradicting yourself.'

I know things he'd kill to know. It's the wanting.

'I'll die, Flora.'

She goes to him, liberated, finally freed from the table with its heavy ledgers of business. She touches his arm, and he looks at her; he is trembling beneath her hand, his gaze is intense and reddened. His hair, the dark ruby of it, his eyes.

Lucian needs consoling.

'I know how you feel,' says Flora, her voice low and calm. 'The truth is, I've felt the same, sometimes. That's how it is with her.'

It's the best she can do.

*

Onward, then, to the house in the country. The only cottage Lucian could secure at such late notice had been closed for months, and was recently subjected to a frantic and ineffectual cleaning and airing, so it is arguably not as idyllic as might have been hoped. Sticky and already fly-bitten, F. pulls the heavy luggage from the top of the trap and, sore-armed, drops it onto the cold flagstones of the kitchen. This first room Lucian is delighted with: he runs from the stove to the great rustic table, then up the stairs to the creaking beds, and laughs as if they've discovered keys to paradise. The days ahead prove to be wider and slower than in the city: they take walks in the pale daylight, read poetry by the fire through the evenings, get up early. The Belladonna even takes to being out in the daytime, protecting her eyes with a pair of small round sunglasses.

As if by mutual agreement there is never any talk of opera, of Paris at all, anything of the city; it is like the whole idea of it has been banished like a dream they wish to forget while here, the better to fully enjoy the country trip; which Lucian, in particular, wants to last. And between Lucian and F. there is never any mention of the conversation by the fireplace.

Knowing for certain how Lucian feels changes F.'s desire for being here, and as a consequence, time at the cottage passes in a grey cloud. She barely notices when after three weeks the trip extends into four, as the Belladonna had whispered in secret to F. that it might. Then again into six weeks, then into eight, then nine.

F.'s mornings are now taken up with letters from Vernon: *Where are you now? These accounts I'm looking at: not sustainable. What, she wants a year's worth of salons to make up for this? Does he realise we're paying by now? Or is she letting him think this cottage is free?* The letters turn to pleading, and eventually address F. directly: *Can you talk some sense into her?*

So, one evening, F. brings up the notion of a leaving date.

The Belladonna only smiles up at her over the kitchen's huge table. 'Let Vernon wait. We're still having fun here.' And Lucian looks happily over the brandy bottle, as if he's the great saviour of the Belladonna from city life; when F.

makes the mistake of mentioning that the Belladonna will already have several commitments to be attended to, he fully takes on the role of La Dame's fiercest protector against Parisian demands, the last line of defence against a society out for blood: drunkenly protective, he leaps up and wields the fireplace bellows like a sword, to peals of her delighted laughter, while F. sits scowling over the account books, penning another delay into tomorrow's letter.

Thirteen weeks have passed, and the Belladonna and F. take a walk together along the river. Lucian has stayed behind to see if he can get the rusty scythe to affect the lawn.

'We'll return to Paris tonight,' the Belladonna says. Her voice startles a kingfisher and it streaks away, rising into the air a vivid blue promise.

F. nods, says nothing. The relief she feels is tempered with some anticipation, and she chooses not to voice it. The Belladonna's mind might change; worse, it might not.

'This,' says the Belladonna, gesturing about the peaceful river that smoothly winds its way along the willow fronds, 'becomes fairly boring, doesn't it? After a while.' She links their arms and leans her head on F.'s shoulder as they walk, and more birdsong reaches them through the trees.

*

The Belladonna's return to Paris is met with the expected flurry of engagements and celebrations, enquiries and invitations, and she flings herself into the renewed attentions of the city like a true star. She attends one gala supper after another before being seen at the latest premiere, she moves on to a fresh circle of aristocratic admirers—achievements come in numbers. Her schedule—and F.'s to match—moves to take up more nocturnal hours. The money is an issue after such a long stretch, as Vernon will remind F. needlessly, but La Dame's concentrated energy and sheer charismatic force fill up the dance-card until it is dense with names, and the endeavour steadies itself. Any questions about her absence are responded to lightly and noncommittally. And now, attending a fitting in one of the more prosperous boutiques in the Triangle d'Or: the haute couture quarter, one of the Belladonna's favourite playgrounds. A fitting that is much overdue, having been extremely postponed. The Belladonna stands inside a dress of sharp black silk, still as a mannequin. In this private space, cool and dark at the back of the shop, she and F. are surrounded by neat cabinets of fabric samples, tilted mirrors that reflect sugary posters of pastel silk and bare shoulders.

The fitting chambers are as well-suited a place as any for the subject F. wishes to discuss.

They are in a temporary lull in the action of pinning and re-pinning, since the tailor and his trio of apprentices have gone for a moment, to gather notes for the next stage, or to fetch more pins, whatever it is they do.

From within the dress, the Belladonna looks plainly ahead, her expression almost melancholy. The silk flares out slightly at the skirt, dropping neatly from a form-fitting bodice with a daring plunge. An elegant line that reveals the shoulders, edged with lace and dark pearls. Now is the time to ask, while she cannot run away without risk of toppling over into an intricate trap.

'Will it be tonight?'

The Belladonna almost looks surprised before rescuing her expression. 'This won't be something I do lightly, you know. And it won't exactly be easy.'

'I understand. But if you need things arranging, in order to achieve this peacefully, we need to be as one on the details of when and where.'

'Where to settle it? Why, nowhere; I didn't imagine it happening in person. I'll write to him.'

'Do you think a letter, after everything, is what he deserves?' F. pictures the Belladonna's swooping signature. It's an appropriate outline for someone's death warrant.

'You needn't be so dramatic about it. I think a measured approach will help.'

'You'll break him into pieces with a letter.'

'Oh, *don't*. He may think a great many things, as it turns out.' She stretches out an arm in front of her, examines the sleeves held up by a few trails of thread. 'I can only be responsible so far. Still. One of the more cumbersome dalliances of which to rid oneself.'

These words have something of a blade's glint about them. F. shakes the feeling off, which the Belladonna notices.

'You may not believe it, but sometimes they cling on. I hate to be harsh. But he's still wrapped up in dreams, and you can't argue logic with someone who's dreaming.'

'He'll turn whatever you say into tenderness.'

'So we will have to be swift and unchanging.' She raises her head slightly, angles her chin at F. with the attitude of a challenge. 'You can write the letter for me, if you like.'

The doors open and the tailors come back in, tape measures

126

already unrolling. F. shakes her head to decline the offer.

The Belladonna flicks a speck of invisible dust from the corset and returns her arm position to one of high grace, to allow for adjustments to the sleeves.

'Very well, if you're refusing. But I know you would find the right words. It's all very delicate. But he should keep his distance and his dignity and if we're lucky there'll be nothing further on the matter.'

But consequences come at a gambling-house in the coming weeks. The dress, duly fitted, has received its successful premiere and similar necklines can already be noted along the Champs-Élysées. And now the Belladonna is seated at a long table gridded into squares by coloured lines. A dozen men in evening dress sit to play, and many more stand and watch politely. She is shaking a fist, the dice rendered silent by her gloves.

F. is following the action, standing a little distance away.

The dice land with a faint clink on the baize, and a moment of silence. Then the crowd breaks into shouting and cheers, and one of the gentlemen flicks a hand to send for champagne. F. is suddenly surrounded by waiters, holding their trays tall—

Oh. A heaviness announces itself just under her breastbone. She has seen a mop of dark reddish hair in the doorframe. *Please no.* She notes the staggering exhaustion as he leans against the wall for a moment, recovers, and lopes in. His steps to the dice table are deliberate, he takes long strides. He has been building himself up to this, she can read it. He is exhausted, or drunk, or both.

The gamblers part as he arrives at the table, and the

Belladonna looks up; she and Flora register the expression on Lucian's face at the same time. He is flushed, his face splotched with pink, his eyes a watery red. None of this is pitiable, which Flora would have expected; rather, his lips are held in a sneer. This is the ugliest, perhaps, that anyone can look. Flora takes a step towards the dice table, her heart beating a push to intervene; not knowing how.

The Belladonna's face opens with astonishment for a moment before closing again, a professional lowering of the shutters. It's a slip and Lucian will have seen it. She presents a careful face to him, a cautious welcome, no hostility, not yet.

With a thick papery slap, a wedge of notes lands on the dice table.

'Sir, I'm taking no more bets,' says the man in the crimson sash at the head of the proceedings. Lucian holds up a hand, and the intensity of the gesture silences everyone.

'I'm not here to gamble,' he says. 'This is a payout. Somebody else has won.'

The Belladonna continues to return his gaze while a low, uncomfortable laugh travels around the dice table.

'Accept my commiserations,' says one gentleman, his fingers fiddling with a counter that represents ten times what Lucian just flopped onto the table. 'That's the risk, mind you.'

'It's why we play at all,' says another.

Lucian stabs the pile of notes with a finger. 'I've come to pay my debts off. That's what you wanted, isn't it? To earn money out of me? Well, here.'

His eyes shine with tears that don't fall.

At the edge of the group, two discreet gentlemen take a

step forward. The Belladonna raises a finger and they remain still.

'You should know,' she says, softly, calmly, eyes on him. 'Payment like that won't be accepted. That isn't how it works.'

His mouth opens and closes. Whatever he imagined hadn't played out like this. Flora groans inwardly at the thought: he has just presented the Belladonna with his neck.

She smiles, a picture of control. 'Payment is generally in advance, and never afterwards. I've got what I needed from you.'

'You never felt as I did.'

'That's right.'

'You made me think—'

'Oh I made you think? Was it really me? Did you expect you were about to magic up a rapid change of lifestyle— years of comfort, was it? *Marriage?*' The word sits heavily in the room, unfitting, ridiculous. 'You had your moment with me but there was never any more than that for us; I choose for my life to be here. If you cannot cope with that, then I'm afraid you've never understood.'

His face breaks into a grimace, an expression that's all teeth. 'You spoke differently once!' He marches towards her, his hands twitching. 'I'll prove it to you—'

The room explodes: those around the table shout at Lucian to get down and stop this absurdity, and then two more gentlemen in crimson sashes march directly to him with faces of thunder. Lucian has time to make one desperate gesture at the table as they reach him, and with a flail of his arms he tosses the contents everywhere: a fountain of coins and counters land on the hard floor and bounce. The dreadful pile of paper notes flutter in the air while Lucian is grabbed and held by the arms, and he flounders against the heavy men who restrain him, indulging in the futility of it.

The Belladonna has stood. He stops resisting and looks directly at her.

'I've loved you. And I've paid for that. So there you go!'

She turns and sweeps to leave, and is immediately followed by an entourage of gamblers and waiters, a crowd which will very soon will include Flora—in fact Flora should be there already, she ought be the first person by her side for this, but she finds herself following the sight of Lucian, who has given in to his captors and keeps his gaze on the Belladonna as they drag him away, as if committing the final sight of her to his memory.

At the doorway he looks briefly at Flora. His expression is blank, as if he doesn't recognise her.

With him gone, the room slips back to light chatter. The waiters speak to one another in low tones as they restore the disruption, delicately replacing the cards and resetting the counters.

*

F. leaves the gambling-house (nodding, half dazed, at the porter guarding the door). She ought to be with the Belladonna, but she cannot ignore what just happened. She steps around to the narrow street behind the building. A low moan is coming from the gutters, which are pooled with pale light from the gas lamps, but they'd be better off left in the dark. The bunched-up shape of Lucian sits, head in his hands and feet ankle-deep in the dirty water.

F. stops beside him, noticing how her shadow looms across him—she could be those men, returning for some more. She waits. She can see marks on his face, the smear of blood about his mouth.

But he doesn't move away or flinch. He peers up at her, moving his head slowly. His eye is red, welted, swelling, and his voice is plaintive: 'I wanted to show her. How it felt. I know you understand.'

F. can feel how sharp her silhouette must be, standing over him: the harsh corset-line, her hands on her hips. She makes her voice to match. 'One final act of closure, was it? Meant to break her heart? It's over when *she* says it is, and she's not to be condemned for it. It's her position, Lucian.'

'Oh god,' he loses his face back in his hands. His voice comes through muffled. 'Why can't I make her as upset as she makes me?'

She bends, the edges of her skirts soaking in the cold water, and for a moment her hand butterflies to touch his head—but she pulls it in.

*

Neither of them mention the incident. The Belladonna is going through an ill spell, and sits in front of the fire rigid with headache and cough. F. herself has a painful thumb and wrist from the constant writing, and a new patch of frozen stiffness in her lower back; nevertheless she constantly rises to fetch her mistress's necessary medicines, holding small bottles out to the Belladonna as she shifts uncomfortably in her chair.

Requests for attendance have been pouring in ever since their return from the country. The Belladonna and her companion, by the fireplace, sort through these various letters. A constant round of invitations, letters, bequests—the usual paperwork has tripled in volume.

And, correspondence from him. A week or more of an avalanche of it. Multiple letters in a day, written in a fever, sent, recanted, re-written, replaced, the replacement sent, paced over and over and thought about, elaborated on, taken back, asserted, sent again: all the while Belladonna sleeps over the course of the day, so a small pile awaits her when she finally wakes to get ready for the evening. He ends it, then he offers her the world, or what of it he can.

La Dame leafs through a collection of these desperate missives in spidery writing.

'He's sent me a dozen more since,' she says, raising a hand to cover her eyes—even the soft flicker from the fire is a source of discomfort. 'Good thing I know better than to be hurt by the crueller ones.'

'Could you say anything to him?' F. asks, watching her. 'If you replied briefly, maybe said something kind …'

The top-most letter is flopped down onto the pile. 'Perhaps. Do you think it would make them stop?' She runs a thoughtful finger down the stack of envelopes.

'I only wonder if it's what he needs. A true ending … though it's hard to separate what he needs or what would be best, from what he *wants*, or what would make things worse.'

The Belladonna looks at F. with a new sternness. 'You're certainly thinking about his every move in an awful lot of detail.'

F. doesn't deny it, couldn't. She is constantly thinking of him, of how he thinks of the Belladonna, obsessively.

One of the letters has an unusual crest, highly elaborate and surrounded by vines. F. takes it up, then frowns as she reads the invitation. Whenever she thinks she has a grasp on this, something new arises. 'A domino ball?'

'The theme is black and white.' The Belladonna takes the invitation from her and thoughtfully examines the crest. 'And masquerade. Tremendous; it's all the better when you mask the guests, people reveal all kinds of other things. Ah! And it's being hosted by the Comtesses de la Rosière. They do like to spring things onto people but they're superb hosts. And my gowns being newly completed at my *maître tailleur*. It all comes together.'

Rosière. The name sprouts like a tree, out through society. F. follows some of the names, reaching poets and actresses as well as aristocrats and heroes of the military and the bar, so yes, they are likely to know Marcelin, and therefore …

'It seems likely to me—' the words are out before F. can stop them.

Belladonna looks up from the paper, her eyes perfectly still. 'Yes?'

No use sugar-coating it.

'*Ah.*' She looks back down at the invitation. The sigh is low down, discrete, but F. senses it. 'Of course.'

The words barely pass her lips. 'May the devil's own patience be with us.'

She leans forwards, reaching for the small bottles of salts—and stronger—that F. has placed on the table. 'I'm sure we can successfully avoid anything we need to, should it be necessary. That would be the kindest thing.'

The act of straining for the bottle has exhausted her. The Belladonna stretches out a leg, idly inspecting the line of her skirt, as a cover for her battle for breath. She tosses the pile of demanding letters away.

'We won't reply to these.'

She gently lowers her body further into the chair. The medicines are beginning to take effect, obliterating the headache with a thick blanket of something stronger, and F. leaves her to sleep.

*

Any masquerade succeeds only by the commitment of its guests, of course, that's part of the charm. And this ballroom is uniquely suited for the event, with its dizzying chessboard floor over which tonight's guests find themselves circulating in accordance with strict rules. The eccentric Rosière hostesses, those formidable sisters, parade across the space in lacquered boots, done up as can-can girls in black and white, silver buckles to match their buttons, their heels squeaking on the perfect floor. They wave and shout to their guests, on patrol with eagle eyes to make sure everything goes just awry enough. No high society event is allowed to go on without strict protocol, and they are on watch for any accidental chaos, the quicker to put it out.

The Belladonna arrives late, masked with a festoon of nightshade leaves. The crowd parts to let her through, along with Flora in a mask patterned with stars and a gown the colour of midnight. Whispers travel across the dancefloor, excitedly declaring who has arrived.

They are approached by a figure in a white cape edged with ostrich feathers. Flora's professional eye knows them to be a distinguished professor of philosophy at the Sorbonne.

'Would my lady care to join me on the balcony? I wish to discuss the very important matter of how I'd hoped to invite you for a drink.'

The Belladonna laughs. 'Ah, matters of import will come in due course.' She waves the professor off; but *later*, her hand says. *Yes, most certainly, later.*

They keep walking across the chequered terrain, the Belladonna issuing further greetings. The crowds press in and the music intensifies—

And now the sudden sight of Lucian, the flash of red hair.

Flora feels the cold pulsing through her.

Of course he is here, but to come upon them so quickly? Worse, her lady breaks into a beaming smile and curtsies down to him, and Flora is suddenly in the way, while the Belladonna lets Lucian take her arm and lead her off to a corner, where they hunch in towards each other, gossiping, laughing...

It is as if the gambling-house had never happened. They have made it up again. As if none of it mattered: the writhing desperation, the tears he let her see. *I'll die, Flora.* And now look at them. They are inseparable.

Flora has no idea what to do and finds herself watching, silent and helpless. He and the Belladonna are dancing, now, closer together. Almost as if there were nobody else in the room, he reaches up a hand and lightly strokes her cheek, then returns his hand to the waltz and they carry on:

135

Flora could cry out. She looks about to see if anyone else noticed, and can't tell. So brazen, so easily done, almost as if neither party involved even knew of it. He touched her, just like that, in the middle of the ball; did they plan for this, have they been in contact? But, doesn't Flora run the letters … ? Flora's too big for the dance floor, she's taking up too much space, she shouldn't be there. She takes a few steps backwards, almost walks into a different group of dancers who deftly avoid the collision then break into abrasive laughter, fluttering their fans at her.

But then she finds herself by the Belladonna's side, gossiping away with a group of lawyers—who tonight are a troupe of Pierrot clowns, all baggy white pyjamas and black balls of fluff—and Lucian is away to the back, speaking with someone else at the far end of the ballroom, and everyone is simply performing the masquerade and she shouldn't be so worried. Surely?

But no, look; even though they are at opposite ends of the ballroom, the Belladonna glances over to where Lucian stands and he turns to her as if possessed by an uncanny knowledge. He is aware of the Belladonna's every movement; Flora isn't imagining it. These people are joined together even in this whirling space, even when they appear to be speaking, laughing, dancing with other people. And Flora has found herself dragged in too, pulled about by desires she didn't know she had.

The masquerade unrolls; the chess game continues. Flora finds herself standing beside him at the edge of the dancefloor, not knowing if they've done this deliberately or by careless accident. The Belladonna is dancing with a great-grandson of the Duc d'Orléans. No reason to feel upset about this: it's a partner swapping dance, she's dancing with everyone. But Lucian is watching La Dame and Flora feels the tension of his gaze, and she can't bear her own lack of impact upon him.

She begins to speak. He turns to her. Flora hears herself say: 'I'm going to leave now, by that door, if you would care to come with me.'

Already stepping away from him she hears his staggered yes—and she makes her way through the crowd of revellers and trusts he follows, she can almost feel him behind, as if she were pulling him along by a wire.

Outside the ballroom, she passes through several heavy doors, finally finding herself inside a dark space with narrow walls. A service corridor, or perhaps a hiding place especially for jaunts such as this. The space is dark and plush, candlelight giving weight to the velvet curtains.

There's too much, it's too much, she can't keep an eye on all of it. The Belladonna and all of society and the endless re-groupings and disguises where everyone is more themselves than ever, she cannot follow them about any more in this ridiculous waltz of seeming.

The space she's in is empty, with the music coming through muffled from outside, and she cannot hear his footsteps. Still, she knows he is behind her and she turns, sees that yes, he is there, he has followed her here, so far so reliable: and she turns fully and leans onto the wall against the velvet plush of a hanging curtain, and the whole space becomes a fuzzy dark red from the candles shining on the velvet, and he is there, she sees his outline, the light giving his hair a red halo.

'Well?' she says.

His outline moves closer towards her. She leans further against the wall.

The first kiss is tentative: an action that checks this is indeed what is meant, what is happening. The second one is deeper, the wall taking the weight of both of them.

He creates a minute space between them. It has the sense of coming up for air. He speaks, and his voice has a tone of triumph.

'If she could see us now … !' he says, a gleeful whisper, and leans in again to kiss her.

And Flora, seeing with total clarity, finishes the thought for him.

She wouldn't care.

Vaguely she feels the gentle push of his mouth over hers, and she opens her lips further to it; but that thought is now the dominant sensation, riding roughshod over everything else. The physical action is far away, impossibly distant, the doings of people who think and feel differently in another world. *If she could see us now? It wouldn't sway her at all! What do you think this is about? It's the power she not only loves, but needs; it's the role she has to play, and see how well she does it. See how brilliantly it works. You're with me, you're here with me, I'm here, I'm the one who's here. I am reaching towards you and all you can think about is her.*

If she could see you and I at this very moment, she'd know this for exactly what it is. Which is more than you can do.

Another thought, a lump in her mind that she permits to form: *All you can think about is her. And I cannot help but turn my mind to that same source. If I love you, it's because of the way you love the two of us, me and you. And you only love that because of the way we both feel about the Belladonna. That's what we have in common.*

The words pass through her mind like clouds racing, as high and as intangible—the world they pass over is her own sun-bursting valley, clammy with writhing heat, damp with desperate tears. She hasn't any emotional attachment to these thoughts, they are simply there, a plain truth of the situation. It doesn't matter how she *feels*.

His hands trace down her arms to hold her waist, and she can feel the heat from him. She is suddenly extremely thirsty: she takes his head, holds it closer to her.

Between her corset and gown, her gloves, and the double-bind of the masks they wear, they might as well be either end of a hallway. The intimacy somehow underlines this distance, makes it even more incongruous. The heat rushing about her body belongs to someone else: she's too wrapped up to feel anywhere near it.

They break apart as sounds come from further down the corridor: party-goers who have promised themselves a tour of the back rooms; the rattle of a drinks trolley and drunken cheers as it gives up its brandy. The two of them flee, rushing as if they'd been caught with their hands on the silver. They return to the ball in silence and once through the great main doors they go their separate ways, not speaking, and are pulled immediately into different worlds.

La Dame gives Flora a small look on her return from the misadventure in the corridor, and for a moment Flora's heart stops—is it written all over her face? Has he left an image of himself there? But the Belladonna only frowns slightly and asks a question about their hosts, the Rosières. She cannot recollect the name of their delightful cousin she was once introduced to, and wants to charm them by asking after her. And Flora plunges back into the ball with a feeling of something sickening, like relief.

At last the fray of dancing turns into a steady stream of goodbyes as the party begins to wear itself out, and Flora stands beside the Belladonna, a quiet onlooker to her grand farewells with everyone. When the time comes for Lucian and his friends to leave, he bows to both of them—deeply to the Belladonna, an exaggerated flourish that speaks too loudly. To Flora, he practically whisks himself away before the bow has begun. When Flora briefly closes her eyes in the carriage, in the red darkness behind her eyes she sees him— the glowing halo of his hair like rusted wire, his features obscured by shadow.

*

At the end of the week, a calm evening brings the final storm.

The night breathes across Paris, the curtains have been pulled open and the city below glimmers like rippling water. The business of the day is done and Flora and the Belladonna sit quietly together at a game of dominoes—the only sounds in the apartments are the gentle ivory clicks of pieces cajoled into line by her thin fingers. Her *fingers*: a rare occasion where the gloves are off.

In the gentle silence of the rooms the thud of the door echoes heavily, and the distinct sound of footsteps mark a sudden steady progress towards them. Identifying it immediately as Lucian they have enough time to look at each other, register what is happening, and for the room to charge with the spike of alarm—when the door opens and he staggers into their presence, jacket open, tie undone, tailcoat rippling, a dour and unwashed staleness. He staggers into the room with a sort of alarmed jump, as if taken by surprise and pushed through. Which perhaps he was.

'What brings *you*?' The Belladonna is already taking steps backwards towards the fireplace. Flora stands too—impossible to do otherwise—but she remains by the table, with its neat line of shapes and dots intersecting on top of it.

'You weren't at the theatre tonight,' he mutters, reaching the table and pushing against the back of the chair as if to prevent himself falling. His centre of gravity is low. His guard, like his attention, is down. 'I thought you'd be there and you weren't and I wanted to come.'

Flora exchanges a small glance with the Belladonna— *We weren't due there, were we? No.*—and the face of La Dame takes on a protective barrier of benign puzzlement. 'There must be some mistake. Why were you waiting for me there?'

'You usually would be …' he stops himself. Tries again: 'Somebody said to me you'd be there.' He casts a desperate glance about, runs a hand across his face. This is already not going how he might have imagined.

'Do you want?' He takes a deep breath in. He closes his eyes, reaches for a piece of information, brings it like a precious nugget from his pocket. 'I thought you wanted me. I thought, at the ball, you'd decided I was important to you again. But then I hadn't had word from you for days and I'm back in this place once more. And then I heard you were in Pigalle tonight and I thought, how sad it is, that you hadn't told me

141

that? That you didn't want to tell me you were going? That you're quite happy being there without me of an evening and didn't wish me with you. Not caring whether I'm to be invited —I'm not enough to you, not enough for you to want—'

The Belladonna almost relaxes, she sighs like a birdwatcher finding the correct specimen in a book: now she can put a name to this there is an action to take, something to do. She steps towards him, her arms opening in a gesture of plaintive soothing. 'There's no conspiracy. And thank you for telling me. I'm sorry for everything. But I can't, not anymore. Absolutely. You need to understand.'

'Your position makes you say that. You don't want to say those things, it's others forcing you to have that life instead of one with me.'

'If you want to put it that way.' There's a sadness to her voice, as if she's letting him glimpse an unholy secret. 'My *position* means I must stop things between us here.'

Flora, forgotten by the domino table, silently shouts at him: *It means she doesn't want any more of this from you. It's as simple as that! Can't you see it?*

But he rallies. His jaw narrows, his cheeks take on a new redness—in giving him a glimpse, in trying to be kind, she's given him a deadly new hope. 'So give it up! Run away with me! If your position traps you so, let us take another. We can try. I don't know how. If you don't really want this to end.'

'But I do.'

His face open, shocked, unbelieving.

She glides to the table, fingers a domino piece. ' That *is* what I want. In fact, nothing else will suit me.'

'But *why*?' His eyes shine with tears. His clenched jaw

makes his neck tight and gives a pinched, narrow expression to his face. His whole appearance has twisted; a cloud remoulded by the wind.

'All right,' he says, with new resolve. 'All right.' And then he is moving again, pushing himself up from the chair to get the momentum. Before either Flora or the Belladonna can move he has burst through the door that leads to the bedroom. The mistake of this hits Flora like a wave: the invasion of space, the evening ripped open. The Belladonna touches her on the shoulder and speaks quickly, urgently.

'Don't call the concierge. I think we can still deal with this.'

'What do you mean *don't* call?' She has wanted to get help since he burst through the door; for this to be so quickly outlawed makes even less sense than his own dreadful spirals of logic. 'You're not going to reason with him while he's like that. You've seen him drunk, distressed like this before. We both have.'

But she is already striding towards the bedroom. 'I didn't say reason,' she says, her bony shoulder moving through her back as she works the handle. 'I said deal.'

Flora takes a blind moment to register this before following them both into the bedroom, where he is just finishing a manic harvest of the nightshade tree, pulling berries at random from the branches, that bend and loosely sway in the deadly breeze that has entered the room. Beneath one arm he holds—*how did he know where she keeps it?*—the crystal bowl, and he is throwing the berries into it, blind to the red blotches and welts already showing up along his hand and wrist.

Hearing the door close, he turns and addresses them both with an air of triumph. 'One last salon then! One last journey!'

The Belladonna's voice comes through smoothly, stopping and starting as if cycling neatly through options: 'You don't really, come on now, this isn't needed, please don't do that, there's no need—'

Flora feels off-balance here, but being in the bedroom has given La Dame aux Morelles a new authority, and she stands peacefully before Lucian, who is still clutching the crystal bowl and steadily filling it with berries. Some have already been squashed between his fingers, staining his hands with dark red matter.

'I can't attend your salons anymore I'm afraid, if I'm not allowed to see you.' His voice has reached a manic pitch and he approaches his words at a rush, as if he must hurry before he loses the nerve. 'And if I can't see you I may as well not see anything, so why not do both? Why not?' He picks a berry from the bowl and pushes it between his lips. 'Why not do both at the same time?' His face contorts with the dry sourness. 'Why not do both…' He swallows; and Flora feels it in her own throat.

One down, the rest come easier: he takes a handful of berries and pushes them all in at once. Through the blubbering dark red of half-chewed berry flesh, he begins to laugh. He pushes the berries in further, his throat resisting the onslaught of bitterness, a dull gagging mixing with the laughter—and putting the berries out of reach of Flora, who is now coming towards him. And then his expression changes with a snap to one of urgent appeal, and his gaze turns to Flora, begging. The laughter has stopped; now his voice is only thick and desperate.

'Please, no,' he says, losing stability, dropping the bowl to the ground. 'Please stop it! I'm sorry!'

The bowl cracks on the thick rug. The sound of breaking glass is muffled by the carpet and there is a heavy thump as his body loses balance. The berry pulp is dark and horrible on the newly exposed innards of the glass, a smooth ribbon of shine, deadly at the edges. Flora kneels in the pulp, reaches a hand towards Lucian to help him—then, her hand is batted away.

The Belladonna in a new rage drops to the floor, heaves him up and brutally clasps his shoulders. It is almost a loving cradle, except she looks made of stone. Her anger is immovable. She looks into his terrified eyes and shakes him slightly with every word.

'You. Chose. What. You. *Wanted.*' At the final word she shakes him deeper, more violently; his head jolts back and forth. His face is that of a terrified boy, smeared with the dark red of the berries.

She holds his face firmly and looks into his eyes, her whole expression a sneer. 'You want to die for love, is that it? But you *don't*, because it's the *game* of it you like. All of you. I've had enough of this.'

In the semi darkness of the bedroom her gaze is all pupil as she stares into his terrified face. Her clutch of him becomes gentle, and she leans in towards him and speaks again, quietly. 'You've embarrassed me in public. You've embarrassed yourself everywhere and now this—what did you want to achieve with this? Because I'll tell you what you *have* achieved.'

His eyes. Flora is watching the scene play out from somewhere far off, behind a curtain, behind glass.

He begins to shake: a deep spasm coming from low down, taking his whole body with it. He keeps his gaze on the Belladonna, who runs a hand tenderly down his cheek.

'Nothing I can do,' she says. 'There's nothing to be done about this now.'

That snaps Flora out of it. Her paralysis cracks like a mirror, like the crystal bowl. She jumps up, staggers away, with a vague plan to head towards where she last saw the water jug. 'If we make him vomit—'

'*Pallidiflora.*'

The Belladonna's voice is so calm, Flora turns back.

His eyes have become glassy and still. Her fingers are stained with marks of the berries. Her hand cradles his face: she is removing her fingers gently from his mouth.

She lowers the body to the floor, stands. Smooths her skirt down, tracing more berry marks over the fabric; it's an unthinking gesture, perhaps she imagines for a moment she's still in her gloves. She looks down at the figure sprawled on the bedroom carpet. Shards of crystal lie beside him. The sour smell of drinking without sleep, of desiring without happiness, now joined by a terrible absence of smell. The smell of dust settling.

'There was nothing either of us could have done,' the Belladonna says. 'It's important that you know that. You take that many berries at once, you go into shock. It can happen and indeed it does happen. Even with a single one, it can happen. With that many...' She shakes her head as if disappointed, then she takes a deep breath in and slowly lets it out, closing her eyes. Her sigh seems to fill the room, as if the whole apartment is tired.

And that, it seems, was his moment's tribute, for the Belladonna goes to the corner of the bedroom, reaching out with her arm. F. is trapped into stillness, understanding that the Belladonna's life contains more depths than she's known, seeing that arm reach forwards, knowing what is going to happen before it happens, her brain spinning uselessly with the implications—as the Belladonna reaches up and gives a single tug to the thin black bell-pull.

There is no sound. When the other is pulled—the strip of purple silk beside it—there's always a distant ring, a confirmation, the reassurance that infrastructure will be called into action. None of that now. The black cord simply returns to its state of quiet stillness, unmoving, like a crack down the wall.

The rest of the room starts wavering in F.'s vision, as if to compensate for the shock. She looks from the bell-pull to the nightshade tree, which appears to her like it is shaking in some dreadful breeze—and the Belladonna is suddenly very near, she has swooped down on her, and her cheek and lips are so close to F.'s own. The Belladonna puts a hand on the small of F.'s back and says kindly that they shan't be waiting long, perhaps it's best to return to the drawing-room in the meantime, no use remaining here amongst everything, don't you think? In F.'s dizziness she cannot tell apart her mistress from the nightshade. La Dame's soft words keep coming ('It's quite all right, there now, none to worry, it's all in hand, let's leave for a moment so things can be put right …'). F.'s head is spinning. So, the second bell-pull. The Belladonna is still speaking, her words floating somewhere above F.'s consciousness as she steers her out of the room ('we'll wait in here now, it won't be long, a matter of minutes, you'll see …') and the Belladonna keeps up the stream of softly spoken words in the otherwise silent apartments, as empty and open as a freshly dug grave.

V

She sits opposite *Her*, the Belladonna, at one end of the table. The Duc, who is hosting this evening, sits beside La Dame aux Morelles, and mostly *She* speaks with him alone, and Flora is safe. The Duc is doing a good job of entertaining this end of the table.

A guest's voice reaches them from somewhere down in the dimness: 'Pass the peppercorns, if you wouldn't mind? I'm not being droll, I genuinely cannot see them.'

They are seated in a dining hall illuminated by candlelight; so many candles the long table blurs beyond a certain point. From the end, where Flora finds herself, it's impossible to see all the guests, though she can tell the table is full, heaving. What it seems all these candles primarily do is reveal how dark everything around them is. The embossed patterning on the black wallpaper shows itself in patches under the sconces, holding yet more candles. The guests all wear black, as requested, and there's barely a sound between them. Speaking is not forbidden—it's a party, after all—but the guests find themselves reaching for quiet: somehow, it seems to match. They move their cutlery silently, like shadows given appetite.

She, the Belladonna, is as leading a presence as ever, a shining example of decorum. She tips her head to laugh at some comment of the Duc's. Flora looks down at her soup. The inky colour does not give much away as to its contents, and the rye Russian bread doesn't offer many clues to it either. The cutlery is silver but the crockery is black, and Flora can't tell where the food begins and the plate ends. She can only deduce the tablecloth by its indistinct satin sheen.

'You didn't choose tonight's theme just to please *me*, I hope,' *She* is saying, and the silence deepens: the whole room has been wondering this.

Flora raises herself slightly as she listens in on the conversation.

The Duc shakes his head. 'Not at all. I was in a mood for something with depth, with shadow, that is all. Wonderful to see how many shades of darkness there can be at a single feast. I should hope the coincidence pleases?'

'Oh, very much.'

'Have you considered this decor yourself? I imagine it would suit your own rooms, would it not?'

Now She shakes her head. 'I couldn't top your own commitment to the theme, having seen such a triumph as yours.' A smile breaks through, and *She* runs a finger down the black ribbon that runs along the shoulder of *Her* dress. 'Besides; how would I find myself?'

'It's a bit funereal,' says Madame Szécheny, a fellow guest wearing a cape of bombazine, her voice strong as a metal bar even through a mouthful of rye bread. Flora winces, but mostly out of social embarrassment; perhaps this guest believes if a comment goes unspoken it has gone unthought.

As if sensing the potential critique lurking in her morbidity, the guest quickly adds: 'Vibrant though, for all that!'

The Duc feigns modest embarrassment, as if he has received a great compliment. 'You're very kind. Sometimes I remember the truth: that I should have visitors more often. I simply get out of the habit, and forget perfect solitude isn't the *only* option. Then every so often I come to my senses, and voila! Open house.'

The Belladonna squeezes his arm—cheerfully but protectively. A gesture of ownership. 'I'm delighted you've done so. The *excitement* when your missive came. We've been so bored in Paris lately. I often wonder how you are.'

There's a brief glint of candlelight on a row of medals pinned to the chest of an off-duty Captain of the Guard.

'Best host in Paris,' he says, smiling as he raises his port glass. 'Even though you're outside of it by many miles.'

'It's most accommodating of you,' says the Señorita Sofía Lopegia, a refined member of the party who speaks through a veil of thick black lace. 'Awkward for the rest of us that you dig yourself in all the way out here, so far from the bustle of the city.'

'Guilty as charged,' says the Duc. 'But sometimes you find you want to get away from it all.'

'Could anyone please pass me the peppercorns? It really isn't a joke.'

Flora looks down at her soup and wishes it were a hole she could drop into. She closes her eyes; it barely makes a difference. *She*, the Belladonna, laughs again, sounding so carefree that it resonates within Flora as a sort of anger. She's heard that laugh before; it doesn't necessarily mean amusement. And

153

anyway, it's not about whether the Belladonna is genuinely amused or not—it's that *She* has persisted in pretending to be. They haven't stopped for a moment since …

Flora feels she is used to the precision and cold calculation. And the visions, the headaches, and their slack faces and absent, empty eyes: but this had been different. This new facet of the Belladonna she hasn't had time to process, as if she's cracked open a stone with a chisel and found the sea inside. Belladonna has barely looked at her and hardly spoken to her since, beyond the brief missives thrown lightly in her direction. Flora doesn't know how much longer that can possibly carry on; and now her own thoughts are turning her stomach.

Flora takes up her spoon and finds some soup; its dark onion warmth has a sweetness that in normal circumstances would be welcome. The blackness of the Duc's feast provides a door into her mind's eye: once again, she sees the dark juice spreading over her fingers; she sees the Belladonna stride quickly to the corner of the room and tug, once, on the thin black bell-pull. And then those few seconds of waiting; the utter silence. Flora's mind full with a roaring quiet. And then the swift entry and the bustle, the dreadful efficiency of the hotel staff, following the Belladonna's directions of a few swift arm gestures, removing the body, no questions. The way she had spoken so smoothly and calmly until they were out of the room, and then clapped her hands together—which for a moment Flora had seen, heart-stopped, as a broken and sarcastic round of applause; until the gesture became clear with repetition. She was getting the act off her hands. Putting it away, into past events.

And then she had looked at Flora, her face arranged perfectly, and made the suggestion that Flora go and wash her face, for they were shortly due to visit a dear friend for supper, and that they would go directly, that they would go now. The quick note, sent ahead to let the Duc know they were coming—her sweeping signature, the looping name in plum-coloured ink. And then—Flora shakes her head, no longer seeing the soup in front of her—how had she gotten into the carriage? How had she physically managed to leave the hotel? Flora recalls huddling into her cloak as they bumped through the night to the Duc's secluded house, and this midnight revelry, and as Flora rocked with the motion of the carriage *Her* voice had fluted along, to prime Flora for such a visit as she went over the Duc's habits, described his eccentricities, summarised the gossip—but Flora's vision had blurred and now here she is, listening to polite chat, while this Duc is holding a wake as a folly. Flora swallows, her throat pained with unmoving granite.

The Duc is proposing a toast, the wine a squat triangle of maroon in the glass. Arms are raised all the way down the table. Flora raises hers but doesn't follow the content of the toast, a strained rushing filling her ears, then hears the Belladonna thank the Duc for the honour.

She should have known. You have to be able to deal with the possibility that those near the Belladonna might die. *The risk of being there.*

'You could never have realised.'

Flora's heart leaps. She turns her head to find out who was speaking—and sees two disappointed guests a little further down the table.

'There's no rescuing your soup now, all the salt's fallen into it.'

'Well nobody warned me! This is what happens when there's no peppercorns.'

'We'll ring for another.'

Flora takes her gaze back into herself, dizzy with something like relief. But it shouldn't feel this heavy: and, sensing something, expecting it, there from across the table, their eyes catch and She is staring directly at her. An eyebrow is raised; it's a challenge to get to work, an instruction to be present. *Your job is to work a little harder than you are. Can you be with us at this party, please?*

It is a look that brooks no acknowledgement of why Flora feels like this.

She had been trying not to look as the body was removed from the bedroom, tugged roughly by a pair of silent, bony fellows whose dark uniforms bore an insignia that did not match the crest belonging to the hotel. There had been a momentary fumble—a problem with the lock, and one of the body's arms dropped while a ring of keys was jangled and dealt with—and she had seen the dead face, the grim flash of a moment long enough to imprint itself on her memory: the smudge of dark berry juice around the mouth, the still eyes. He looked so crumpled up as they took him out, and so easily done, like he was nothing but newspaper.

The Belladonna shifts her gaze back to the Duc and asks after his former pet tortoise, whether he intends to have it stuffed and mounted, or what?

'Shame to let something that beautiful go to waste,' she says.

The Duc is pulling his beard into a point. 'When he was

first brought here I thought the messenger carried the shield of Achilles; that's the size of him. His shell all gilt and precious stones, patterns shimmering in all that gold. I wish you could have seen him alive. I'd like to keep him about, but I fear it's not the same now.'

Chatter passes across the table, into the distance that Flora can only see through the waxen blazing prison bars of candles.

The Duc nods. 'Our dear Belladonna is correct—there might well be something further to be done with the shell.' He turns to her. 'Would you want it?'

She looks at the Duc with the perfect combination of flattery and modest refusal, allowing the gift to be passed on to someone more worthy, the job done in an instant.

Something shifts inside Flora, a new low feeling that brings a sensation of dread. It's not so much what happened as how calm she's being now, how engaged, how sociable, how perfect.

The Belladonna is saying, 'Of course I'd very much like to get a close look at its shell—'

'It seems a shame,' says Flora, her eyes firmly cast to the table, 'an awful pity it had to die.' The words are out, into the silent dining room, her legs are shaking. She scrapes her spoon across the bowl, where it seems to reverberate like fingers down a blackboard.

And the Belladonna taps the Duc on the shoulder and asks if he attended the most recent ballet gala at the Comedie, and on finding that, no, of course he didn't, for he was holed up here—to ask if the *Duc*, of all people, had been at the gala! what wit, to ask this of a man forever away from the city's pleasures—she launches into a description of the company's special performance, a masterpiece of artistry. She tells them of the first soloist's routine, a dumbshow, set by a moonlit lake, of a gosling first learning to walk. Soon the whole table is listening to her story, which manages to convey the humour of the dancer portraying a bird waddling around the stage insecure on its feet, and all the virtuosity this entails. Laughter follows, and the Duc claps lightly in delight as he imagines the broken high-kicks and tottering spins. It leads to an agreeable chat across the table about the role of technique in fostering illusion, the question of a performer's impulse to hide their own craft, the details of various dilemmas in the art of depiction, and Flora's comment is left behind in the dust.

F. finds this humiliating, more so than the silence she was trying to summon: she had felt a need to puncture the evening somehow. But the Belladonna had swooped in, quicker, cleaner, with her own incision and the more successful. In making them laugh, she let them realise that the funereal solemnity needn't be everything, and F.'s remark is read as a display of impertinence, a lack of understanding. Of naivety: among this company, the worst of all. Dishes of rice laced with squid-ink are served with promises of dark chocolate desserts to come later, and F. barely feels her own existence as she floats silently through the rest of the evening: the laughter, the refined conversation bubbling over, the remaining courses of the meal, the tour of the house, the show of his prized paintings, the jewel collection, the orchid hothouse, the library of rare books; the final round of drinks, the goodbyes.

The night lifts as they rattle back to Paris, facing each other within the close wooden walls, further weighted down by an angry silence more pronounced than any admonishment might be. To save the Belladonna's eyesight and headaches the carriage is being kept deliberately dark, the curtains drawn, and for a long time F. can't even tell if her mistress is awake; when her eyes finally adjust to a sketch of her face, the eyes seem closed. When they flick up and look into F. she is startled by an expression of such exquisite anger she wants to shrink away into the lining of the seat.

But no words are spoken, and the carriage returns them to the Paris apartments. The Belladonna swoops through the salon room and into the bedroom, with F. following behind.

'My head,' she says, removing her cape, flinging it to the ground—it hits the chaise longue briefly then slithers to the floor, the silk pouring over itself. Still behind her, F. nods invisibly, not knowing whether she'll be reprimanded.

The Belladonna is unscrewing a cordial bottle in the dull light.

'I can see you're disapproving, my Flora,' she says. 'I can tell you now, none of that is for the good. If you want to follow my advice you'll lose it.' She places one foot on the chair before the dressing-table and pulls off her opera gloves in two clean strokes.

She is going about all this so casually, as if this were any other night, when a few hours ago something other than her cape was discarded on the floor.

She looks up at Flora, one hand on the top of her boot, the process of unfastening hinted at, not quite begun. 'Loosen these emotions, let them run off. There shouldn't be the slightest interruption. That's how it's done.' She brings her ankle higher. It's almost a coquettish display of leg. 'If you or I felt the attitudes on display by the Duc or his guests tonight were a little wide of the mark, given recent events, or that dreadful theme of his, you may well be correct. But you can't let it distract you from the purpose. Mustn't let it stop you being the life of the party. Are you familiar with the phrase *"to move wild laughter in the throat of death"*?'

Flora does know that phrase. She finishes it: ' *"It is impossible."*'

La Dame swallows, and looks briefly thrown off. 'Well, yes. But my point is: for us it mustn't be.'

Flora nods. She moves towards the dressing-table, with a mind to gather the empty perfume bottles.

Leaving her shoes fully fastened, the Belladonna rises, and walks towards Flora.

'You're not going out again *now*? Surely—' and suddenly a great scratching pain plunges down her arms and she is rocketed back, a slick shadow whips around her and now she is there right in front of her. She wonders if she has *ever* been this close to the Belladonna's face—her nails are bared, pressing into Flora's arms, and with strength of conviction she is marching Flora backwards, pushing backwards, walking them together towards the nightshade tree whose branches lean out with an attitude of deadly thirst, and F. has hit the wall hard, and the branches of the plant spring about at the edges of her vision, and F. is pinned into place.

'Now you listen,' says the Belladonna, and her lips snarl around the words. 'Why do you think they come here, what do you think they see me for?'

F. finds it difficult to breathe. She pushes herself back into the wall, as if she could get further away from the woman who grips her to it, secure a slither of space. At the other side to the nightshade plant is a wall-mounted lamp, turned down dim to save her lady's vision of course, but still bright to be this near: she can feel the heat of it on her face.

'Do you know what those people play at when they come and see me?' Her fingers scrunch harder into F.'s arms. F. is silent, gasping. 'What's the worst thing they have to lose? Many of them already flaunt the worst society could think of them; they'll always find understanding in my company. They only have to look down at their shoes on my carpet in one of my salons and they may rest assured they are right where they should be. It's work, that's all. I give them everything: every moment, I perform for them. Occasionally there is one, cushioned by life, who decides that for some reason *he's* one to take me out of this, who wants the assurance that he is special.'

'Let me go! Please!'

She scrunches her nails harder and slams F. once more into the wall.

'What was it to him? True love or a dalliance? What was he to you? They think I'm enjoying it just as much as them, they don't understand. It's not even about those ridiculous berries. They play at the fact they risk their lives, but the *real* risk for them is nothing to do with what berries they eat: they lose themselves to my construction. And they enjoy that. They forget by force of their own will.'

'Aren't you playing a game of your own?'

'You see the anger when they realise they do not, in fact, possess me. They think they are risking their lives when they

161

dally with me—*what would father think? might I still be called to the bar? Do I lose my chance of a good marriage?* What kind of danger is that? They think that's what they risk: their lives. Well, I can ensure that they are. I make it so that they are.'

In the hot light of the lamp her face is sharper, it has more edges—the snarl of her lip, her nose and cheekbones have become like chiselled stone. Her eyes, larger than life, have taken on a new hard shine, bright as marbles. As statue-like as she seems, energy is practically visible, like the white glow around a full moon.

The Belladonna tightens her fingers again. 'Between one heartbeat and the next,' she says, 'anything can change.'

In that moment, Flora remembers—before she came to Paris—a party in an attic. A hole in the ceiling letting the cold in, the landscape outside ravaged by the snow. A young man had stolen from the medical school one of the fancy new innovations of the day: a kit including a great syringe, its silver tube coming to a point, and a new substance to fill it, for the numbing of pain. Well, Flora had been the first to volunteer and had laid down, felt the piercing into the top of her arm and suddenly, instantly, her body opened itself and revealed a truth: that it had been, all this time, merely a web of connected lines—she could feel it in action, a comet-flash of sensation running down the arm, back up again, into the chest, instantly woosh! down the legs, down her thighs, up and back again, with each beat of her heart sucking the liquid halfway around the loop of her body: and now, pushed against the wall by the Belladonna, the beating in her chest, feeling just as it did then, again she closes her eyes with the sensation of it as she remembers—in that attic, before

162

losing consciousness, she was just about able to think: what a powerful pump the heart is.

She is held there, pinned to the wall.

The Belladonna sighs.

The grip on Flora's arms is released. There's a brief shine of silk as the Belladonna turns to leave and a neat movement of shadow as she goes into the adjoining room, the door clicking behind her. Flora does not see her again while she tidies the remaining bottles as if in a dream. She retires to her own room, collapses onto the bed without even getting into it, and there, wide awake, she scrunches her eyes shut and waits for time to tick by, go beyond this moment and take her with it.

*

Flora must sleep, because at some point she wakes in a cold ball, still and tense on the bed where she landed.

It's morning: light comes in clean shapes from the half-drawn curtain. Flora creaks herself up and wobbles coldly through into the drawing-room, where the air feels empty and sodden, with no fire yet lit, and her feet tread the hard floorboards. The neat space seems almost reproachful; the furniture, not expecting to be used during the day, stares back at her as if interrupted from pursuing its own business. The door to the primary bedroom is closed, and in any case, Flora won't be going in there. Instead she pulls one of the curtains over the great window, to let more light in. She sits barely awake on one of the divans and watches motes of dust playing about. Two spin around one another, almost

163

as if they're dancing a waltz. She quickly stands, shakes her head to dislodge the vision, goes to the smaller washroom to splash her face.

She has the feeling she is being followed, not by any person but by the relentless ticking of time at her heels. This pause in the moment, this sitting in the light, the domesticity of washing herself—it all marks some kind of time.

When she returns to the drawing-room a tread is coming down the corridor, then she hears a slip of paper being pushed under the door. She reads the missive and her hands shake. It is a summons to a meeting at the Opéra.

She is quick to dress and quicker to travel, with a rising dread the entire time. Flora's heartbeat now leads the timing of things. The carriage ride goes by at a clip, and she notices only the roaring in her ears. She enters though a shadowy door at the side of the building, hurries through the labyrinth of passages to the upper levels with their faded carpets, up the velvet staircase and, without knocking, enters Vernon's office.

The Belladonna is there, standing with Monsieur Vernon at his desk, pouring over an unrolled piece of paper. She is pointing from one part of the diagram to another.

'The orchestra may enter from there—'

They stop and look up at Flora. Fully dressed and elegant as ever, the Belladonna must have not slept at all—did she come here immediately? Flora frowns, tries to piece it together. The Belladonna's bedroom door had been closed all morning, surely Flora would have been able to sense whether or not she was inside. And yet here the Belladonna is, up before noon, unthinkable the night after a party, especially a party *out of the city.* A wrap over her shoulders is the sole acknowledgement of the earliness of the hour, the lightest possible indication of a delicate state. Vernon with a red cravat and a matching glass of wine already in his hand. Flora is out of breath, and aware of how rushed her own state must appear—her layers pulled on without thinking and her hair, frankly, shambolic.

'Good morning, come and take a look at this.' Vernon beckons her over. 'Forgive the short notice.'

'Some things won't wait,' the Belladonna adds, then goes back to looking at the plans.

'We wanted to include you as soon as it was looking like a done thing.' Vernon is performing as host; a wine glass is pressed into Flora's hand. 'Here's to the newest scheme. My lady is right; it's been far too long since La Dame aux Morelles did anything for a wider audience. And the people are clamouring!'

'You put it too strongly, Vernon.'

'Not in the least. You've convinced me. She convinced me, and as you know,' he adds for Flora's benefit, 'I take some convincing!'

He chuckles as he refills his glass. 'We've been chatting it over. Originally I thought it might be a little too much— set the wrong precedent. The Belladonna doesn't *perform*. We tantalise. But then it was pointed out to me—we needn't give much away! A single concert, we can push the rarity of it, add an exclusivity to the ticket-holdings, people can be in the Belladonna's presence who wouldn't usually and so on. Build a nice programme of *highly* exclusive salons off the back of it: long story short, my mind is totally turned around.'

Flora opens her mouth to say *so it would seem.*

Vernon gestures to her to drink. 'We're finding a way to make it work—and the money! Imagine it: fill the theatre and easily match salon takings.'

'This is where we differ.' The Belladonna marks a place on the blueprint with a finger, reaching for a pencil. 'I still want to do it at the hotel. Not on the Opéra stage.' She is still not looking at Flora.

'Details.' Vernon claps Flora on the shoulder. 'She tells me a lot of this is down to your encouragement. We'll need your help, of course. There's a lot to do all of a sudden.'

Belladonna looks up from the stage plan and seems to see Flora for the first time. Her expression approximates a kindly smile and, whatever she has been doing for the last few hours, she has not refreshed the eye drops: the thinnest ring of hazel is visible.

'Don't let his excitement intimidate you,' she says, her voice soft, explaining. 'You'll be relieved to hear I favour a select audience. Vernon says the Opéra but I'll convince him otherwise; he's gotten too excited thinking about the money. What do you make of it? You said so yourself, just the other day—do you remember? "You should perform"? Well, I've decided I will.'

Vernon laughs triumphantly, tightens his grip around Flora's shoulder. 'Such a brilliant idea, and aren't you pleased—isn't it wonderful to get what you wanted!'

*

'We really shouldn't host it at the Opéra. Too big, too much. I don't want to look like I'm after anything—what's the word?—vainglorious.'

The Belladonna looks ahead. In a great change from usual, the two of them sit beside each other. The city is rattling by outside the carriage, morning light pushing against the damask-smothered windows.

'I'll make quite a spectacle, don't you think?'

F. sits quietly. She is no more able to interrupt this elation than she is to shatter the windowpanes with a breath. Best to let it go by, wear itself out.

The Belladonna is making plans. 'We'll start circulating rumours ready for the next salon. No, we're going to cancel the next salon, make it the performance itself. No need for a full orchestra; I must speak to Franz … '

More plans stream out: which song to begin with, where in relation to the piano to stand, which character is best evoked with a brooch or a quirk of the hair, which are best not evoked at all.

Back at the apartments she swoops through towards the bedroom. 'I've barely slept since the Duc's dinner. I'm indisposing myself. Please send any visitors away.'

F. had been expecting this. There's a way of walking, of frowning, that indicates one of the Belladonna's headaches is oncoming. A day and a half lying down in darkness will be the minimum she needs. F. nods agreement not to interrupt, thinking of all that time with only her own self for company, with only her own head to be in. At least she won't have to enter the bedroom.

The Belladonna is standing at the door. When she speaks, the softness of her voice comes as a surprise. The enthusiasm has been shaved away.

'I can count on you, can't I?'

She is framed by the entrance to her dark bedroom. 'I don't want to put on this show without you. I won't grovel, but I believe I need you.'

F. looks down at her feet as she considers. 'Wait,' she says.

With only a light trace of impatience, the Belladonna does as she's been asked. A delicate balance between them.

F. looks around the apartment. 'What does Vernon know?'

Her face does not change, but F. can sense the Belladonna's surprise in being asked this. 'He knows what he needs to. Vernon agrees with me; it's a great shame, young men can be impatient for sensation.'

'What does he know?'

'Vernon and I have a relationship of absolute trust and discretion. The only questionable link in the chain, as we see it, is you.'

The open door behind her.

'I need you, but I need to know I can count on you.'

F. could walk away. A single chance to leave.

And go where?

There's a long, low room with a printing-press; or perhaps a high attic, with the damp smell of desperation; a dark room with a stone floor; a snow-battered barn with hay to keep the chill out. Well, yes, she would be perfectly free to go to any of those places.

F.'s face falls for a moment, and then immediately she composes herself.

'I'm here to help you. That's what you brought me in for. So I'll help you.'

A victorious smile, a quick turn, then the bedroom door shuts behind the Belladonna. F. is alone again in the apartments, and she isn't going anywhere.

*

The necessary preparations are going to keep F. busy: her list of errands doubles, triples. But there's a moment that stands out: it's centred around an item among the outgoing post, a thin letter. A black border sits at the edges of the paper.

Something about the address: Trouville, Normandy. By habit she calculates the length of the ride: eight days, perhaps ten depending on the weather. The name of the village is familiar but she can't tell why. It takes a moment to realise what this letter is about, despite the black border. Now she sees exactly what this is.

'Took me a while to find out who we needed to inform,' says Vernon. His voice is kindly, the words chosen with delicacy, the tone there to lead her gently across the situation. 'We didn't have the usual paperwork of the salon. Quite remiss of our lady, there.'

Should the worst occur, there is a letter to be written. Normally, this sort of thing would be her responsibility. Wouldn't it?

'Shouldn't I have written this?' asks F.

'Oh, shoulds and should-haves.' Vernon takes the letter and slides it calmly back into the outgoing pile, like a magician hiding a card in the deck. 'As long as it gets written, and received.' He drops his voice. 'She mentioned the incident left you wavering a little.'

He proffers the pile of letters to her, and she takes it from him, stretching to keep the tower of envelopes from falling since Vernon snuck some of his personal correspondence into the pile, and she must do the same with her voice: work hard to keep it steady. 'Thank you for your concern but

I am feeling much better.'

'You know there was nothing either of you could have done.'

His voice seems kindly, but Flora knows him well enough to detect its deliberate nature. He has an open and generous expression, but it says *this is all you are going to get from me on this.* He is laying down the foundations of an immovable story.

F. nods to accept this version of events, and the black-edged mourning letter vanishes into the dark labyrinth of the postal system.

VI

F. overhears things in the gilded foyer, words spoken in muted tones along with the phrase *terrible shame*. The concert has been announced and is making news, but it is not the only thing being gossiped about. A great lady in white fur is conversing loudly with her circle.

'Which of us hasn't lost ourselves like that for love, for obsession? The tragedy is he hadn't the discipline.'

A younger man frowns in thought. 'Which salon was it? That's what's confusing me. I thought I'd been at the last, but I hadn't seen him.'

'A private one. You can get them, you know.'

'What, just you and *La Dame*?'

'Can you begin to guess how expensive they are?'

Two more keen-eyed patrons of the opera join in the story.

'He was insistent, I heard.'

'Too quick for her to do anything about it.'

'The poor thing.'

'Imagine how horrible it must have been for her, seeing him go too far like that. Having to watch it all.'

'Couldn't be stopped, they say—mad for the grief of it. It's no surprise to me it went the way it did.'

'You're only supposed to take one, if you eat more on your own head be it—'

F. hasn't heard these details spoken about before, not in public. Not so openly. She hasn't been asked, hasn't said anything at all about it. It will happen eventually, and nerves tighten their iron grip on her insides. The knowledge is certain: when the questions do come, she knows exactly what she'll say.

*

Behaviours change as preparations continue: there is a knock on the door of the Belladonna apartments and a guest is freely admitted, right in the middle of the day.

'I'll show you through to the piano,' says F., gesturing at the singing tutor—leather roll of manuscript under one arm, beard neatly combed for a new client—and he follows her into the salon room to wait. They sit awhile, the tutor not initiating conversation, merely looking around, not seeming put out by the wait; in normal circumstances F. might ask something to make a show of interest. Instead she stands awkwardly and wonders if she should be announcing him. Finally she sweeps through into the room, with the ghost of an apology drifting lightly from her like a cloud of mist, to take her place standing by the piano. The Belladonna has arrived; she and the tutor busy themselves in the business of ignoring F. Jet beads on a necklace are adjusted, a piece of sheet music is looked at, set aside, chosen over another. The tutor sits at the piano, opens the keylid, and makes a minute adjustment of the placement of the chair.

Ready to sing, or perhaps not quite. *She* glances at F., then back again to the smooth midnight lake of the piano surface.

The tutor stands, which scrapes back the stool too loudly. He clears his throat, goes to sit with a bend of the knee, stands again, politely, awkwardly, still refraining from beginning. Waiting for some permission from *her*, which doesn't arrive.

When the realisation comes, F. is too surprised to be hurt by it. *They're waiting for me. She's waiting for me to leave.*

She doesn't want me to hear her.

F. tugs the purple bell-pull to initiate a summons for the carriage, and can feel the tension in the room dispel as she goes.

She takes a journey to the centre of town, on no specific errand. If the Belladonna had taken her aside and whispered: *I'm a little self-conscious this first time, haven't wrapped my tongue around a phrase for a while. Perhaps you might go out?* Yes, of course. F. would have fully understood. Why embarrass her instead? The awkwardness of it continues to heat her face as she blankly leafs through costume designs in the couturier, residual unease that keeps her mind occupied and prevents her from negotiating on the price.

When she finally returns, the singing-tutor is mercifully absent from the apartments; so is the Belladonna, who since the lesson ended has been indisposed with headache and shivers. It is a while before F. can speak of trivial matters rather than whisper essentials into the tormented bedsheets. Eventually she is sitting up in bed, looking wilted and tired in the dusk of the bedroom.

F. brings more salve for her forehead. 'How did it go?'

'It's a long time since I sang properly.'

F. nods, feeling inwardly vindicated. 'It will fully come back eventually.'

The Belladonna manages a smile, raising her hand to adjust the silver nightshade leaf pinned into her hair. 'I must get myself up. My head. Oh, why are there always more letters to write?' Her expression pained, she looks at F.

She will be loyal. She cannot be anything else.

'Most of them can wait,' says F. 'And I'll do the others.'

*

Franz, the pianist, waits like a cat at the door. F. allows him in and thinks idly about giving him his own key, he seems so at home. Franz keeps an aura of success and energetic charm about him whether on a private visit like this one or entertaining a whole salon's worth of admirers.

He finishes a great flourishing set of scales at the piano, frowning through the motion of it, curling up against the keys as he plays. Eventually he sits up, and looks the keyboard up and down with a sad shake of his head.

'It might be about having a new piano for the performance.'

She is having none of that. She slaps him on the wrist and smiles. 'Don't even attempt it. This has been the piano for other recitals at my salons and it was perfectly fit for purpose then.'

'No, think about it. A showstopper from you, a brand-new piece by me, on a whole new piano! An unleashing in triplicate, do you think the world can take it?'

'You're getting overexcited.'

'You're not excited enough! What do *you* say?'

This last addressed to F. Her mind's eye writes new figures in the correct columns and adds them up. 'It could be called an affordable expense,' she says slowly. 'But only because we've already increased the allocated funds.'

The pianist claps his hands. 'There you are then!'

The Belladonna frowns and asks him to play something again, to further examine this piano's capabilities. She is taking it seriously: and now, there is a possibility of getting a new piano. The parameters keep changing. First it's a private salon performance, then a small audience but only of invited guests, then perhaps we *could* use a small public stage … ? Then suddenly it's the whole Opéra again, and it always was.

Franz finishes trilling a flourish over the keys. 'That's how they do it in Vienna, you know!'

F. watches the two of them. She doubts very much this is how they do anything in Vienna.

'Yes, of course,' she mutters. 'Whatever you want.'

*

Tucked away within the Opéra, one of the building's greater secrets, is the foyer de la danse with its soft smell of chalk. It appears wide, spacious, warmly golden—it's the room for patrons to mingle with the ballerinas, in the luxury of the great gilded columns. There are sparkling chandeliers, plush chairs, busts of great composers displayed under regal arches in the brick, carvings and paintings wherever you look. To balance this splendour it has a large bare floor, and a barre runs along the walls. A great mirror stretches from floor to ceiling, doubling the hall's already considerable size.

The Belladonna speaks into the mirror, addressing the rehearsal director: 'I would like to try it again. That entrance was too fast. Lifting me in is quite a distraction.'

The huge mirror reflects a dozen women in white dandelion-clock skirts, standing by with their hands on their hips. A few more sit on the floor in varying degrees of attentiveness.

'I need time to reach the front on my own, I cannot be plonked down centre stage like a bottle of wine. Let me do it.'

The rehearsal director makes a note in a yellow-paged notebook, and the ballet school's dancing instructor bangs her cane on the floor, where the dandelion clocks dutifully re-assemble into a loose line. Two male dancers, white tights moulded to their bodies, walk towards where the Belladonna stands in the space indicating 'offstage'. She casts an eye towards a rehearsal pianist who sits at the appalling rehearsal piano; Franz slipped out earlier for something and has been gone for several hours.

The mirror wall is reflecting all the foyer's usual social furniture, a dozen coffee tables and a set of chaise longues, pushed for now to the sides and covered over with sheets. Vernon and F. stand among these, together at the back.

The music begins again, rousing from the piano. The pair of ballerinos take her hands and lead her onto the stage space.

'Quite an entrance,' whispers Vernon. 'And her all in black, the corps in white.'

The ballerinas are entering from either side, crossing into and between themselves, weaving intricately across the space in pleasing lines. In the mirror the numbers all double, and the foyer is filled with featherlight motion like snowflakes on the wind. The dancers reach their final position, in an evenly spaced grid framing the Belladonna. They kneel, extend forward with their arms, and the rehearsal pianist prepares a flourish … and all eyes on her.

She takes a deep breath in:

'And *that's* the point where I begin singing.'

She looks around at the cast. 'Yes. It could work. I could see this being effective. I'd like to try it again.'

'Whatever helps her, of course,' Vernon says to F., as the dancers silently retake their places. 'If she's comfortable, it is fine. But that's all the dancers have to do the entire performance. What she really needs to rehearse is the singing, and if she can't do that here … '

F. steps onto the dancefloor.

The Belladonna's hands go to her hips as F. approaches, and she frowns her frustration at being disturbed. The dance mistress leans against the piano, happy to watch; the interruption, after all, isn't to any passion project of her own.

'If you're tired,' F. says, 'we can call that finished. We can schedule Franz to join you later for private rehearsal of the songs.'

Sensing this conversation will begin winding down yet another day, the rehearsal director clears his throat and speaks up. 'We really ought to go through the whole thing at least once. It will help the dancers to know the amount of time they'll be on the stage.'

Her face sets icily. 'That will depend on the repertoire,' she says. 'Which so far has yet to be finalised.'

*

What she wants: for everything to be done. Ideally by the time she has finished formulating the request.

A routine establishes itself. Flora slips out when the apartments become a flurry of decisions about hair and dress for the concert with the daily arrival of the *coiffeuse*. She is usually not required to attend the full company rehearsals: the Belladonna dismissed her from that duty with a wave of her hand, her fluting tones the only giveaway of her nerves. La Dame will not be attending any social events until the performance: time is now reserved for practice, preparations in her rooms. Progress is slowly being made: the repertoire has been decided upon—more or less (what about the *Addio, del passato*, the heart-rending aria for Violetta? 'I'm not touching that. Nothing against Verdi, but it's not very *me*.') and she at last allows her singing to be overheard. While F. is in the apartments, soprano notes lilt through the rooms, silver and fluid, and although guests are not being received, they are hardly left alone with each other: the deliveries and visits by stylists and tradesmen are constant. Franz the pianist is regularly in, charming her with tales of world tours and planning her own for when this debut is over, with himself in the manager role as well, for only a modest percentage.

F. looks forward to errands at the department store, a precious interval in all this where she can be alone amongst the city bustle. Arriving through the wide doors—opened for her by gentlemen in white gloves with gold buttons—and up the staircase with the metal railings that weave a soft pattern. She likes the gridded glass ceiling, the anonymity of the crowds. The cut of her dress and cape indicates she is lady enough to pass through without being bothered or stopped: and here she is, at the dress store. Rows of leather gloves, furs, stockings and corset-hooks. Only the look of the attendant reveals her chosen ensemble is inadequate: an assistant can recognise another, even if under a hat and veil. Then it is simply a matter of explaining who she is here on behalf of. And there is still pleasure to be had: she is surrounded by mannequins wearing the latest styles; the Belladonna house is always at least a half-season ahead. F. has the assistant bring out various options and arranges for the sending of any packages, while looking forward to later when she'll treat herself to a bun in the tea rooms.

F. signs for a consignment of corset bone with the official signature of her mistress. There: quite a name to write, isn't it? The flourish, like that.

She has been staying up late some nights, trialling the marks on the thick paper, over and over and over. As she is increasingly busy at rehearsals, and often ill in between, it makes sense that her letters are written, signed and sent in her absence.

The first time F. signs *Belladonna* and gets it right is quite something: a thrill like the woman herself, the black ink staring back at you. But after the joy of it comes the truth. There's no need, not really, to use her signature in the department store—the assistant doesn't know what it looks like. She's simply someone who's learned to copy.

Next, the chatter of the tea-rooms, and then the dark apartments beckon her with a new round of tasks. And also the Belladonna, with her own tasks that may well contradict or cancel out the others. F. lets herself admit this much: she's sure it's good for them both to have something to think about.

*

What the Belladonna wants is to rehearse. This time an interruption can't be helped.

Flora lets herself in to the foyer de la danse at the back of the Opéra. She manoeuvres past a dancer pulling her ankle level with her ear and a few more who are gossiping at the barre. Unsure where to best be of use in the bustling space, she instead looks for somewhere to sit, and eventually perches on the edge of a rigid oblong: a dust sheet covering a chaise longue.

The Belladonna, at last, is moving with more confidence. The rehearsal director and the dance instructor are gone. She gives suggestions of her own, sweeping a whole corps de ballet one way or the other with a wave of her gloved arm. She casts glances to the piano and smiles at Franz. No wonder she is so able to lead the room: her second in command is here.

'Again!' she says, and the dancers take their newest start positions.

A flourish emerges from the corner of the room, Franz managing to perform on the inferior rehearsal instrument. The dancers hit their marks; the entrance is effective; the song's chords swoop and rise; the whole thing is starting to get somewhere.

The song stops. Franz stands and calls out from behind the piano: 'The section with the lifts at the back! Might we go again from there?'

In the resultant organised chaos of resetting, Flora approaches the floor, clutching to her chest a list of questions. The Belladonna's voice is light, almost floating.

'What do you think of the new sequence?' she asks, not

looking at Flora directly, although she never quite does, these days.

A pas de deux has been added, to be enacted behind her entrance, instead of two dancers escorting her down to the front.

'They work well,' says Flora. She starts to say: 'I had an update about the flowers … ' when her voice trails off, as if the words lost themselves in the large room.

Two new figures have entered the foyer. They stand calmly at the back. They are ignored by the dancers, who flit their eyes to them and hurriedly pay attention back down at their legs, arms, the mirror; not their business to be noticing such people.

The uniform of the *policier* is immediately recognisable: the trousers, the navy cape, the hat. The shorter man beside him wears a light grey suit and waistcoat, apparently nothing but a modest gentleman. They stand patiently, quietly, wanting for nothing.

Flora's mouth moves a while before the words come. 'What are they doing here?'

The Belladonna's voice is still airy, but there is a tightness to her words. 'They've been coming and going.'

'They've been to more than one rehearsal?'

'They told me Vernon sent them. Something about my safety. A security measure, for me! Can you imagine! Go off to the side, would you, we all have to take our places.'

The dancers begin again and the strangers leave silently, letting themselves out. The Belladonna watches the door closing behind them. Flora's heartrate has increased and she stares blankly, willing her nerves not to expose her.

The chandelier hangs twice above her, once in the room and once in reflection. Then she begins pulling her list of things to do into thin paper strips.

*

Later the same day, after the rehearsal has juddered to a halt and the dancers have been dismissed, back in the apartments. The Belladonna has gone out—alone, Flora arranges a display of deadly nightshade flowers and thinks about the visitors. *They're doing it on purpose: to wrongfoot us before we've even begun.*

The Belladonna's full-length mirror calls her attention. Flora stands before it, takes in the vision, which is not unlike a younger version of La Dame aux Morelles but made forever childlike in the short wrist-length gloves. She remembers a discussion—a memory from another age—about fairground mirrors. Wouldn't it be such fun, one of the poets had said, if such a mirror was your only access to reflection? You'd go about life entirely differently if your view of yourself was so pulled and distorted. How lucky this poet is, to think you need to twist a mirror to develop notions like that.

'Mademoiselle,' Flora says, making her voice low and deliberate, 'there is no need for alarm. But we would like to ask you a few questions.'

Even pretending the scenario tightens her throat. She takes a few steps closer to the mirror. After all, the Belladonna's not acting worried, so why not try adopting the face?

It takes a few goes to really master it. Even when dropping all her features and thinking to herself, *don't move, don't move*, she simply looks overly serious—or like she's waiting for something. She takes a step closer until she is nose to nose with the mirror.

And:

There she is. That's the expression: utterly impassive, read into me what you like. Love? If you wish. Guilt? Hopefully not. But it's entirely your decision, and on your own head be it.

In any case, it's worth being certain about why those men appeared. There could be a perfectly ordinary explanation, and Flora knows where to get those.

To the theatre then, where she catches Vernon as he stalks past her in the foyer, striding, as he usually does when managing operatics, from one crisis to another disaster.

'Vernon! I must ask you—'

'My dear, can't it wait? The orchestra are threatening to strike and I've been informed the new set's too big to get through the stage door and only God knows why, the trap's malfunctioning, and in the props department they've misplaced that Jokahnan head again though that feels like a joke and I'll replace it with the stage manager's own if it doesn't bloody turn up, so help me—'

Try the face: the flatness. That sense of absolute, utmost importance. You did it for the mirror. 'Perhaps this can't wait either. There have been two men, Vernon, coming into rehearsals—'

Vernon shakes his head, sighs and leads Flora to a space overcast with stone arches. 'All right, then. I can see this matters. Tell me what I need to hear.'

So, it worked. But don't get ahead of yourself. She calmly describes the situation.

'Unbelievable,' Vernon says, when she has finished. 'I instructed them very clearly to back off and away, to go the whole damn way out of it.'

A sinking feeling in her chest: the real world is raising its head to snarl at them through their carefully crafted work of theatre. Vernon and Flora hold this certainty between them, not needing to speak it. Regardless of her own reaction, the important thing now is to focus on the Belladonna's welfare. 'Does she know the truth?'

'Of course she must; but she hasn't mentioned anything.'

'She only talks about the show.'

'They're under strict instruction not to bother her until then. Assuming they follow strict instruction, which I'm beginning to bloody doubt.'

Flora twists her fingers together. 'They'll approach her afterwards, then?'

'My hope is to somehow lose them in long grass. But heavens if I know how.'

Flora looks down at her feet. Vernon's shoes shine like oil.

'Look,' he says. 'Keep her afloat until after her recital; after that I'm convinced we'll have her full attention. In the meantime, any upsetting business about that whole thing can wait. I don't want her fretting about this before the performance.'

Flora nods agreement, and the idea that this spectacle should perhaps not be happening at all hovers as a spectre between them.

'And who knows?' says Vernon carefully. 'Perhaps the whole thing is overblown and *we're* the ones overthinking it. I'm sure it's routine; they'll only need her assurance she's completely innocent. It was a surprise to me they're bothering with enquiries at all.'

If you're so sure about all that, why are we making them wait to approach her? Why do we both know that's the right thing to do?

Back in the apartments, Flora composes at the writing-desk while the silver voice of her mistress floats again through the scales. Invitations to the opening night are signed personally, of course, with Flora handling the Belladonna signature. But beyond the scented paper and the ivory seal for the envelopes, Flora sees a less comforting image. It is flickering over the warming fire: she sees it wherever she looks. Not long to wait, the event is almost upon them, and after that, those two men will … Flora blots a signature, the pen makes a crooked mark on the paper of its own accord. She swears quietly, reaches for the blotting paper, stains her sleeve. She dabs away at the ink, looking at the smudged, ruined Belladonna name.

VII

The carriages are rolling up, releasing expectant patrons who stamp their feet into the cold and, in the foyer, clump together waiting to be allowed to take their seats. Their combined voices are a rumble like thunder that Flora swears she can hear all the way from her position in the wings.

The Belladonna is pacing across the stage, going around in choppy, hesitant circles: not ready to retire to the dressing-room and wait for the audience to file in; not quite ready to say, formally, that all possible preparations have been done. Flora is standing in the wings, waving, trying to get her attention to say, formally, that now it is time for the show. The Belladonna goes to the piano, positioned at the centre of the stage. That is all it will be, the piano and her. The ballerinas who rehearsed for weeks making up the background picture are gone. She decided—it was decided—that a certain simplicity would be more impactful. But now she seems dwarfed by the vastness of the stage. Hanging at the back is a painted backdrop of a moonlit lake, surrounded by a shadowy forest and with a mist-shrouded château high in the distance, something supplied to evoke mystery and charm. With one hand resting on the piano the Belladonna looks up at the château, as if working out how long it would take to run up there.

Flora calls out: 'They are about to open the doors; we must let them in now,' and is surprised at how small her voice sounds. How uselessly, she thinks, it would fail to fill the great yawning velvet emptiness out there. Granted she hadn't been trying to reach the whole theatre but saying anything at all underscores, with a vertigo-inducing spin, the scale of the singer's task. The Belladonna nods and comes to her, her face closed.

They go through into the dressing-room and here the Belladonna's physical pacing, at least, stops. Instead a sort of mental pacing takes over—Flora can almost see her thoughts tumbling about, spinning like loose wheels. She grips the back of the chair and stares into the tinted mirror. The vision that looks back at the two of them is a low and golden depiction of the Belladonna, a romantic picture, surrounded as it is with flowers that further soften the light. Only Flora, knowing her well, can see the determination in the mouth. It's a vision of control.

But also: there is something else palpable in the room. It has a metallic smell like copper, like blood, and it takes a few moments to place it as the presence of absolute, unquenching, unspeakable terror. Only when she detects the slight trembling in the Belladonna's arms does she fully realise, see it on her. Flora has known her to be anticipatory before, of course: hosting the poison salon, dealing with an insistent acquaintance, arriving at any party when she is feeling ill; such things usually require a certain gathering of resources. But this is an entirely different kind of tension.

Then the Belladonna raises her eyes and now both women are looking at the reflection. The edges around the Belladonna seem to harden and become more precise, by force of her own will: and when she turns to address her companion directly her voice is steady.

'My future is out there; I suppose I must go to meet it.'

Time is briefly disjointed: Flora finds herself addressing the frightened person she was looking at a moment ago. 'They are ready to love you! Give them a taste of something that could have been, a different world, a glimpse of you ruling it.'

A flicker across the face. 'Thank you.' Unimpressed; offended, even. It seems that was the wrong thing to say.

The roar of the audience can be heard even in the dressing-room.

'What I mean to say is you'll be exquisite,' says Flora, trying to offset a new mild panic.

'I understand.'

'You're already a star soprano in their eyes.'

Her face tightens again, a door closing. 'Yes, yes.'

Finally the pianist, Franz, adjusting his diamond collar-studs, pops his head around the door to check on them.

'Remember,' he says, 'This is only an opening night.'

The Belladonna waves her hands to the heavens. '*Only*!'

'Only. The audience *expects* some nerves. Remember, they know you. Think of this as a private salon on a different stage.'

'You can say all this. *You've* been doing it your whole life.'

'Listen to me then. They will support you, I promise.'

They are out of the dressing-room, making their way through the darkness together and into the wings. F. hangs back, keeping some distance, searching for a space she won't be seen, tripping into a flyman at the ropes and gaining a disapproving grunt until she eventually finds a spot to watch from.

The orchestra plays a long vibrato: taking its cue, the whole theatre tucks itself under a blanket of silence. The Belladonna holds herself tall in the wings as she stands there, examining her hands, alternating them between fists and spread fingers. Then, as if tricking herself into it, she raises her head, looks into the glare of the light on the stage and steps out into it—and F., breathing out suddenly as if released from a spell, watches the Belladonna moving steadily through the waves of applause. When the pianist joins her from the opposite side the applause deepens, and F. feels the temptation to relax; but to do that would be bad luck, wouldn't it, surely.

*

The Belladonna, standing by the piano. She places one hand upon it. The applause becomes quietness, turns into waiting.

Her dress, that eternal Belladonna cut that reveals her shoulders and neck and makes a straight blade of her. Its elegant sheen is articulated in the theatre light. Keeping her hand on the piano she lowers herself, making a gesture that's half-curtsy, half-bow. The gesture is pitched well for a greeting: knowing, aware, but not overly grand. It does not shout *here I am* but rather whispers, *this is me*.

The orchestra are pulling some low introductory notes from the strings, famous notes with a subtle bounce to them. The audience, recognising the tune as Bizet's *Habanera*, will now know more of what they're in for, and the Belladonna's shoulders move with her first inward breath, and in the wings F. breathes along with her.

The music comes steady and rhythmic, and opens the space for her to begin.

There: the first gentle words, the melodic defiance of them. The lilting down-the-steps tune, flirting with certainties, forging confidence.

F. feels a friendly warmth at the choice. It's the aria they had sung together that night in the apartments, where F. had made the offhand comment: *you should be on the stage.* It's an ode to the unpredictability of love, a strong, joyous song from a character who is, at this moment in her story at least, fully in command of herself; raucous, untameable, untouchable.

There is a quiet clarity to her voice, and like a reflection in the desert it shines out over the Opéra House.

A fearless choice, this musical work. It has a bravado all of its own, it suggests a kind of solidarity. *If you applaud the character, you'll surely cheer for me.*

The audience is quiet, difficult to read; it's a silence that suggests appraisal, of waiting a little longer to decide, as if to say, *you are not out of the woods yet.*

The Belladonna raises her hand and bends slightly with a corresponding note, and makes a gesture of running a hand down her skirts. It reads almost as a complete undressing though all that happened was a slight twitch of her fingers. It's a risk: the Parisian taste might decide it prefers something more refined.

She finishes a phrase and, as she goes into the next, snaps

her attention to the other side of the stage, singing with a slight lowering of her head, looking outwards and to the back. Everyone in that part of the audience will think she is looking at them and them alone, and the Belladonna is loving the whole pack of them, daring them to love her back. Even seeing the performance from the side, there in her tight spot in the wings, F. sees the power of this strategy. Only if it works.

Still silence from the seats; if the Belladonna is thrown by this, it doesn't show. The song seems to stretch out ahead for miles. She smiles going into the next verse, and the lyrics move though her voice, and—oh! what is this! a steady ripple of pale laughter comes over the stage. F. feels hot with relief, the sound echoing into her ears. It's a miracle—a *laugh*, they are with us! When did they choose, how did they decide to be with us? But there it is, the verdict is made: they are onside, and now the job is only to keep them there.

The Belladonna knows this. She casts an eye across the stage again and finds her light. She steps into it, which takes her away from the piano, loosens her from the anchor. There is a different energy to her now, F. can see it.

She has taken a small item from its hiding place on the piano and when she reaches her point downstage she snaps it open. A pericón in black—there is a smattering sound over the stalls as the audience clap. The Belladonna fans herself, languidly, leaning her head back—deliberately overstating the gesture: *this* is exactly what I'd do, in this situation, isn't it?

She allows the prop in her hand to move down to her side and leans into a rising melody. Her smile to the audience is knowing. She glances at the pianist, and they share a mutual flash of enjoyment, and her face breaks in a way that suggests her laughter is real, is coming through the song, is a crack she didn't actually intend. It endears her to the audience further.

She spreads her arms as the final notes soar up to the ceiling. The orchestra reaches that finishing musical passage with a pronounced levity, trotting along beneath the Belladonna's triumphant note which turns into: laughter! She laughs, half in character and half as herself, closing her eyes as if she can't quite believe it—the heroine of the aria and the demi-mondaine on stage: two women laughing as one.

She snaps the fan closed, becomes fully herself, and it's done. The first impression has been made. And the rest will follow.

She curtsies again, deeper this time, into the applause. She puts her hands out towards the audience, gesturing to thank them, then moves elegantly to give the pianist the focus—he stands and nods, then salutes their adoration back to the Belladonna herself, as the one who has earned it. She closes her eyes briefly and her smile seems ghostly, the relief of someone rescued from somewhere dark and eternal.

In the wings, F. watches the Belladonna briefly look down at her fingers. It seems a private moment, as if she is checking to make sure she's really there, to keep a dot of calm within herself among the swirling applause from the audience. But F. reads the gesture differently. The Belladonna is looking at the palm of her hand, and thinking: *here's where I have them*.

*

'I ought to send a note to those boys backstage, the whole team.'

The Belladonna puts her wine glass back onto the table, a little too heavily so the wine jumps; she makes abstract shapes in the spill with her fingers. 'And thank *you* for everything.'

'Of course.'

'I do realise I'll have to see everyone eventually.' She rubs her head, shivers a little; shakes a coughing fit away. 'They'll think me rude for leaving the theatre so quickly.'

'A memory by then. Let them ruminate on it,' says F.

'That's true.'

'If there's a wait between the audience seeing you on stage and off it, the stage version will seem all the more special.'

'Exactly. Good idea.'

They are on their own, thanks to F.'s quick thinking. She had sent a messenger clattering down the theatre stairs to let it be known the Belladonna was suffering from one of her headaches, an all-consuming attack, and that she had finished her performance and was leaving the theatre immediately. Once this note was duly dispatched, they had snuck out the back way and come swiftly home in the carriage. Now they sit at one end of the dining-table, where a single candle illuminates the wood and glistens off the waxy fruit display.

The Belladonna picks up the wine bottle, sighs at how light she finds it. 'I'd forgotten, you know, that's the interesting thing. How much it takes out of you. I thought it wouldn't be much different from a salon or watching from the box. I'm just as on show there.'

F. nods. 'It went well,' she says, for the two-dozenth time that evening. The words have taken on a rhythm of their own.

The Belladonna leans towards F. and speaks in a tight, efficient manner, using the clipped phrases of an objective professional. 'No dancers was the correct call. Yes. And a good repertoire of the pieces, this song drifting into that one. It all worked.'

She picks a single olive from her plate, examines it and replaces it. 'The crowd were nice and warm, too,' she adds. 'This may sound odd but I really felt we grew into each other. Good responses; especially from the balcony. The fan got a laugh.'

F. nods. The Belladonna is saying nothing that isn't true.

And yet there is something, a cracked stone edifice hastily papered over; there is *something* tight and unhappy in the Belladonna's debrief, as positive as it is. F. watches her carefully, tries to puzzle it out. It really hadn't been a disaster. There was no croak into deathly silence, no running offstage partway through a line. The audience had been supportive; the feeling that filled the auditorium like heady perfume was that those present wished her well. Perhaps this was merely the anti-climax of it being so suddenly over.

'It went well, I thought,' says F. again. It isn't any kind of a lie.

It had been better than fine. She had ruled the stage, just like any other soprano visiting the city and putting on a small concert to announce themselves; perhaps it was clear she hadn't sung for a while but it was hardly a dead duck either. This brittleness; anti-climax or something else? Something *more*? The Belladonna announces she is going to bed, but F. hears her pacing well into the early hours of the morning.

The next day begins normally enough: the Belladonna

wakes in the afternoon to a nice pile of supportive letters: a gentle onrush of notes and missives that have been arriving steadily through the day. She sits up in bed and leafs through them, smiling distantly at the raft of congratulations and jovial calls for an encore.

Cards are arriving, bringing with them the threat of visitors. For most F. writes a brief note of regret.

The pianist, though, he may enter. He dashes into their presence and bows almost fully to the floor. 'Lady of the night! Queen of the dream-like jewels of the gossamer aria! Singer of divine phrases into the stars joining their number!' He carries on in this vein, seemingly oblivious to the slight winces he's getting in response.

Eventually he comes to the point: 'I'm dashing off, I'm afraid; sudden call to lead a performance in Krakow, so I'm journeying to Poland.'

They stare at him, as if he just spoke an unintelligible garble instead of French. *What do you mean, you're dashing off?*

The Belladonna speaks after a moment, her voice brittle: 'How exciting for you.'

He claps his hands together, relieved, energised. 'Excellent; I hoped you'd be pleased. Would love to stay and relive last night with you endlessly of course. It'll probably turn into a longer tour, it usually does once the rest of the continent gets a taste; so shall I say, see you next season?' And he is gone; the two of them sit there, stunned, left only with his faint aroma of lavender.

The Belladonna blinks. 'Charmed, I'm sure,' she says.

She rises, goes towards the dressing-table. F. watches her reach towards the vial with the amethyst crystal.

'He didn't even ask how I thought it went!' says the Bella-donna, but her voice is more amused than offended. Still, there is that brittleness somewhere. The world beyond last night's performance is continuing to go on, whatever she may prefer.

She has retired once more to her bed by the time Vernon visits, so F. receives him alone.

'How is she feeling?' he asks, leaning back in the leather chair to reach into his waistcoat pocket.

F. thinks about it. 'Steady,' she says. She doesn't add: *unnervingly so, the steadiness of one who mustn't think too hard about what's keeping her upright lest it all crumple.* 'I thought her performance was excellent,' she adds.

Vernon has found his pipe; he sparks a light for it. 'But what does *she* think? Has she mentioned wanting to do another show?'

'I haven't broached the subject.' The smell of pipe smoke makes her eyes water. 'Do you think we'll be seeing more of those men now—the ones from the rehearsal?'

He doesn't speak for a few moments.

'I can't shake them off,' he says. He gazes into the fireplace and avoids looking at F. directly. 'I saw them again this morning. They tell me they're just checking everything is all right. That's why I've come; I want to talk about her peace of mind. Congratulations with flowers I can offer later. So. What do you have for me?'

'She seems disappointed. I can't think what about.'

'Can't you?'

F. considers. 'She built it up so she would have to be the best soprano in the city, in the world. And then go off and sing forever, I don't know. Instead she was just as brilliant as she rehearsed herself to be, and that's all there is to it.'

She doesn't want to voice her theory that the Belladonna is disappointed because the concert did not, after all, help her forget recent events. The applause was not enough, in the end, to close the door upon those thoughts.

A triumph is what the Belladonna wanted, rising with fire-tipped wings out of the ash, half believing the pianist's talk of world tours and an enraptured public and the whirlwind life that never requires coming down to face more prosaic things.

'Perhaps the problem was being too sure of success,' says Vernon. 'And now she's wondering how she could ever live up to her own expectations.'

'I'm not sure we were ever certain of success. By the end she was positively frightened—she wavered at every point'

'And if that happens again, you must hold her still.' Vernon pauses, having pivoted again to the subject that stretches out beneath them like a dark river. 'Perhaps I'm being pessimistic, or if I'm right, we might still have cause to worry.' Vernon sighs and slumps down more heavily into the chair, as if forcibly pushed into it. 'My concern is if she grows careless of the wider risk. She'll need to be even-tempered.' His gaze is piercing. 'I cannot hold them off for much longer.'

'When should I expect them?' F. pictures the bottles topped with crystals on the nightstand. 'How soon are they planning to come to us?'

'Very soon.' His voice is level. 'If you sense she is wavering, about anything at all, you will need to help. That's the role we require of you. She's going to need to be level.'

'I understand.'

'I cannot hold them off for much longer.'

*

'How much longer are we going to be in this carriage? I've never known the city so busy. What's going on?'

Flora adjusts the tasselled curtains to peep out. 'We're on the quai de la Mégisserie,' she says. 'It must be the market.'

The horses draw to a halt in the face of sheer density of crowd gathered by the bridge, and the carriage bounces uncomfortably as the driver attempts to turn. After a third jolt and bursting whinny from the horses the Belladonna gives the roof a hard thump.

'Oh, I can't bear this. Let's get out here. And I want to eat; let's have some frites. There's a man does frites in a cone, have you ever? You must...'

Flora follows her out of the carriage—which continues its incremental turn, to go home with no passengers— and together they step onto the wind-whipped bustle of the bridge. A row of stalls stand beneath brightly-striped awnings, piled high with fruit, cakes, fat ropes of jewels, small books with marbled covers, novelty crockery claiming to be etched with detailed maps of the city. As if following a clear route to treasure, the Belladonna heads towards the stall where a man in a greasy apron operates a pot from which rises a crackle that sounds like applause.

The bridge is busy; as usual, the crowd parts a little at the sight of the Belladonna's striking profile. People go around them with bags of goods, casting glances at the enigmatic woman in the cloak. Flora walks behind, trailing invisibly in her wake.

As the Belladonna heads towards the scent of frying potatoes Flora sees someone on the bridge and the recognition stops her still, sends a tingle up her neck and over her newly hot scalp. Those shoulders, the shape of a back; the way an arm moves a certain way to choose from a stall: unmistakable, even after all this time. That creaking bed in the attic, a tiny window of pre-dawn sky. So, her lover still exists. Well, of course, it shouldn't be a shock. Still, hadn't Flora considered the possibility?

The turn of a head; and if there is recognition, it can't be detected from here. The distance between them is more than the width of the bridge. Flora gets a smile usually reserved for neighbours or distant relatives, and acknowledges the truth that there is nothing to say. Her lover quickly ducks behind an argument that has broken out over prices, and disappears.

Reeling, Flora walks at a pace further down the bridge, to catch up with her current life.

The Belladonna is being served up her paper cone, clutching it closely like something precious while Flora reaches into her own skirts for the coins. They cross the bridge and lean out over the stone edge of the wall, the wide Sienne below them and the city stretching out along the sides.

'I don't know how I'd manage without you,' the Belladonna says, the wind taking her words away and over the water. 'I may never have said this outright, so,' she looks down at the cone and smiles sheepishly, 'I do appreciate having you here.'

With a hunger like a child she eats a frite, immediately followed by a few more.

'Before you came along—how did I ever do it? I suppose people act the dear friend well enough around me, but few are in a position to be sincere.' She digs into more of the frites. In spite of hearing words she would once have given the world for, Flora cannot help but wonder at the sight of the Belladonna on the Pont Neuf with her paper cone.

'I'm here to help you, so I help you,' she says, and she feels the words coiling around her like rope.

'My world is more exciting than your printing press? Thank you for saying. I know we've had our—how to put it?—ups and downs.' She speaks quickly, between bites. The smell of salt whips over the river. 'I've placed you in difficult situations, I know this. And you haven't always been prepared for them.'

'It's no trouble.'

'You make it no trouble.'

The Belladonna crumples the empty cone into a ball, tosses it casually from hand to hand. 'There's a way you can further help me. I know there are rumours going around about our former friend, how he died.'

Flora becomes alert.

'I know you've been going along with the tragic accident, all that,' the Belladonna continues. 'I want to thank you for your commitment there. But I know there are people circling, preparing a list of questions. You've been kind enough not to mention it to me.'

The Belladonna presses against the stone of the bridge and leans over as if craning to look down at the river, so the wind takes her words as soon as she utters them: 'If things come to the worst, if *truth* must come out, we might consider *which* truth it actually is.'

'Which truth?'

'If it suits me to change the story, I will. I might decide it is better framed differently. That someone in particular was responsible for his death after all.'

Better framed. The words are suddenly around Flora's neck.

'I can't be seen to be going about killing my friends and lovers, Pallidiflora, you know that. Accidentally or on purpose.'

'But I didn't—and nobody thinks you have!'

'I know what I am, Flora. But compared to you, my word carries a modicum of weight. I'm sure you agree?'

And there it is. They are bound tightly together now; the Belladonna's message is clear. The river is dark and cold beneath them.

IV

VIII

Invitations come and you accept them: there are still dinners, receptions, first nights, private views, carriages to ride along the promenade. It is February: Carnival season. There are more Opéra balls to attend than ever before. More jaunts. More offers.

'They want to gawp,' says Belladonna, pulling her cape to her throat against the bitter air. 'They think it's better to have me, lest they miss anything. It's what we wanted, wasn't it—more of an audience?'

Flora doesn't respond: she's just been knocked backwards by an ashen-faced old man, bent at the hip, carrying a bulging sack. He spits into the gutter and keeps walking. There's pain across her ribs, but now she must trip ahead a few steps to keep up. Belladonna has not glanced behind—she hasn't even noticed, still speaking instructions over her shoulder.

'We'll arrive at the ball in a moment; remember at all times to watch everything. The whole time, as we go.'

Watch everything. This is becoming her constant instruction. Flora cannot even be sure what it is she is supposed to be watching for. It's almost as if La Dame is talking to herself. However, it's true that they are both ever more aware, these days, of the looks that happen around them: the quick snatches of a glance, there and back again.

Perhaps as a consequence, they enter the ball with a sense of gritted teeth.

And the day after, in that carpeted office high above the Opéra, Vernon speaks in tones that are edging up to desperate: 'Can't you talk some sense into her?'

'I can but try,' Flora says. Half an hour earlier she had left the apartments to the sound of smashed glass, a voice risen almost to screeching.

Vernon sees all this in her face. 'What was it this time?'

Flora shakes her head. She hadn't folded a silk scarf the correct way, or she'd put the wrong earrings in the wrong box, or heavens, she'd walked across the carpet too loudly and a headache had chosen to descend.

'Honestly,' she says, 'I don't know if sense can be talked into her at the moment. By me, or anyone. I worry she's becoming …' Flora casts about for the word. 'Reckless.'

Vernon, holding his head in his hands: 'But last night at the ball. Are you telling me nothing untoward actually happened?'

'It depends what you call untoward, and by whose standards.'

They both permit themselves to laugh at this: what is or isn't appropriate becomes contorted in the context of Belladonna's activities. But then Vernon nods a curt encouragement. Go on then, keep telling me.

'She's brittle; I was forever flinching. Not the usual social butterfly with everyone grateful to have her there. It felt like she wanted to bend the event to her will instead.'

Beneath her silk cloak had been a dress of the usual glittering black, with the (less usual) sense that she had chosen to wear every jewel in her possession. In her hair a whole spray of deadly nightshade was recreated with black diamonds for berries, silver leaves and silver thorns. Intoxicating, shimmering, bold: starstruck guests had said all these things, and Flora felt there was no other word for it than *brilliance*. The soft aura of all those jewels framed a face more than usually determined. Belladonna's sharp features were pinched, her face carrying the spectre of illness. Her expression spoke of a low-carried and barely contained anger. She had seated herself on one of the small sofas and watched the crowd at the Opéra Ball with an air of silent challenge. Like a statue.

Vernon shakes his head, making the calculations. It's clear he almost daren't ask: 'And she stayed there all night, or did she dance?'

'Eventually she did,' says Flora. 'When the musicians played to her liking.'

And then it had been an overwhelming burst of energy. Belladonna had reached out her arm to the nearest soldier and spun around with such apparent rapture and passionate giddiness it made Flora dizzy to follow it, standing there among the crowd along the edge of the dancefloor. It had been like watching fire roar over kindling.

Vernon leans forwards, looks at Flora very carefully. 'How is she today?'

Flora shrugs. 'The headaches are more frequent, and she's low of patience. I'm doing what I can. More invitations arrived off the back of last night, so if anything she's receiving more interest. Since the show.'

Vernon's intense gaze hasn't let up. It has a wrongfooting effect.

'I'm wondering,' he says. 'What is it you're not telling me.'

It's a relief, almost, to broach the subject. 'I think she's waiting for it all to begin.'

'She knows what's coming?'

'Exactly. We don't speak about it, but she's hardly oblivious. Why else would they have been there, hanging about, following us?' She pictures it, again: those *policiers*, standing calmly through the rehearsals, waiting for a cue of their own.

Vernon looks at Flora, then casts a glance down to the accounts on the desk. There is a pause as both of them weigh up the situation.

Flora speaks first. 'You're seeing a trap?'

'Perhaps she'll think of it that way,' says Vernon through a dry throat, his voice gruff. 'More likely she'll view it as a dull chore to be done with eventually.'

Flora nods, but what she doesn't, *can't* say to Vernon, is that this is because Belladonna will, if she has to, think nothing of laying the whole disaster at Flora's feet.

That's the real trap, and it's laid for Flora. And there's a deeper trouble: the knowledge that their fates are tied together and this—still, impossibly, soaring above and beyond everything she's seen and known—makes her *lucky*.

Later, then, back in the apartments, Flora passes over the ointment pot, rimmed with gold. Belladonna takes it from her wordlessly, places it down on the dusty table and reaches for Flora's hand.

Even now. Even this close. Even knowing the small things, the order of the bottles on the jar, the way she prefers her hair combed, her preference for one necklace over another, her opinion on vital things, tiny things. The small textures of a personality, that another person had died wanting to learn. With all that information pushed aside, known, internalised: still, the feel of Belladonna's hand over Flora's own, the privilege of it. Belladonna looks at Flora and a sheer pull of *need* between them. The full force of Belladonna's attention still has the power to knock her backwards.

'I have some concerns,' Flora manages to say.

Belladonna looks surprised; and all concern for Flora, even with her own headache pressing down like a low ceiling. And then a barely visible finch as she freezes, waiting for the rest. 'What's scaring you?'

'A storm is gathering around us.'

'Ah.'

She almost sounds relieved; oh, we can talk about anything but the concert.

Belladonna gives her only a bright smile, a squeeze of the hand.

'If you're sensing storm clouds,' she says, 'it's just as well we keep the curtains closed.'

*

It feels like an ambush, because Vernon asks to see Flora for matters of usual duties: there's a premiere coming up, you'll be wanting the usual box and please confirm how many guests, where to for supper afterwards. But as soon as the door to his office swings open the meeting is thrown off-kilter, as Vernon steps backwards to bring her in, gesturing grimly into the room, his eyes cast down as if ushering her some-where he can't bear to be himself.

'This is Monsieur Théophile Davignon,' he says, his voice flat, hinting at a furious argument only recently lost. 'He's an *enquêteur* who comes to snoop around all the way from somewhere ghastly in Normandy.'

She recognises him instantly, of course, from the back of the rehearsals. The same neat waistcoat and aura of patience. As Davignon extends a hand she feels his charisma, the sensation of suddenly being up close to a face she knows well only at a distance. She takes his hand briefly. As Davignon bows, her eyes meet Vernon's, whose face is as flat as his voice was.

'I informed him you're very busy with your duties, Flora,' says Vernon. 'But I'm afraid he insists on making your acquaintance.'

'You must forgive me,' says Davignon. He pats his waistcoat pocket, looking about, lost. 'No pipe it seems. So I cannot play the full part of settling down informally. You'll forgive that, as well?'

'Monsieur Davignon,' she begins, but Vernon interrupts:

'I am also busy,' he says. 'If you must be here, let's at least pretend I am allowed to rush you.'

'Of course! Of course,' Davignon smiles at Flora and taps his nose. 'I'm sure this place requires more maintenance to operate than I can imagine, and I won't keep you from it longer than I have to. Given your patience, I would like to ask you a few things.'

Vernon quickly becomes a skulking shadow at the window, his outline emphasised by the winter light pushing against the glass. She can feel the energy radiating from him: *don't tell him anything.*

'I've seen you before,' she says, seating herself on one of the chairs before the desk. 'You were with another gentleman.'

'Oh yes! You weren't always there though, were you? I did enjoy watching you rehearse. Not much of a thespian, but love getting behind the scenes. All those people busy at work, a big team pulling together, doing their duty to pull the whole thing off.' He sits on Vernon's desk—right across Vernon's desk, with one leg dangling. 'Remind me please, what *is* your role in the whole operation?'

It is amazing that Vernon has not already shoved him off the desk and rolled him like a barrel out the door. There is a small bronze model of the movement of the spheres on the desk, and Davignon spends a second looking at it. He moves a hand towards the brass planets, then thinks better of getting it spinning. Not pushing his luck all the way.

Flora speaks. 'I'm a companion to the Belladonna. I accompany her.'

'You live with her in the hotel. So you're with her all the time?'

'Most of it. I am her assistant.'

'What do you assist?'

'Most everything, really.'

'As I said, I'm not of the theatre but I love learning how it works. Can you break down most everything for me?'

'It's, well ...' she begins counting on her fingers. She makes herself frown in thought: *that's it, try to look easily confused. Make it seem as if even this question has thrown you, that you lose your composure when you concentrate.* 'The Belladonna is a high-profile

211

person in society, even if it's the *demimonde*. She has many demands on her time and on her company. So I am someone who assists with that. I arrange her social calendar; invitations to events, for example, I send out, and we might discuss who's coming, what the fashion for furs is, so, what to wear to any events; then I'll arrange for the necessary visits, help her dress, solve any problems; if her plans change I make the necessary excuses. Like I say, I'm there for nearly all of it.'

'And why might her plans suddenly change?'

She gives him a smile. 'Mainly, reasons of her health.'

For a moment, they hold that look there.

Eventually he nods. 'Understood: secrets of the trade. You must be privy to quite a few of those.'

'It takes a lot of work for her life to seem so effortless. It's not actually a floating palace, I help with the foundations.'

'And the two of you, along with Monsieur here, work together to keep up the illusion her life is naught but flying through clouds? I believe I'm coming to understand.'

Vernon breaks free from his stasis and makes for the desk. 'Right, time is upon us. I've got a great deal of work to do before this evening.'

Davignon stills him with a raised hand. Vernon stops, midstride, and she almost wants to clap: she's never seen anyone do that before.

'I don't want to outstay my welcome,' says Davignon, raising himself from the desk. 'But I have to confess. I'm here for more than learning how you manage the backstage arrangement. I put my enquiries on pause, as requested, until after—a certain performance, wasn't it? I have empathy for such a request. *The show should proceed*—even I know that one.

But my employer is keen on a short timeframe for wrapping up this business. And I'll be honest with you, because I can see you're being honest with me, and I put my cards on the table, waiting suited me anyway, as I had other enquiries to pursue.' He pats his pockets again. 'Damn pipe. So. You help your mistress run her social calendar.'

Flora nods—by the window she sees Vernon shake his head, and fancies she can make out the strain in his neck. She leans back a little in the chair, casually. The question sounded similar to the others, but she senses their conversation has reached a summit, that they are about to dive downwards.

'Yes, I help my mistress run her calendar. That's a fair description.'

'Do you assist at these, what do you call them, private salons of hers?'

'Of course. They're the most important event we run.'

'How does one get to attend?'

'Well, it's a little complicated, because it's exclusive.' *Frown again, look as if you're reciting things you've never questioned.* 'There's a referral system, a sense of who'll be suitable. We don't allow just anybody in. There's a waiting list. It can be very expensive.'

'And people are really doing this? Lining up to poison themselves?'

Vernon interjects. 'We don't call it that.'

Davignon raises his arms to the ceiling. 'Doesn't matter to me what you call it!' He returns his look to Flora, with great concentration. 'What if somebody dies?'

'People don't,' she says. 'A small amount, a single berry, really isn't strong enough.' She swallows.

213

'Yes, yes, and they sign a piece of paper stating if they *do* die, it's not your lady's fault? It's all taken on their own risk?' He pats his pocket again, draws a piece of crumpled paper out—Flora recognises the seal, even through the haze of panic that's floating down before her. 'Can't find my pipe but I do have this. This sort of document, isn't that right?'

Flora waits for Vernon to say *that's a private thing you have no right*, but nothing comes. Perhaps he is as surprised as she is, and Vernon having ambushed her, now Davignon ambushes both of them.

'That's right,' she says carefully. 'That sort of document.'

'This one in particular is signed by,' he squints theatrically at the signature, then holds the paper out before her. 'You knew this one?'

'Yes.'

'Regular attendee?'

'He saw my lady often.'

'At these salons?'

'Sometimes, at the larger ones.'

'But he's signed the disclaimer for the smaller one?'

She shrugs, but otherwise holds herself very still. She does not look at Vernon. *Hopefully, Davignon will take this as distress remembering a tragic episode; not the panic of having never seen that damned document before.* She speaks slowly: 'He did sign that, but in the end, he decided not to attend the nightshade salon.'

'And were you friends with your man here?'

'I was fond of him. But that's the profession, I don't become close you see.'

'He and your lady got particularly close though, didn't they? And what happened to him?'

'He took too many berries. Heartbroken; they'd argued. It was accidental.'

'That's the story I've heard. But here's where I get confused.' Davignon rolls the contract into a tube and puts it under his arm, as if it's as common as wallpaper. 'It doesn't add up to me. Don't you have all sorts of stringent policies, practices, rules and so on, to prevent that sort of thing happening?'

'We do. But, I don't know how to tell you. People can still overdo it.'

She can feel herself flailing. She feels as if a pair of hands, sleek in black opera gloves, have just given her a shove from behind.

'The other odd thing is the date of his death. I've asked around; and that was a difficult task, mark you, so please be impressed. Not many people want to talk about this nightmare of a death salon the two of you run, I had a devil of a time putting together who was where and why and when. It's like trying to get blood out of a stone. But here's the upshot of my enquiries: nobody else has testified to being at a poison salon on the same date as our late friend. It's almost as if he never went to one.'

'I just told you. The one where he had the accident was a private salon.'

'Just the two of them present? Her, and him?'

'Well, I was there.'

'*Ah.*'

Davignon pulls up the second chair, takes the contract from its absurd position under his arm and leans forwards, as if soliciting advice from a friend. 'So, here's my dilemma. My employer wants to know what happened—what really happened—between the three of you. How do you suggest I find that out?'

Her gaze flashes to the stricken outline of Vernon. No help from there, no movement either: he may as well be painted onto the wall.

'Well, you can ask me,' she says. 'But I'll tell the same story as everyone else.'

'I'd expect nothing less! The story had to come from somewhere, didn't it? Perhaps I have found the mouth of the river?'

She shakes her head. 'Davignon, I can't do this. It was terribly upsetting for both of us. But if you already know he ate too many, and his death came fast, I don't know what further I can say.'

'How about the medical college?'

'What?'

'Our friend abandoned many courses of study, to his family's eternal chagrin. Including, mark it, a line of medical training at the surgeon's college. Are you telling me a lad of his experience wouldn't know the result of putting a half-dozen of those in his mouth? Or that the two of you, without a room full of lolling aristocrats to serve as a distraction, wouldn't immediately plunge into action to save him?'

'He was distressed! He *knew* it was too many!' In the corner of her vision Vernon reels backwards. She's let something go that she shouldn't. 'He was heartbroken by her, everyone knew that. Did your line of questioning take you to what happened at the gambling house?'

Davignon leans back in the chair, as if stretching out by a comfortable fire. 'I did hear about that. We're talking a heartbroken suicide, then?'

'Perhaps. He arrived in a blur, it was very difficult to stop him.'

'Wait, I thought this was a privately arranged salon?'

There it is. She has run heartbeat-first into the yawning trap. 'I mean—'

'Was this a private salon with all the pre-arranged accompanying paperwork, or was it a spur of the moment lover's tryst?'

Her fingers are tied into knots. Sweat down her back. 'I—'

Davignon leans forward again. His voice is kind, almost consoling. 'It might not matter. The paperwork doesn't specify a date, does it? It's more a general contract some choose to enter into. It's the danger they dance on, in the entertainments of the great Belladonna.'

He stands. 'You've been a huge help,' he says, folding up the contract and tucking it somewhere in his jacket. There's a pocket-watch chain visible on his waistcoat. Flora thinks: *if you casually check the time, I may scream.*

Mercifully he doesn't, but he does frown in thought. 'I may have to speak with you again. Would that be all right?' He stands over her, looming, until she nods her assent. He beams at the both of them. 'Thank you so much. Very kind of you.'

At the door, he turns back.

'I am sorry for putting you through all this,' he says. 'You see, it's my employer. They simply want to get to the bottom of what happened. They don't believe he had it in him, however heartbroken he may have been. Now, I may find the ultimate answer is that sadly he did, and my employer is mistaken. It's possible. And I don't mind being a conduit for somebody's desperation if I have to be. Answers are what I need, it doesn't matter where they fall. But my employer—and it's their theory, mark it, I've nothing against you personally —they think their young man wasn't as protected as he might have been. They're provincial, I'm afraid, so that's the out-look. Terrified of the *demimonde's* corrupting influence, you know the type, can practically feel the rot stretching outwards from Paris and coming to ruin the soil of their little farmstead. Now I don't mind it. I know plenty of *demimondaines* myself. But that's a sketch, for you, of what you're up against. It seemed polite, at this juncture, to provide you with one.'

And with a click of his heels, and a click of the latch, he is gone.

Flora immediately stands, and although she aims to be quiet the anger makes her voice a furious stage-whisper. 'What are you doing? He never signed any contract! How on earth did Davignon get that?'

Vernon sits at his desk heavily, bearing the weight of the world. 'We thought it would be a good insurance policy. I didn't have time to tell you.'

'I nearly lost sense of the story.'

'But you didn't. Ultimately your word of what happened, combined with hers, is all he has to go on. He was just testing you.'

'Well, it worked,' Flora runs her thumb down from her hip to her skirts, her mind a looping mess of signatures and ink. 'A fake contract is worse than none at all for the story that he died by accident, you do know that?'

Vernon shakes his head. 'It proves she's not responsible,

whether it was a salon overdose or dramatic gesture gone wrong. We're in a much stronger position, to have it.'

You and she might be, but I'm not. Once again it's before her: something opening up at her feet, a great hole in the world. And the sensation of someone waiting to push.

*

The door gives an inch, revealing a butler with a face that's all sternness and bristle. 'We're not expecting a delivery.'

F. flashes the envelope. 'I bring a letter.'

'Give it to me, then.' He holds out a hand in a neat white glove.

She takes a moment, then plays her card, laying it as carefully and unambiguously as she can. 'My apologies, but the Belladonna has requested I deliver it personally.'

The door swings fully open.

Her name will do that.

The *cercle* is a prestigious one, *très fermé, très élitiste*, where silence is preferred and discretion is demanded. Not the sort of place Flora would usually expect to find the man she's looking for; his activities at the salons and the balls and the parties would suggest he never sits still, that he would surely rot away in the quiet and respectable; that without anyone next to him to be impressed, why exist? Yet, the spurred boots reveal his presence by the fire, and what she can see of his legs suggests he is sitting sprawled out. The chair has a high back, so Flora does not come into his vision before she's nearly on top of him.

Marcelin Capet is staring glumly into the flames, ignoring the newspaper on his lap. A plate of veal sits beside him, also ignored. The bottle of wine, though: that has his full attention. When he looks up at the shadow of Flora standing over him, his face sets into a grim expression, with sorrow etched into it.

'We've met before,' he says. 'I remember that evening, of course.' His mouth contorts as if chewing on something bitter. 'Is it you I'm seeing, or are you here representing that woman?'

So, he knows how it works. He looks exhausted. His eyes are ringed with shadow. Without his jacket and epaulettes his shoulders appear small and his whole body hunched. 'Frankly I don't care which of you it is. I wish you'd both be gone.'

'She doesn't know I'm here.'

His eyes widen a little in surprise. 'You don't do a thing she doesn't instruct you to. Why would you be sneaking off now?'

'Because I like my letters and my information to be in order, as the person who runs her house. At the moment there is something missing.'

'Don't talk to *me* about such things,' spits Marcelin, flailing for the wine glass. 'I introduced the two of them; I knew he'd be taken by the artiste, but I didn't expect he'd unmake himself over it. Or that you'd sit by and watch, and not help him. I knew he was a romantic, but—' He fumbles the glass to his lips.

'I know you've spoken to someone about what happened,' says Flora. 'Someone hired especially.'

'I don't talk to people like that.'

'You may not remember making the exception but I assure you, you did. His name is Davignon. He told me he's been asking around, anyone remotely connected to those involved. He must have met with you.'

For a moment Marcelin looks completely blank. Then a memory dawns; Flora can see it coming over him, slow and steady like a delayed hangover. 'Oh, him.'

'What did you tell him?' says Flora, reigning her impatience in.

'Just what I knew of the old boy's character. That he was the romantic type, and probably did try to eat all those berries, in a state of romantic agony or whatever he claimed to enjoy, but that it shouldn't have actually killed him. I believe your lady killed him and I know Davignon thinks the same.'

No dashing repartee here; no jokes, no playing with language. Certainties only. He stares up at her with eyes shadowed by grief and exhaustion, and his confidence has the impact of a concealed weapon.

She tries not to show how bruised she is by it. 'Davignon is in the pay of a relative. Do you know who it is?'

'His father is long dead. It must be his mother.'

Flora shakes her head. 'God knows what she's paying Davignon with. Her son's expenses on the country house all but cleared the family finances.'

Marcelin doesn't question this: they both know Flora has seen the accounts, that she would know. He winces as if the whole affair is an affront to him and lifts the wine bottle again, visibly distressed by its lightness. He signals into the shadows for someone to bring him another, then leans in and whispers: 'Why are you here? Doesn't she have a victory dance you'll need to dress her for?'

Flora ignores the comment. 'I want to express my condolences.'

'How very thoughtful.' Marcelin is sitting in the chair like he can never get out of it. This close to the fire, the heat is beginning to come through Flora's clothes, making the fabric scald her legs and back. Too close.

'Well, you've found out what you came to find out,' he says. 'So what will you do?'

And here is the question. Flora looks into the flames and sees two paths ahead. She turns from the fire and looks down into Marcelin's expression.

'I'm going to look the truth in the eye,' she says.

'No doubt. And then what do you suppose you'll do?'

*

It's an unthinkable collision of two worlds, Monsieur Vernon in the salon room: both sides of the transaction, an unpleasant combination of the business and the pleasure. The sight of him makes Flora want to reach for the account book, but there is also an urge to settle across and offer a glass, the way he lounges about as if he owns the place.

Not that this is a comfortable meeting. He had to come here: Belladonna refused to go to him, citing headache, even though he'd sent letters suggesting her presence was urgently needed. So, hat and cane donned, here he sits. Flora watches as Belladonna paces and snaps at Vernon:

'Can't you stop Davignon from all this infernal poking around?'

'What ought I to do,' Vernon says, 'ask him nicely? It doesn't work like that. I'd have more luck telling the ballet corps not to sneak off to the can-can bars after hours.'

'What happens at my salon is none of anyone's business. *Especially* his.'

'Ah, but our situation wasn't a salon, was it? You were being paid a visit.'

'It shouldn't matter!'

'And yet.'

She turns, tutting, and keeps pacing the length of the room. Flowers move gently in her wake as she passes: bouquets fill the apartments, given in thanks for attending one Opéra ball or another. And since this is Carnival season and all invitations have been accepted, the space resembles a florist's showroom, or an undertaker's.

Flora watches Belladonna's obstinate expression. *Why did you think you could avoid reckoning with this?*

Belladonna turns again, pacing back, making more flowers wave. 'I still say that what happens to my clientele, and to my friends, is none of his business.'

'You know who's employing him, don't you?'

At this she stops.

Vernon looks at her. 'Yes, I assumed you wouldn't have thought about that. He may be gone, but his family are still with us.'

Her mouth has dropped open at the mention of his family. As if Vernon just unleashed a tide of mud onto the carpet.

Vernon speaks carefully, aiming the words down to his shoes. 'Not everyone is cut from their roots, as we are. His darling mother has come to Paris, and requests an audience with the last person to see her son alive. It's just as well I'm telling you; Davignon was going to give you the news himself.'

Belladonna sighs with relief, having imagined a way to avoid being summoned. 'Last person to see him alive?' She glances at Flora.

Vernon smiles, his face tight. 'Clearly that is not who she means. I fear you ought to grant the mourning mother an audience. She'll feel very short-changed if your right-hand woman turns up instead of the real thing.'

'Well, I certainly won't see her. Why should I?'

It's such a dramatic tableau they make: when Belladonna's full arm extends in Flora's direction, it's as if a painting has suddenly reached out from the canvas to grab at her throat. And those words: *Why should I?* Flora's pounding heartbeat has suddenly risen.

Vernon's voice is calm. 'Madame deserves to be seen by somebody. And it might make the whole enquiry stop.'

Flora is ready. 'I can go. I'll speak to the mother, put a stop to it. If it's emotional closure she wants, I can provide it.'

Belladonna pounces on the opening: 'See? Flora is happy to do it. She represents me, she can carry the message.'

'That's enough.' Vernon stands neatly. 'I won't hear more of this. This woman isn't trying to trick anything out of you; she only wants to know what happened. Go and tell her how upsetting the whole thing has been. She wants to hear it first hand, not in rumours and whispers.' He finishes pulling on his leather gloves and for a moment, with his fingers spread he looks like a stage magician, all conjure and coax. 'The carriage will be ready in one hour,' he says. 'I've arranged somewhere you can meet in private.'

Belladonna arches a cynical eyebrow. 'Not at the Opéra, you mean?'

'Better, while remaining suitably dramatic. We don't want you trapped, nor speaking anything you shouldn't. So I've arranged for a very brief conversation to happen at l'église Saint-Eustache.' It's an intimidating idea—a grand setting for a casual conversation—but Belladonna keeps her composure. Vernon smiles, clearly relishing the plan. 'This way we can say it's coincidence: you simply met each other while praying.'

'You beast.' But Belladonna smiles too. It's almost a smile of recollection, as if they've made this kind of arrangement before. Flora, her heart still pounding, looks between them, lost within their mutual understanding.

When he has gone, Belladonna speaks urgently, flinging fabrics onto the bed.

'I'm not going,' she says. She beckons and Flora comes closer, following the fast turnover of dress options with their various shades of black. At this proximity she can make out Belladonna's slight tremble, like an orchid in high wind.

'I can't do it,' she says. 'I won't and I *refuse*. And you don't think I'm capable either, do you? I saw the look on your face just now.'

Flora shakes her head. 'I wouldn't want you to go, but that's not the same thing.'

'We are in agreement, then. I don't want to look on her; I don't wish to dwell on the poor dead boy anymore, and what of it? Why should I? You go, but we can at least put you in something formal. Which of these do you like?'

She holds up a gown with an iridescent turquoise shimmer

over the bodice: aphid wings sewn into an intricate pattern. 'This one?'

Flora does not respond to the dress, which they both know full well could not be less appropriate for church. Instead, she says: 'I might have an idea.'

Belladonna waits, her face expectant.

Flora silently runs through her proposal once more: she can see no problem with what she is about to say. 'What does his mother know about you? What does she actually expect?'

She shrugs. 'What does anyone know? Has many friends, wears black, what's your point? She'll be expecting a murderess, probably, and if that's what she wants she'll get one.'

Even as she speaks this, the anger rises in Belladonna's voice. There's no way she can meet the mother and keep her temper.

So, Flora takes a deep breath. 'Will she know about your eyes?'

'What of it?'

'It's indeed possible for someone else to have your eyes.'

'And?'

'I'll wear the drops too; you were about to give me your gown. Why don't I go?'

'As me?'

'If I wear the eyedrops, and your gloves, and if I don't say too much, or say nothing at all. Why not?'

A pause breathes through the room while she considers. 'Vernon will know,' she says. She's taking it seriously, weighing it up. 'We don't want him acting strangely.'

'He may not like it. But if I'm the one who gets in the carriage we'll just have to go through with it, won't we?'

So. Flora, sitting at the dressing-table, Belladonna standing over her, one hand a friendly silken warmth on her shoulder. A bared shoulder: Flora has already been tied into one of the evening dresses La Dame aux Morelles wears all the time, even in the middle of the day and yes, even at church, dresses cut wide to bare the neck, the shoulders. Not the aphids in the end, a simple design of silk covered with lace, and Flora will wear a hooded cloak over this, so it will be enough to scrape her hair back; the shining black hair and elaborate style of La Dame will not be missed.

The eyedrops bottle sits there on the dressing-table, as ever in its place, the amethyst gleaming purple at the stopper. Belladonna picks it up, shakes it slightly. 'Look up,' she says, and Flora cranes her neck into the light, Belladonna's hand at the back of her head: it's gentle, almost a caressing hold. Although such a hold from her is not to be confused with affection. Another was cradled in her arms like that.

'This will be uncomfortable for a moment.'

Fat wet smudging spreads across Flora's vision and blurs everything. Then, sharpness: instant tears. Flora holds her face still, resists the urge to close her eyes; she stares up at the lamp on the wall, while warm tears stream down her face.

Belladonna lets go and Flora scrunches her hands at either side of her face, blinking uncontrollably.

'Don't rub.'

Flora pushes her fingers into her cheeks, as if soothing her eyes by proxy.

'The burn will fade. Wait a moment.'

That voice, kindly offering instructions from beyond the realm of discomfort. Flora is taken back to her first salon.

And then to a more recent memory, the cradle in her arms … all at once, images overlapping and recomposing in the sore dark space of her eyes.

The burn fades. She blinks a few more times, willing the oozing shapes in her vision to resolve themselves back into her reflection. It forms eventually, and when it does, Flora leans in with fascination towards the mirror. She stands— and the chair moves loudly, scraped back over the floor. She gets her balance, then leans in further again towards the new image.

Her eyes have become great black dots on white, and her face is shiny with tears: an eerie parody of herself is staring back at her. The edge of her sight blurs into chaos she can't recognise, and direct light is going to be most unwelcome until the drops wear off, that much is clear—she is uncomfortable even knowing the lamp on the wall is there. But for now, any relief must wait. Flora stands back, putting herself fully upright before the mirror, and there—the dress, the eyes, *the gloves*—the effect, she must admit, is startling.

'I should think you'll pass for me,' says Belladonna. 'Just: you mustn't say much.'

Flora smiles, still looking into the mirror, and she catches the effect of the smile, how it changes her face. She means to express that she is happy, genuinely so: the plan is going well, it has promise. But the effect, with those eyes, is enigmatic and opaque. She does appear pleased—but it's a total mystery with what. The eyes give her an expression strange even to herself. It's off-putting, a gaze to misdirect, confuse, to keep on top of the interaction.

To show she agrees with the assertion she mustn't say much,

Flora nods and smiles again, deeper, at her reflection, and Belladonna starts with something like alarm. It's an exaggerated response, for Flora's benefit, but it has a core of something real.

'It's convincing,' she says. 'And frightening, you silently nodding at me like that.'

Flora smiles again. This time, she shows teeth.

*

The jolting carriage ride begins to flatten as they reach the facade of l'église Saint-Eustache, and her eyes have grown more accustomed to the wide, wet strangeness of the eye-drops. The outline of Monsieur Vernon looms up before her. The top hat, the shrub-like beard, the crisp line of his shoulders: surely it could only be him, but how strange to have her sight distorted so she must ultimately guess. Vernon had recognised her instantly, of course, barely batting an eyelid as the sight of the wrong black-robed woman. His voice comes to her from the other side of the carriage, and yet seems far too close.

'You needn't give much,' he says. 'She wants to ask some questions. Platitudes: that's what will win it for us.'

Flora nods. 'Does Davignon know this meeting is happening?'

'I couldn't give a damn. As long as he's not here now to get a good look at you.'

He sighs with the deep weariness of the long-suffering and murmurs something about making the best of it.

Outside the great church people are passing hurriedly with

purpose. It's daytime, though the grey skies are giving little away. This isn't a pleasure garden or part of the gaslit nocturnal promenades. No romantic trysts here, no mindless circuits; just people whose existence, in the moment, necessitates crossing her path. Flora sees it mostly as a series of jarring shapes beyond the hood. No chance of getting to know the feeling, then, of the crowd sweeping back on your behalf, bowing as you pass. Vernon holds her at the elbow, leading her through the heavy doors as if taking an invalid to prayer. Flora closes her eyes as they enter the place, and if Vernon notices how she flinches as they cross the threshold, he doesn't say anything.

Their footsteps echo across miles of stone, and soft blue light spreads over the floor from the tall stained-glass windows—that no doubt would be pretty enough to look at directly, if she could bear it.

'There's been a change of plan,' Vernon murmurs, turning a new direction across the stone floor. 'Thanks to this little scheme of yours I don't trust you to be in the pews. So you'll meet Mother in here. As you won't be doing much talking, you're going to be on the priest's side,' he adds, pulling the open the velvet curtain. 'That's just my little joke.'

Flora has a moment entirely alone, boxed in. She closes her eyes. *I'd offer a prayer of my own, but given what we're doing here, I don't want to think about who'd hear it.*

Her senses are relying on sound in the darkness. There is a rustle of heavy fabric from the other side as the curtain moves, and some low steps as a new presence comes into the box. A heavy thump as someone sits down; a moment of breathing.

The breaths are heavy, laboured in the darkness, and quiet, almost as if someone is sobbing. Flora thinks of how to affect her own performance: Belladonna's breathing, when Flora has been close enough to detect it, is shallow and frequent—taking delicate sips at existence. This person with her now seems to find the action almost unbearable.

A woman's voice, creaking somewhat. 'Are you there?'

Flora moves forwards so her face is visible through the fine mesh of the grate. She tries to keep herself in profile, to disallow the full view of her face, but the temptation is too much, and she looks through the wooden lattice at the woman who sits opposite.

The mother's eyes are red-rimmed, and fill with tears as Flora watches.

'You, they tell me,' she says, with a voice carefully kept low, 'are the last person who was with my son.'

Flora nods. She knows the effect of such a gesture, with these eyes.

The mother keeps speaking. 'My name is Henriette.' She swallows. 'He was always a free-spirited one, and we often quarrelled. I swore I would never go to Paris; he swore in turn I wouldn't want to anyway, that I would hate it here. But I kept up with him how best I could. A friend of his would send me letters.'

Flora nods again, as if all this were well known.

Henriette shuffles herself closer to the latticed grille of the confessional. Even through it Flora can see the painful effort on her face. 'You know he has a younger sister,' Henriette says. 'Due to be married this year. She's been terribly rocked with this news. His friend Marcelin told us he might have meant to die.'

Flora notes the name with a grim thinness, and hopes this hasn't been visible through the grille.

'All of Paris knew what was happening, that's what Marcelin wrote to me. And that he might have meant it. *Meant* to die— that he was sick for the love of you. That you'd been close to marrying—but when I heard his life was gone I thought: no. Not him. He knows a thing or two. And even buffeted about by love, he wouldn't be so thrown as to do that. My boy always found his way through things. He made his way, left Normandy for Paris; he got out of every course of study that failed to please him. Even looking upon you now, I don't believe you could have been one he would take his own life for.' She waits a moment. 'Why don't you speak to me?'

Flora moves a half-inch and feels a sudden sharp pain over her breast. The silver brooch of nightshade berries she is wearing, with the spiked leaf, it's come undone somehow, and the needle has managed to pierce through the top of the gown and the chemise as well, and now it hovers delicately over her skin. If she moves it'll go in: even raising her arm to move it away will risk it.

'I'm not one,' Henriette continues, 'who would usually make demands. But if you're at all sorry for what happened to my son, perhaps you'll stop the salon.'

She pauses; is clearly waiting again. Flora bites her tongue.

The pin of the brooch, just beneath her collarbone.

Flora's voice sounds weary when it comes; low, tired. 'Forgive me,' she says.

And she hears the sudden jangle of the curtain being pulled aside, and the heavy movement of Henriette pulling her skirts out of that small space. And then, worst of all, Flora's own curtain is being pulled open. In the sudden light, she raises an arm against what is newly bearing down on her.

'You ask me to forgive you …'

Flora is trapped in the box, cowering.

'As far as I'm concerned you killed him,' spits Henriette.

Flora has to take control of this. She stands, pulls herself upright.

She knows how: she pulls the hood to further shadow her face, as if about to leave in a swirl of fabric. She keeps her gaze level, knowing the power of those eyes. Above all, she mustn't rise to it. She has to stay strong: if she's been pulled out into the light she must stand and face her there, as if she won't let herself be pulled anywhere else.

When Flora speaks, her tone is decisive. 'Your son was heartbroken,' she says. 'He ate the berries to take his life. I was there, I saw everything. I didn't act in time; I cannot forgive myself for it. Though I know that will be no consolation.'

No lie spoken.

A movement in her peripheral vision: Vernon coming to the rescue, to bat Henriette away like a bluebottle. No need.

Henriette stares into the black eyes and Flora can practically feel the charm working. It sounds as if Henriette were reciting a script from years ago. She speaks softly. 'Davignon told me my boy ate too much poison by mistake. I didn't believe that.'

'You were right not to. He was too clever to do that. It was passion.'

Henriette pauses, as if thinking it over.

'He has always been a passionate boy,' she says.

It's working; she is hypnotised. Flora's voice is coming out low and controlled, it takes Henriette by the hand and steers her towards where Flora wants, needs her to go.

'Now you know this, you will need to leave us alone,' Flora says. Then she thinks: who is this us? She's made it sound as if Belladonna speaks on behalf of all goddesses.

But it is working. The mother, shaking with silent grief, seems to believe what she is hearing. Flora's control implies a cavern of her own sadness, doesn't it? So perhaps they reside there together …

Here's Vernon arriving with a bluster, pulling up beside them, practically skidding on the stone. 'Our gracious *La Dame* is obliged to be somewhere this afternoon, I'm afraid I shall be taking her away. I trust you got what you need?' He reaches out to take Flora's arm.

The movement breaks the spell, and Henriette comes for Flora, claws raised.

'You have much to answer for,' she says. 'The woman who drove my son to death! I'll have those eyes!'

Vernon lets go of Flora to commence the more urgent task of grappling with Henriette at the arms, securing control as she sobs and spits. Two concerned priests like white bobbing tablecloths arrive breathless from the far side of the church. Wide-eyed and slightly hostile, they are investigating matters: the agreement with Vernon was for no interruptions to the service. And certainly nothing like this.

Henriette, stilled for now, her face red and open.

'Justice is coming for you,' she says. Her voice echoes through the church.

Vernon takes Flora's arm once more and steers her away towards the doors. 'That did not go as planned,' he hisses.

Flora keeps her gaze on the flagstones as they hurry off.

The dominant sounds are the muffled cries of Henriette, dropping onto the shoulder of one of the priests, as they step through the grand threshold and back out into the square, to face again the bustle of outdoors.

IX

She will keep on this until the bitter end.' Vernon is angry.

'How are you so sure?' Belladonna says wearily.

She holds an empty wine glass at an angle over her lap, her skirt spread as if she'd been plucked loose and dropped into the chair. A stack of ledgers sits open and blank on Vernon's desk. He is behind on the calculations.

And Flora sitting silent, feeling the blame roaring off both of them.

Vernon is pacing. 'She's had Davignon back here again, damn him, slinging cigarillo ash all over my desk and asking more questions. And they're going to keep applying pressure until you admit what they want you to.'

'Well then they'll never stop, will they? The boy killed himself, he overdid it. Everyone knows.'

Vernon shakes his head. 'No use putting up that defence now. The mother intuits another truth, and we can't account for your not taking care with the nightshade. It adds up, at the very least, to wilful abandonment of a body in need, especially with the two of you there.'

His argument builds a wall, each word blocking Flora in.

Belladonna runs a finger over the rim of her empty glass. A long oval of dusty red shows where wine used to be.

'We could put out a new story,' she says, calculating. 'To try and slake the appetite. Like throwing a piece of meat out for the dogs. We might somehow turn this scandal into something useful.'

Vernon's voice is calm. 'We can't have death on your hands, for the sake of the business.'

Belladonna says: 'Her companion, however. There's a person who can make a mistake, and be dealt with.'

Vernon nods. 'That is true.'

The final brick sealed into place. Flora is trapped.

She closes her eyes a moment and sees an image of her mistress's face, closely lit by gaslight and sharp with fury. Then a memory, of Belladonna opening a door for her, ushering her through into a world of unfathomable glamour and ease. Letting her in. Showing her how it all worked. And the way she had wanted it all, a pull she'd felt through her whole body.

Flora is thinking it through. 'And if I did come forward? Then what happens to me?'

'We protect you.'

'How?'

'We'll say it was accidental.'

'I'll attest to that.'

Vernon and Belladonna, staring. Flora, silent, feeling the pressure from both of them, a pressure that could squash her into nothing, leave her an empty set of skirts and a pair of worn-out leather shoes. Which is what they're suggesting, almost.

Vernon, precise as a scalpel: 'This is the only way we're going to make this stop.'

Belladonna: 'I need you to do this for me.'

'But I'm innocent,' says Flora.

Belladonna's face becomes very still. 'Remember the conversation on the bridge.'

Flora stops, understands. They can put it about, one way or another, that she's responsible. Agree, and they'll protect her, say it was an accident. And if she doesn't, they'll say she did it deliberately—out of jealousy, or petulance, or whatever they like—and her life will be ruined and over in that order.

Many years ago, long before she came to Paris, in an orchard in late September, there was F.: surrounded by many friends, all scrabbling about, climbing along branches, throwing leaves above their heads, bursting into snatches of song. And then they had come upon a tree absolutely loaded with plums, dark purple and bulging and slightly dust-bloomed. They had immediately fallen on the fruit; it was perfect, and there was so much of it the branches hung low with the weight. F. had taken at least half a dozen and put them into her mouth whole. Great juicy fleshy things, the moment was too joyous to think any further—if one were a bit dry, why, she'd simply move on to the next; now *that* one. F. had gone about the tree, greedily reaching for one and then the next—the sight of them, so many and so purple, plump with the juice of the flesh straining against the skin— and suddenly F. heard someone screaming. F.'s friend, in the spirit of being more discerning with the fruit, had torn a damson in half; as they all gathered around her, she held the fruit open in her cupped hands and showed them all there, among the yellow-brown flesh, dozens of tiny white piec- es of living thread, moving about, flopping with interrupt- ed life, their world torn clean in half. Everyone but F. had made sounds of disgust, cried out in alarm; several more damsons were plucked down and pulled open. They didn't all contain worms, but many did: enough for it to be obvious that if someone had eaten several … and F. started running, sprinting out of the orchard, her eyes focussed on her feet as they kicked through the leaves, noticing the sheer green of the bending grass, in fact noticing everything obsessively to avoid thinking about the consequences of what she'd just done. Her mind protected itself. When the greedy harvest of the afternoon tried to enter her head, her imagination allowed her to simply bounce away from the horror of it. And now here she is again, head down and heart racing, looking into the face of Vernon and Belladonna standing there together, working to protect the most important thing to them: that the business of La Dame continues. F. has torn apart that gorgeous world of unfathomable glamour and ease, and found its exposure repulsive; but she has not admitted that to herself. To do so would be to confess she has internalised far too much of it already.

'I'll do it,' she says, her mouth dry. 'We can say I killed him.'

Belladonna's voice reaches Flora from somewhere far away. 'We can say you'd taken a shine to him; were jealous of him and me.'

Flora continues, her mind purposefully blank. 'We can say he arrived speaking of his heartbroken love for you, and hearing it, I couldn't stand it. So I got rid of him. *Him*, since I still needed you.'

'Very good. That's exactly what we can say.' The story agreed, not even questioned. The confirmation sits there, grey and dull: they're perfectly happy for her to do this.

Vernon looks relieved. He pats Flora on the back: 'We'll

have Davignon bring the constables; they'll want to make a show of arresting you. Or considering it at least; you won't be taken away, we'll see to that.'

'This will work in our favour,' says Belladonna. Her voice has a bubbling quality. She almost sounds cheerful. 'And let them have their excitement.'

'Better it be me.' Flora, innocent of murder, eater of maggots.

*

Shadows and light.

The usual gloom of the Belladonna apartments where the gentle gas lamps are always kept low, to save her eyes and provide relief from the headaches. Flora's trip to the church has her thinking about how the Belladonna's work requires entire nights of suffering like that, still able to charm and be the sparkling host, tell the right jokes and whisper the wrong ones, keep in balance a whole number of delicate social situations, while all the world hurts her with its glare.

In the room where salons are held Flora faces her mistress and tries to stop herself from shaking.

Belladonna is perfectly poised. She says: 'Are you telling me there are fools in uniform outside? Where's Davignon?'

Her expression is closed. Belladonna stands before the fireplace, a full spray of nightshade leaves in her hair and a matching corsage of dark green spikes upon her dress. Her jet beads are polished smooth, shining without sparkle.

She arches one eyebrow to perform her displeasure. 'Well?

Answer me! Are there policemen coming?'

'Yes,' says Flora, and with this she has the confidence to continue: 'They're on their way. They'll be here in minutes.'

'Why haven't you done as I told you? You were supposed to give the story to Davignon.'

'I did see him but I told him the truth.'

She stares into Belladonna's dark gaze.

As the pause between them extends, Flora fancies she can hear the wooden clicking of a scene change. The splendid backdrop of these grand apartments is raising into the flies. It isn't yet clear what will drop in next.

Belladonna speaks into the silence. 'No, I don't think so. Look at you, you're shaking, you're lying to me.'

'You don't think they're coming? You don't think that's what I've done?'

'That's right. You couldn't possibly have.'

The scenery stops in place; perhaps this is as far as it goes. Flora does everything to control her nerves. 'Well you can believe it. I won't send myself to hang for you. I told Davignon everything.'

'No, you wouldn't do it; it's not worth this whole world.'

Flora wonders if *this* is how she will remember the Belladonna: waiting by the fireplace for her companion to turn herself in, with a conviction that such a thing is right.

'I told Davignon it was you,' says Flora. 'He knows everything.'

Belladonna looks at the bouquet of lilies over the fireplace, the gold clock with its stilled hands. 'You wouldn't cast me beneath carriage hooves and wheels like that.'

Flora holds herself steady.

Suddenly, Belladonna laughs. '*Oh*. I see!' She lets out laughter again. It seems carefully measured out, like a shot of fine brandy. 'So that's why you're trying to scare me, this is about that boy? Loved him, did you, all in secret? Is that what this is about?'

For a moment it could almost be true: but, no, cast all that aside. As if she could feel for *anyone* more than she does for this woman laughing at her by the fireplace. Any love for him was for the charming parts, before any of the human mess starts showing through. And when she had seen some of his private ugliness, the main result had been an unwilling recognition. Belladonna inspires a loyalty that runs deep with emotion, luring her, the steady pull of it. *This* is where Flora's love belongs.

'He certainly loved you,' says Flora, speaking slowly. 'And that wasn't easy.'

Belladonna's head raises slightly. It's as if they're talking about a much more innocent affair: all this might mean only broken hearts. It might not mean murder.

'Yes, it comes with the territory, you know this.' Belladonna's words lightly dance around the phrase. 'Besides, you've been perfectly happy keeping your distance up until now. You know full well what I do to people.'

Flora sticks to her own territory. 'Davignon is coming. He's bringing the constables, and it's you they want.'

If she doesn't believe you ...

Belladonna takes half a step forward. Her fingers twitch a little at her side.

'For you to do something so stupid ...' she mutters. 'You'd really try to save yourself with such a miscalculation?'

Flora's throat is thick, she's desperate to swallow, but she has to carry on. 'I couldn't tell the lie for you. Not that one. I told the truth, that's all.'

'*That's all.* You make it sound so small, so easily put right. But does your *that's all* have to come at the cost of destroying the both of us?'

Flora shakes her head. 'I've never wished for that. But I couldn't lie.'

'I judged you so wrongly? You would really do something so misguided, so against your own interests? But look at you: you really would do it? Even though you're nothing without what I've given you? Even though without me you'll be back to some mud-splattered gutter somewhere, dead in a few months if you're lucky? Even though I let you share a life most of Paris dreams of? Gifted you secrets you didn't realise you were dying to know? Even though I saw you, recognised you, gave you exactly what you wanted? Your darling boy cannot thank you, you know.'

And then the Belladonna's face is suddenly, completely, hideously open: all rawness underneath, her teeth are flashes of bone.

Flora backs away until she is almost upon the glass table. She must be careful not to lose balance and fall backwards through it; with one more step its sharp edges will be pushing against her legs. There is nowhere further to go: she must resist the urge to keep retreating, to run from the teeth bared, eyes locked, sheer animal of the Belladonna now, who whispers something, her voice a hiss:

'For the wretched woman who falls but once, the hope of rising is forever gone.' She takes another step towards her former companion. 'What a traitor you are.'

Traitor she thinks: Flora remembers Davignon in the cafe earlier that afternoon, a time that already seems a whole life away.

'Busy season?' he'd said, the cigarillo in his hand sending up plumes of pale blue. 'Tell me about it. Throw a pin at a map of Paris and I've stared at a blank expression in any street you hit. How is your mistress?'

'She's ill,' Flora had said. 'Tormented by headaches.'

'It's the eyedrops, isn't it? One of her friends from the theatre said she should stop taking the drops. Thinks the stuff's going to be the death of her.'

'It's managed. Some headache is inevitable but we control it. She isn't herself without her eyedrops.'

'Well, *being herself* will be the death of her then. Look, delightful as this chatter is, I'd rather tell you where I am in my enquiries relating to your mistress.'

And Davignon had blown out more smoke, dropped the cigarillo and ground the ash under his heel, and Flora had prepared herself for the worst.

But then Davignon had put his head in his hands.

'I've reached just about as far as I can go,' he said. 'Henriette has her suspicions, but there's not enough evidence. There hasn't even been a body.'

Between one heartbeat and the next. 'What do you mean, no body?'

'For whatever reason, it wasn't deemed appropriate for our young man to lie before the throngs of sight-seers at the city morgue. The surgeon's school clean got rid. Or whomever's job it was to disappear him completely managed it. God knows it's probably not coincidence. But here we are. I can't gather enough evidence to call her guilty. She's untouchable and she knows it. So this is the part where I tell you to go home and give your mistress the good news. I expect you'll have a party to get ready for, soon as her head clears.'

And Flora, dazed, had risen and walked away, and her last sight of Davignon had been him lighting a new cigarillo and closing his eyes, happy to be free of this whole business.

And now.

The Belladonna pushes Flora into the bedroom then locks the door with a neat click of the key. They face each other either side of the bed, the low lamps casting a shine across the silk sheets.

Flora hadn't known, until the moment the lie settled into the room like a bird on a high branch, whether it would stay or immediately flit away. She hadn't known just how deeply the Belladonna would trust in her honesty.

The Belladonna looks down at her hands, as if considering her options: these are the tools, now how best to use them? What is she capable of?

She mutters, 'Of course, if you're dead by the time he gets here …'

Flora's heart makes itself known in her chest as this new hideous possibility rises into the charged space between the two of them.

'No,' she says. 'Don't say things like that.'

'Whyever not?' Her voice is casual, as if she were discussing something of absolutely no importance at all.

'There's no point in getting rid of me, it won't stop anything. You're either guilty of one death or two. That part of things can't be undone now, it's over.'

She finds herself becoming steadily more trapped, backing away towards the wall, caught between the nightshade leaves and her slowly approaching mistress.

'I'm sure Vernon will try to do his best to protect you,' says Flora, provoking her. 'Knowing Vernon, he's already off to make plans. Probably he's invited half of society to attend a benefit towards clearing your name. "Wrongly convicted murderess"? You never know.'

She looks disgusted. 'Let me guess. He promised not to take you down if you threw me into it, yes?'

'That's right.' Goodness, she hadn't even considered that. Her mistress just gave her that on her own, a gift. So now she thinks Vernon is against her, too.

Those hands—and what they're capable of.

'There are ways to keep you by my side,' she says. Her eyes flicker as she calculates: it's as if she's rearranging a house of cards. Is it all coming down now, however she orders things? She must work it out. 'Let us say we convinced each other it was the only way, we acted jointly, then you got frightened and threw the whole thing onto me in a panic … no, that doesn't work.' Her voice is pulsing with anger. 'Perhaps it won't be necessary to do anything so drastic. I can simply tell Davignon you've been lying to him.'

'Try it; tell him when he gets here. He won't believe you.'

'Which of the two of us do you think the world wants to listen to? I could have you on the gibbet before the sun rises.'

'And then go on to do what? Do you think there's any more "Belladonna" after this?'

'Vernon—'

'Will cut you loose. It's only barely understood he has anything to do with you.'

The Belladonna looks down at her hands again and her stillness is absolute. She looks completely alone. Flora has seen that air of steady concentration before, that ability to be her own best company. For an instant she is suddenly back in the foyer de la danse, in rehearsals held under the shadow of dread, and she remembers how the Belladonna would stare at the empty floor, unmoving and silent for so long that the dancers would begin to whisper. When that happened it was tempting to wonder if the Belladonna has forgotten everyone else was there with the stress of her artistic ambitions coming undone, or the hubris of the project sinking in and bringing doubt to any closely-held confidence in herself, or whether, simply, the spectre of stage fright had spread its terrible wings and caught her in its shadow: and then, suddenly, the Belladonna would look up, decision set into her face, to speak with absolute certainty.

As happens now. 'I won't tell you just how greatly you've disappointed me.'

'That I slipped from your control?'

'Oh, but you haven't. Not really.'

Her face is sharp with a red pulsing rage. It's a distortion, her beauty wrought into something fearful. It's the closest thing to colour Flora has seen in her and it gives a dreadful flush to the shine in her eyes, that marble-like sharpness she acquires when she is certain and strong and furious like this, when the Belladonna transforms herself by her own will into this incandescent statue—this blazing marble figure. Flora finds she is holding out her arms defensively before her, as if this rage could be placated.

'There's nothing to gain from killing me.'

'What about my own satisfaction?' She takes another step closer. Flora's heart is beating faster than she thought possible. 'You were helping to run the whole show, all of it, before and during and after. Don't think you're not culpable. Don't think you haven't been any part of this. Don't think this will be enough to get rid of your own guilt.'

'My guilt will never leave me, I can assure you of that.'

'Very well, then. I suppose there's nothing left I need to know.'

'It's over,' says Flora, but what she means is: 'I'm sorry.'

The Belladonna speaks then, her voice lifting in a rising tide of power. She has gathered it up from somewhere deep within herself and when it comes all at once it's overwhelming: 'I'm afraid it's over when I say it is. *Not when you decide.*'

She has performed the final calculations, looked over the contract and seen a bloody clause where promises used to be, and she's still in control. Flora is aware of the danger in the nightshade leaves just behind her, the knowledge of what her mistress is absolutely capable of doing, and a sense that she has sealed her own fate.

Those dark eyes flash. 'You think you've ruined me but you haven't,' she says. 'There is something I can do. A thing that I decide. *You'll find you've only ruined yourself.*'

She moves, and Flora is so certain she is about to come towards her, but no: the Belladonna's decision has propelled her in a different direction, and she turns away with a ripple of dark silk.

She is going to the dressing-table. Her attitude is purposeful and distant, as if running an errand. She goes to the dressing-table and Flora realises this isn't a snap decision. This is the contingency plan—has always been so—and this is a final performance, the most intimate possible show for one.

The two bottles on the table, each filled with clear liquid. They have been there from the moment Flora first saw this room, even as all the other powders and jewels endlessly change and swap about. The vial with the purple amethyst contains the eyedrops. The other has its black setting, topped with a large opal.

'If you've unravelled my life,' says the Belladonna, picking up the second vial, 'I'll not see it. Not with these eyes.'

She takes out the stopper, takes its store of clear liquid in a single deep drink, then drops it. The empty vial lightly bounces on the floor and rolls to a halt.

She looks into Flora, keeping her attention. Flora knows what the Belladonna is saying in this moment: *Think of this as a final message, from me to you. I won, at the end. I've won: see it.* And so Flora is looking into those dark eyes as the Belladonna neatly unfolds, and her eyes take on the same strange hardness as the jet beads at her neck, and her face sets itself into a new world of shapes, becomes a new expression, its last one, a sharper arrangement of skin and shadow, with the ghost of a smile.

It is a steady collapse, graceful almost, how she performs the impossible transition from standing at the dressing-table to lying on the floor beside it.

A new silence enters the room.

And Flora knows what she must do as neatly as if she had the libretto open beside her. Still, she succumbs to the magnetism: *that* certainly hasn't gone away, and she cannot resist, as she approaches the body, looking closely, really *looking* at her now the gaze goes one way only, and the thought dimly registers that she is truly alone in this bedroom for the first time, and she cannot help herself from staring down and examining the arrangement of dark cloth and pale skin and her expression, checking over the details as if they were about to leave together for a ball, taking advantage of this brief moment of appalling new intimacy to gather some final secrets for herself before she reaches up with a steady hand to tug on the thin black bell-pull.

X

The curtains have been pulled back and all the windows are open, letting the gritty bracing air of Paris through the rooms.

The tied-off fabric slouches heavily against the walls while beams of daylight stretch in like greedy fingers, sparkling with motes of dust. The light shines obscenely onto things once shrouded so elegantly. Now exposed, the dark wooden surfaces show themselves to be scuffed and in certain places practically gouged ('Wasn't she careless with her hairpins!')—and the floor betrays a route, over carpets and floorboard, trodden uncountable times from salon and parlour to bedroom and back.

This is the second day of the great unveiling, the week-long display of wares before the bidding starts. The rooms are open to the public. Everything in them has been put up for auction.

F. moves like a ghost across the parlour, where people have crowded in to see what's here. Most are not planning to bid, of course, they are simply here to look at what was until recently so remote.

F. moves into the bedroom, where a pair of fashionable women are investigating the dressing-table.

'Look! That must be her skin powder. So she *was* using a lavender tint.'

'How ghostly she looked.'

What fun they're having, getting as close up as this. Only a few days ago they could have asked her mistress directly. Ah, but they would *never* have been able to get into her company, would they? F. would have smiled at the very idea. Now she cannot bring herself to.

Half-finished pots of cosmetics won't be going up for auction. The two women are still poring over the make-up, their hands hovering in greedy assessment over the dressing-table. F. wants to snap their calfskin gloves away and stop the ridiculous frittering. The bottles of creams and powders now appear so dusty in the brightness, and they are more messily arranged than she remembers. The cut-glass bottles have a worn appearance where she might have expected refinement, and the mirror and brushes' silver handles are tarnished. At the back, standing neatly together as if on guard over the chaos of the table, are the two vials topped with the black and purple crystals. They look utterly inconspicuous and F. knows that today they contain nothing but lavender water.

The women move on and for a moment F. has the bedroom to herself. She notices thankfully that the bed is made: if the sheets were messy and appeared recently slept in she might not have been able to bear it.

The deadly nightshade plant has been pulled back and restrained with twine so no visitors risk passing too close. With its expanse reduced the bedroom has more empty space that it needs, extra yards of floor with no obvious context or use. Not that the plant itself looks powerless, strapped away like that. A danger that is caged only temporarily.

An elderly woman comes in to peer around the bedroom. F. focuses her attention down to her own skirts, not wishing to tolerate any more of these sweeping appraisals.

The lady is looking at the chaise longue, and she grumbles her disapproval towards the worn patch on the embroidered seat.

F. feels a flash of anger. *Look at you. Fox fur and embroidered gown just like one my mistress wore at least two seasons ago; look at you, holding your eyeglass up, wanting to know but acting above it all. This is the world we made and kept together, she and I; and let me tell you, I wouldn't have let you in.*

The woman's gaze is put neatly away along with her glasses, and she doesn't look at F. as she sweeps out.

The apartment has become a place of constant traffic. A nervous-looking couple stand in the doorway to the bedroom, shy to venture beyond the threshold. Recently married is F.'s best guess, from the way the woman is constantly turning that nice ring on her finger. She busies herself looking at the feathers in the new bride's hat (slightly too many, insecurity perhaps, marrying up) and is surprised to be addressed directly.

'So exactly where is she supposed to have gone?'

The bride's voice is as blunt as the question she poses, and brutally loud in that unmuffled space. Before now, even during the busiest salons, there was an understanding, a respectful discretion. This new approach grates on F.'s nerves.

She responds bluntly: 'Away to the country.'

The feathers on the bride's hat quiver, betraying a flinch, perhaps of scepticism. 'Only they're saying she's dead.'

Here the gentleman who must be the groom pipes up: 'Nonsense! She can't. My father says she's practically immortal. He tells this story, that he knew her, and—'

'That's right,' F. leaps onto this idea, grateful for the intervention. She'll take the superstition and scandal sheets when she has to. 'Of course she isn't dead. Can you imagine death telling her what to do and getting away with it?'

This is the official narrative. News of the auction has been posted about the city and the story encouraged to spread: *she is away for another country break; yes, I know, so soon—yet another! But there's no man in tow this time (at least, not that I know of …) and she has decided she longs for a change, and so her rooms are open to visit—it's a charitable act, if you ask me: displaying a famous interior to the curious—and, as she is planning to take new rooms and dress them with the most elegant of fashions on her return to the city, an auction will be held, selling off her current effects, which will raise money for compassionate causes through Paris.*

There's something about the incredulous face of the bride beneath all those feathers. It shouldn't be necessary, but F. wants to add something else: something to explain her own presence.

'Just let us know if you have a question about anything here,' F. says.

The woman in the hat casts another glance around the room, then shrugs—somehow, impossibly, all this is boring her. 'Thank you. Let's go, darling,' she says. 'We've seen it now.'

The rooms will soon be closing, and the couple join the

others who are leaving the apartments. F. is alone in the bedroom, and of all the spaces changed by the daylight, this room suffers the worst. As if the new glare brings everything vividly before her eyes. If she looks *here*, she sees the work of those berries—a crumpled shadow motionless upon the floor. She cannot look *here* or she'll see the dressing-table—a plinth for the eyedrops, for bottles of poison; *there* is the nightshade, strapped back against the wall; and looming before her is the bed, a huge square dominating the room in bolts of black; most of all, she cannot look up, cannot look into the ceiling, towards the picture-rail where, tied in a knot, is the terrible black bell-pull.

As she closes her eyes she sees her mistress falling to the floor.

'Not exactly *cosy*, is it?'

Vernon.

He strides in, brisk as ever, but his voice is kind when he says: 'Strange to see it stripped this bare.'

She finds her voice. 'I know what you mean.' The room is empty, yes. That's exactly it. 'It's as if there's nothing in here, just nothing at all.'

'Makes you wonder.' He opens his pocket watch, idly inspects it. 'Now, that should be the last of them. Thank you for keeping an eye on the open days. I know it's appalling, having everybody burst in.'

She finds something to focus on: the chair at the dressing-table. She sees a pale hand resting on the back of it, but overall it's a relatively harmless memory, one that allows her some way to continue to speak with Vernon as if all this were normal. There, the hand douses both eyes with the drops—and now a shadowy figure is racing towards the table and reaching for the vial. Do not picture the bottle, picture her hand. Remember, you were one of the few who got to see beneath those gloves. Let that be the focus.

Vernon clips the pocket watch closed. 'A word,' he murmurs, not asking a question, and with a single syllable the memorial turns into a meeting, right here in the daylight of her bedroom.

Very well, F. can speak about business. 'I'm negotiating some of the particulars with the auction house—' she begins.

He waves his hand, dismissing her words and all her work with them.

'She's gone,' he says. 'She has left us. It's unthinkable, yes. But, and you'll follow me on this, perhaps it needn't be *so* unthinkable.'

He doesn't look at her directly; instead he follows her gaze towards the dressing-table. They meet each other's eyes inside the mirror.

'As has been said, a new apartment will be required, of course. I wouldn't put you through any less. But in terms of a total redecoration … the interior might not be so terribly different to this. I'd be a fool not to expect an individual touch. But a sense of her broad taste might remain.'

He keeps talking, low and level, staring at her in the mirror.

'I've an eye on some rooms across from the boulevard de la Madeleine; I know the lady who runs them, in fact. We've a little history together.'

She doesn't rise to it; she focuses on breathing softly. 'New rooms?'

'And when she returns to those rooms, for all the gossip

about where she's been, I don't expect her to be much changed.'

'People have seen me,' she says. 'I'll be recognised.'

'Oh they've *seen* you?' he grins. 'Your hair, of course, will have to be restyled. There's a method I've heard about, using egg whites I believe. And the make-up, the wardrobe of course, the eyes—'

'The eyes.'

'And when it's all in place, nobody sees the assistant that once was.' He shrugs. 'Sometimes we have to take what we can get in this world.'

But. Surely not, it's not true, it can't be true.

Vernon sees her having that thought, waves it away. Always waving things away—you can only do that when you're confident something else will be along very shortly.

Vernon smiles at her in the mirror. 'I'm not averse to ringing the changes. But that's mostly, you understand, because nobody is interested in picking up on them.' He fiddles with his watch chain. 'You know what is involved. You may not fully appreciate the emotional toll of the work. I don't say that to underestimate you. But it's one thing to be close to the action, another entirely to embody it. When she comes back, as I hope she will,' a smile flickers across his reflected face, 'I want to feel confident she'll rise to the role.'

Their gazes catch in the mirror.

Behind him the tightly bound nightshade tree moves, a few stray leaves finding whatever breeze has made it into the room.

F. faces a dizzying possibility. To come this far and realise you're not cut out for it at all … her answer must be plain to read in her face.

But her face, she realises, is giving away nothing: staring back at her in the mirror is an expression that is perfectly neutral.

She hears Vernon say: 'Well then. Are you looking at Belladonna?'

The rhythm of one waltz after another, the music of those high society balls, hands meeting over a game of cards, night-time dashes in the hansom from one appointment to another. The power of having the final say. Could it be so easy? Being the one who can decide? She's already answered to the name, why shouldn't it be the truth? Doesn't she deserve this? To be at the Opéra, all in black, up there far and away in the grandest private box, to be known, to be acknowledged, to look out over the stalls densely packed with society in its evening dress, its black and white, its feathers and diamonds, and to know that someone is staring back up.

Between one heartbeat and the next.

'I am.'

Acknowledgements

A huge thank you to Antonia Ward, Fay Lane
and Ghost Orchid Press for supporting this book
with enthusiasm and expertise. My immense gratitude
to Laura Pires and also to Manon Thomas for advice
on all things *en français* (any deviations, of course,
are my own). Thank you E.J. Swift and Claire North
for ongoing moral support and insight—here's
to many more walks in the park. A thank you to
Arts Council England. And thank you Keir Cooper for
being my closest reader and life and art collaborator,
across this project and many others.

About the Author

Rose Biggin is the author of *Wild Time* (Surface Press) —a punk revision of pleasure and power in 'A Midsummer Night's Dream'—and academic work *Immersive Theatre and Audience Experience* (Palgrave). Her short fiction has been published in various anthologies, made the recommended reading list for Best of British Fantasy, and won the Dark Sire's Gothic Fiction Prize. She lives in London and works as a performer across theatre and live art, and teaches with the Creative Writing department at Birkbeck.

Milton Keynes UK
Ingram Content Group UK Ltd.
UKHW011811260923
429400UK00005B/171

9 781739 611668